For fifteen days the wind held fair, and we sailed on, always westerly, working and resting in shifts. Although I had lost hope of seeing the Floating Isle again, everything I had heard or pieced together from remnants of legends told me that our ultimate goal must lie in the west, though it might be further than man had ever sailed before . . . to the very edge of the world, if need be. This didn't frighten me. I have always felt most at peace on the open water, and its vastness never seemed empty or lonely. Looking around at the men I guessed that roughly half of them were of the same temperament: but some of the others were obviously frightened, and in the evenings they spoke of the World's Edge.

One day Conn, our youngest brother, and who hailed from Erin's wild northern mountains, finally gave voice to the imaginings of some of the less experienced sailors.

'Father Abbot, how far west can we sail before we come to the edge of the world? And if we reach it, will we be able to stop ourselves falling off? What of the huge whirlpool that sucks everything over the edge? And what about the monsters that swim in the sea. . .?'

'I don't believe there is an edge to the world,' I said quietly, but firmly. 'No one, not even the fierce warrior-sailors from the northern icelands, have yet reached the edge of the world, and they have sailed further than any other men. Even if we had the strength and provisions to venture in search of it – which we do not – God would not allow us to stray so far from our true goal . . .'

Navigator

THE VOYAGE OF SAINT BRENDAN

by
MICHAEL SCOTT
AND GLORIA GAGHAN

A Methuen Paperback

A Methuen Paperback

NAVIGATOR: THE VOYAGE OF SAINT BRENDAN

British Library Cataloguing in Publication Data

Scott, Michael, *1959–*
Navigator : the voyage of Saint Brendan.
I. Title   II. Gaghan, Gloria
823′.914[J]   PZ8.1

ISBN 0–413–17350–X

First published in Great Britain 1988
by Methuen London Ltd
11 New Fetter Lane, London EC4P 4EE

Copyright © Michael Scott and Gloria Gaghan 1988

Printed and bound in Great Britain
by Cox and Wyman Ltd, Reading

For Anna and Peter
navigators both

In the evenings when the sun dips towards the horizon and burns colours into the sky and sea, the clouds take on surreal and fantastic shapes. Then mountains with tall, soaring pinnacles, slender towers and palaces of ethereal beauty appear on the misty horizon.

It is easy then to believe in the magical haunted islands in the seas off the west coast of Ireland.

Preface

How quickly they forget.

How quickly they allow the memories to fade; how quickly the fear takes them; how quickly time takes us . . .

They lie to me now. They can look me in the face and lie, saying that I will soon be hale and well again. But they cannot conceal the lies in their eyes, nor the pity, nor youth's instinctive shrinking from age and certain death.

I have known death. I do not fear it. If I have any fear, it is only that they will forget and then all that I have done will have been in vain. I have done many things and seen more, and I have travelled further than any other man in the known world.

If they forget, it will be because they do not want to remember, and the fear of what they do not comprehend will blind them.

Those who sailed with me are gone now; some to their reward, others to spread the Word. Now only I remain, and I remember everything.

I am Brendan, sometime called the Navigator . . .

Chapter One

A monk's life is regulated by the bell. Its rhythm becomes a part of his life, regulating it as surely as the sun's passage regulates the natural world. And when it tolls suddenly, unexpectedly, the shock is almost like a blow. It was tolling now, and it was only late afternoon. There was still an hour or so to go before vespers, when the bell should properly call our community to prayer.

I straightened up slowly. I had remained bent over for far too long and my back had locked. Black and red spots danced before my eyes and the thin, high sound of the bell was drowned by the pounding of blood in my head. The throbbing had returned to my chest also, and I leaned on the hoe which I had been using to weed the small and still-struggling herb garden.

I was just turning back towards the few wood-and-stone buildings which would one day grow into a monastery when Fiachra, one of the younger monks, appeared and ran across the garden towards me. He was pale beneath his weather-tanned skin, and his eyes were wide and shocked. 'Father Abbot . . . Father Abbot . . . there's a man here, a fisherman from Dun Rath. He's . . . he's come with news of Fionnbar!'

I dropped the hoe and began to run down the pathway that led to the gates. Suddenly the afternoon seemed very still and the crunching of the gravel beneath my feet sounded unnaturally loud. 'Fionnbar, my cousin?' The question was unnecessary – I only knew one Fionnbar.

'Yes, Father.'

'What has happened?'

'I'm not sure,' he said, his brown eyes avoiding mine.

'Well, what did the fisherman say?' I demanded.

'A wreck . . . washed up onto the beach . . . near his village,' Fiachra answered. He was panting, short of breath; he

1

had only recently come to the order from a wealthy family, and had not yet adjusted to the harsh regime of the monk's life. 'Perhaps it would be better if he told you himself,' he added lamely.

Becoming conscious of the pounding of my heart against my chest, I forced myself to slow down and walk at a measured pace towards the monastery gate. The bell ceased as abruptly as it had begun, but on all sides, monks were hurrying in from the surrounding fields, obeying the bell's insistent summons. I breathed deeply, preparing myself in my heart for news of Fionnbar's death, knowing that I must be seen by my brethren to be able to accept it with a measure of calm and dignity.

At the gate the fisherman awaited us, standing with his arms folded and a quiet dignity that proclaimed him a leader in his own community. He was short and stocky, with a broad, open face and clear grey eyes. He might have been only seven or eight years older than Fiachra's five-and-twenty, but the latter seemed a fresh-faced boy beside him. The sea and its harsh disciplines had tempered and moulded him. Clear grey eyes met mine as an equal. I bowed slightly. 'I am Brendan, abbot of this community,' I said, sounding surprisingly calm even to my ears. 'You have word of my cousin, Fionnbar?'

'Aye, and more than word. If the gods spare him for a short while, he will be with you – though he is not long for this life, I think.' He said it almost casually; but in his own gruff way, I realized, he was trying to be kind. 'Four of my kinsmen follow bearing him on a litter. I came on ahead to bring you word.'

'I thank you for that. He is gravely ill, then?' I asked.

'His boat smashed against the rocks – the currents are treacherous in the seas off Dun Rath, and the bay itself is guarded with a jagged line of submerged rocks. He clung to part of his craft for nearly a whole day, until eventually the current carried him to the shore where we found him.'

'How long ago was this?'

'Three days. There is damage to his ribs, and one leg, and he was a long time in the chill water. He has no feeling in his hands or feet.' The cool grey eyes considered me steadily. 'I did not want to move him, but he pleaded with us to be brought back to his own kind for Christian burial.'

'You follow the Old Faith?'

The chieftain nodded briefly, his eyes never leaving mine. 'My father followed it, and his father before that, back to the Age of the Fianna and beyond. Our faith has served us well and we remain faithful to it. But we have no quarrel with the followers of the White Christ, and we respect the ways of others and a man's desire to die with his own kin.' He paused, and then added, 'Your kinsman called out your name many times when the fever took him, and your name is not unknown to us. Your kinsman – I think he feels a great need to speak to you . . .' His eyes left me, looking over my left shoulder, and I turned and found Geoffrey standing behind me. Beyond him, half a score of the community's youngest and strongest men had gathered.

'There are men coming along the road from the coast, bearing Fionnbar.' Geoffrey's face was stone, but the tremble in his voice betrayed him. He was one of my staunchest allies and had helped me found the community at Clonfert, but Fionnbar had always been his closest friend. 'He is fearfully injured, and . . .'

'I know,' I said quietly.

'I will go down to meet them,' he continued. 'Ultan, Barran and Ruarai will accompany me.' He paused and then added, 'With your leave, of course, Abbot.'

'I will join you.' I turned back to the fisherman. 'You have had a long journey. Will you take your evening meal with us? You are welcome, of course, to spend the night.'

The grey eyes flickered from mine to something behind and above me. Without turning I knew that he was looking at the tall carved stone cross that dominated the centre of the courtyard. He shook his head. 'I thank you, but no; my kinsmen and I will return to Dun Rath. We will go to sea again on the evening tide – the sea's harvest is plentiful this year.'

'As you wish.' I turned back to Geoffrey. 'Perhaps we should go and meet Fionnbar . . . ?'

None of us spoke as we went out along the path to meet the villagers bearing Fionnbar. The pace was quick for men whose steps are normally measured, and time seemed to press upon me, dragging out that short walk to an eternity. But the sight,

3

at last, of the four men carrying Fionnbar on a litter spurred me to a fresh burst of speed, and I reached his side before the others.

'Fionnbar?' I said softly, touching his hand.

'Brendan?' Fionnbar's eyes flickered open briefly and his own fingers sought mine and squeezed them tightly. His skin felt waxy, soft and chill. He tried to raise his head.

'Don't move, lie still,' I said, as forcefully as I could. 'We'll get you up to the monastery . . .' I looked up at Geoffrey, but he anticipated my question.

'Naise will be waiting.' Brother Naise was our herbalist and healer.

As the brothers took over from the fisherfolk, I turned back to my cousin. 'What was so important that you had to risk your life to come here?'

Fionnbar's grip tightened painfully on my fingers. 'It's the Promised Land, Brendan,' he whispered, his eyes wide and much too bright, 'the Promised Land.'

My face must have registered something, shock or pain, because I saw the same look mirrored in my cousin's eyes. I nodded as impassively as I could. How badly injured was he, I wondered, and how far gone into fever? As gently as possible, I pulled open Fionnbar's robe to look at his wounds. I guessed that he had been thrown up onto the rocks first, breaking most of his ribs, although there seemed to be only one cut – a gaping hole low on his left side. The villagers had cleaned it well and applied a poultice of herbs and dung. This had kept the wound from festering, but I doubted that it would ever heal properly. I reached out, my fingertips tracing the jagged impressions of his ribs through the taut skin. Most of them seemed to have been forced inwards, and there was the telltale sign of blood on my cousin's lips. I had seen similar injuries before; they promised little more than a painful, choking death.

'The Promised Isle,' he whispered again. 'I've been there.'

'Rest; not now,' I commanded, glancing up at the brothers, who had taken up positions around the litter but were waiting for my command to lift it. Such talk was dangerous, and could inflame even the most sedate of men into doing something foolish and futile. No man knows this better than I.

4

With a sudden effort that brought blood to his mouth and pumping from the long gash in his side, Fionnbar sat up. His fingers closed on my robe, and he brought his face close enough to mine for me to breathe in the tart copper smell of blood on his breath. As he spoke, he spat red spittle in my face. 'Believe me, I've been there,' he cried urgently, and then his voice ended in a gasp of pain. 'I've been to the Isle of Promise!'

Suddenly his eyes rolled in his head and he slumped back into the litter, unmoving.

In the silence that followed, one of the brothers crossed himself and began to pray audibly.

I bowed my head, numbness beginning to creep up through my throat and behind my eyes. The throbbing began again in my chest. But there would be time for grieving later; now, Fionnbar must be given the Rites of the Dead . . .

I bent and caught his body around the chest to lift him to me – and felt the weak pounding of a heart. It took a moment to realize that it wasn't just mine, and I could only whisper, 'He's alive!' I looked up at the brothers. 'He's alive; we must get him up to the monastery. Quickly now . . . quickly, and gently,' I warned.

The brothers each took one of the poles and, on Geoffrey's word, lifted him. Though he seemed unconscious I thought I saw Fionnbar wince, and red-black blood began to drip steadily from beneath the litter, leaving a spattered trail behind us as we hurried back to the monastery. The brothers did their best to carry the litter along as smoothly as possible, but the pathway was rough.

I followed on behind, feeling every jolt and jar; but I forced myself to keep silent. It took an age to reach the monastery and by that time I felt older and more weary than I had for a long time.

'How is he?'

The old monk wiped his bloodied hands on a scrap of cloth and then slipped them into the wide sleeves of his robe. He looked over at the figure in the bed and silently shook his head without meeting my eyes. He hesitated a moment, but then bowed slightly and eased his way past me out of the small, chill stone room.

The brothers had put Fionnbar in my own cell; it offered little in the way of comfort, except that it was dry, and sheltered from all but the most persistent wind. I crossed to the pallet where he lay, and knelt beside him on the rough stone floor. Fionnbar's face was now the colour of old butter and the skin seemed to have slackened. His breathing was laboured and his eyes were sunken and withdrawn, as if they looked inward at other things. I closed my own eyes, remembering him as I had last seen him – a month, two months ago – a strong, stocky man in his prime, his face plump, his eyes bright and alive, the colour of fresh earth. I have counted more than sixty summers, so my life is generally considered a long one, but Fionnbar would be five or six years younger than I. Now, he had the look of an ancient. What had happened in the past season to change him into this wreck of his former self?

The rhythm of the dying man's breathing changed, and I opened my eyes to find Fionnbar staring at me. In the muted light of the cell, his eyes shone bright and feverish.

'Brendan.'

I reached out and took his hands. They felt cold, the skin a casing over brittle bones. 'I'm here.'

Brendan, you must believe me,' Fionnbar said slowly and carefully, every breath tightening his eyes in pain. 'I was there!' His hands closed into fists. 'I've been to the Isle of Promise . . .'

I smiled tightly. 'Later; we'll talk about it later. You must rest now. Brother Naise tells me that you'll soon be well,' I lied.

Fionnbar grimaced, the skin on his face tightening against his cheekbones, making it look suddenly skull-like. 'Don't risk your soul with falsehoods for me. I've seen men die with less severe wounds.'

'Rest; you must rest,' I tried to soothe him. 'I'll come back to you . . .'

'No!' Fionnbar sat up on the hard wooden cot, and the woollen blanket fell away, revealing his sunken chest and broken stick-like ribs. Brother Naise had bound them as best he could with strips of linen, and he had also covered the

6

gaping wound in his side. But the sudden movement opened this again, and the fresh bandage turned a bright sticky red. 'No,' he persisted, colour draining from his face, 'you must listen to me now, Brendan.'

I was about to shake my head and insist that he rest, but there was something so desperate in his voice and behind his eyes that I just nodded silently.

'I've been to the Island of Promise,' Fionnbar said simply. 'This is not a dream or some fevered imagining, nor am I the first to go there. You remember Mernoce . . . ?'

'A young man from the west, bastard son of a lady in the royal court. Yes, of course. You and he were very close.'

'He was my son.'

I nodded briefly, not wanting to acknowledge that which I had guessed a long time ago.

'Aye,' Fionnbar's eyes glittered with moisture. 'Aye; well, he went in search of the Promised Land . . .'

'Why?' I demanded.

Fionnbar smiled and attempted to shrug. 'Why not? You tried it also, remember?'

'I remember,' I said, then added, 'I remember we found nothing. What made him think he would be successful where I had failed?' I was unable to hide the bitterness in my voice, and it surprised even me.

Fionnbar touched my fist, which had clenched around the blanket. 'Don't blame yourself; you just weren't meant to find the land.'

'And the men who died? The men who trusted me?'

'God's will,' Fionnbar said simply.

If I closed my eyes, I could still see the faces of the monks who had died on my voyage in search of the Promised Land that was said to lie off the west coast of Erin. 'And your bastard son thought he could find it?' I asked him.

'There is a monk on Aran,' Fionnbar said quickly, his voice beginning to come in harsh gasps. 'He has seen the isle; he gave him directions, told him where he would find it – and he did!'

'The Land of Paradise, the Promised Land?'

Fionnbar nodded. 'He found it. He found Paradise,' he

7

repeated. 'Mernoce first. He founded a community on an isle off the south and west coast. From it they caught glimpses of the holy island on certain days. Eventually, they decided to sail towards it. He sent for me.' Fionnbar paused for breath. 'I've been there, I've stayed there. And from its rocky shores I've sailed to Paradise . . .' His eyes dulled and he shook his head. 'I've been there.'

I nodded silently. How many times had I stood on the cliffs and stared out across the waves at the distant horizon? How many times had my heart suddenly pounded at the sight of what I had thought to be an island, only to have the wind resolve it into a cloud? How many times had I prayed to God to allow me to visit the Promised Land?

'What was the name of the monk on the isles of Aran?' I asked my cousin eventually.

'Enda,' Fionnbar said quietly. He coughed then, and his lips were stained with dark red ichor. 'He was once a warrior, selling his sword to the highest paymaster, but then he heard the Word of the True God and repented. He has spent his declining years building a church on the largest of the isles of Aran.'

'Enda of Aran,' I said slowly. The name was vaguely familiar to me, conjured from half-remembered tales and whispered rumours. 'He too has seen this island?' A fit of coughing took Fionnbar and he shook off my hands. I stood up slowly, and backed away, until my spine touched the cold stone wall. I welcomed the discomfort as a sort of penance, allowing the chill to push back the sharp pangs of anger and jealousy I was feeling now.

Fionnbar coughed again, blood spattering the blanket. 'He has seen the Land,' he whispered. 'But he has not visited it; he does not think himself worthy.'

'And you do!' I snapped, and immediately regretted it. My temples began to throb and I pressed my hands against them before kneeling on the rough floor beside the cot. I clasped my hands together and bowed my head. 'Forgive me,' I murmured. 'That was unworthy.'

The monk lay back on the hard pillow. His wizened hand with its stick-like fingers rested briefly on my shoulder, and then I felt it fall away. 'There is nothing to forgive,' he said. 'But the Land is there. I was coming to tell you myself when a sudden wave . . .' He coughed again. 'The Land is there,' he said suddenly, urgently. 'Visit it, Brendan, visit the Promised Land . . .'

Some time passed before I realized that my cousin was dead.

Chapter Two

I glanced up into the heavens; the sky was lightening towards the dawn. Thick wreaths of grey fog wrapped themselves around the monastery's tumbled stones and drifted across tilled fields before rolling out to the edge of the cliffs, where they seemed to pause for a moment before dissipating in the valley below.

A few brothers were standing quietly on the edge of the cliffs, shivering as the chill ate slowly into their bones; but it was a chill I didn't feel. Fionnbar's death had left me numb. I had hurried through the service, not only for their sakes, but for my own. Even so, by the time the final *Amen* had been intoned, our robes were heavy and sodden with damp. Two of the brothers had gathered together a pile of flat slates and shales with which they had built a simple cairn over Fionnbar's remains. Later, I promised myself, when all the buildings of Clonfert itself had been raised, I would see a fitting monument made to honour him. Suddenly there seemed to be nothing more to do or to say, and I turned away, heading back to the monastery chapel.

A breeze from the north sprang up and began to shred the fog, and soon shafts of thin morning sunlight were breaking through the clouds. In the distance, I could see some of the brothers already working in the fields, their brown robes almost merged with the colour of the earth. It was a perpetual struggle with the hard, rocky soil, and the results, every harvest, were painfully meagre; but I found the discipline useful for the younger men. In the opposite direction, some brothers were rebuilding a wall that had tumbled down in the night, and, if I listened carefully, I could make out the chip of stone on stone as the rest of the community helped to raise another portion of the monastery. Everyone seemed to have something to do – except me. Fionnbar's story of the Isle of

Promise had brought back memories – memories which, while they had never been forgotten, I had managed to suppress for a long time. I don't know whether I would have accompanied him to the Isle if he had lived – but his death had changed that. It had decided me, and there was now no question but that I would go in search of the Isle of Promise. I would walk its shores!

Most men have a secret desire, a goal, a longing that calls to them for fulfilment. Some desire one woman above all others. Many seek wealth and lands and power. God has spared me the lust for women, and worldly possessions mean nothing to me. My dream was to visit the fabled Isles of the Blest, the Happy Isles, Tir na nog, the Far Country – call them what you will. The legends of every race told of magical, mysterious, haunted lands in the uncharted seas – pagan lands, lands that had not yet heard the Word of Christ. But I, Brendan of Clonfert, would bring it to them. This was my dream, my destiny; and all my long waking life was but a preparation for it.

I had first learned of the magical isles that lay off Erin's wild western coast when I was still a wandering monk. Then, I tramped the crude roads, owning nothing, keeping nothing. I ate what I was given, and in return I gave my blessing. The stories I heard whispered around the firesides and camp sites were all fabulous and fascinating: there were islands to the west of Erin. Islands of gold and silver, of crystal and precious stones; islands with creatures of myth, spirits, ghosts, fetches, fairy folk. These were the strongholds of the Sidhe, the Devil, God, demons, spirits, angels . . .

The stories differed in many respects, in all respects but one – that the islands were there; the tales agreed on that.

While still a young wandering monk, I had stayed and studied with Jarlath at Cluainfois. Jarlath was then a very old man, how old no one knew. He was rumoured to have come over to Erin with Patrick, but when I asked him, he only smiled his toothless smile and shook his head. By this time the years were beginning to take their toll on his incredible memory in the way that is common with the very aged. He couldn't always remember events that had occurred in days just past, but events and happenings of decades gone were still crystal-clear and sharp. His knowledge of the Scriptures, as well as the lore and folklore of our own land, was enormous, and I often spoke to him of the magical isles. In a way, he was the first to suggest that it might be possible to visit the isles, and bring the Holy Word of Christ to them.

It was a dream that was to grow over the years; a dream impossible for a young monk to realize. In time, however, having advanced in the service of the Lord and found myself an abbot, I sailed upon my first voyage in search of the isles. Accompanying me there had been sixty men, in three currachs, and enough supplies for half a year. But from the very beginning the voyage was dogged by ill-luck and bad weather, and the wood-and-wicker currachs soon began to founder in the Western Ocean. In the end we were forced to turn back and barely managed to reach shore again. One third of the original crew and equipment were lost.

In time even I began to doubt the existence of the islands. Until now. The islands were real; they were there to be visited. I had sworn on Fionnbar's deathbed that I would walk their shores.

Brother Nevin was waiting for me along the path that led down from the cliff. Like Geoffrey, Nevin was one of the men who had helped me to found the monastery at Clonfert. He was one of the oldest monks in the community, and his memories spanned nearly a hundred summers in the service of God – and scores more he didn't care to remember, he would say drily.

'You'll be going, I suppose?' the old monk said, his voice thin and cracked like his skin.

'I must,' I said with a touch of defiance. Although Nevin was one of my closest friends, he always managed to make me feel like a boy.

Nevin smiled without opening his mouth. He had long since lost all his teeth, and even when he spoke, he did so with the minimum of lip movements. 'I thought you might.' He hesitated, looking back along the path towards the cliffs, before glancing sidelong at me. 'He visited the Isle, then?'

'He did.'

'You're sure?' Nevin asked. 'It might have been the fever, or maybe he swallowed sea water – sea water leads to madness, you know that?'

'Do you think I don't know that?' I asked wearily.

'Maybe as he lay dying he was comforted by an image of the Isle, a vision perhaps, a reward for a life of contemplation, of service,' Nevin suggested.

'I think he was really there. That's why he was coming here. He was going to show me the Isle of Promise.' I coughed; for some reason my chest felt tight, and my throat was burning. 'His . . . friend Mernoce had founded a small community on an island that is in sight of the Isles of Promise . . . within sailing distance, certainly.'

Nevin lay a withered stick-like hand on my sleeve. 'Don't go yet. Think about it, pray on it, fast on it if you will.'

'I have to go,' I stated. In the silence that followed we walked down the thin pathway towards the round stone cells of the half-built monastery. 'Fionnbar mentioned a monk on Aran . . .'

'Enda?'

I nodded. 'Do you know him?'

Nevin shrugged, his bony shoulders poking through the thin cloth of his robe. 'I know of him; we met once – briefly – many years ago. He was a mercenary, a hired sword, before he found the truth of God. He has a small company of followers on the isles of Aran. They are an austere and very poor order. Why do you ask?'

We had now reached the low stone walls of the monastery, but I found I didn't want to go inside just yet. So I led Nevin off the track and followed the curve of the low wall. The morning was unnaturally still, feeling almost as if it were waiting for something. Even the birds had ceased calling, and we walked in silence for a while. At last I said, more to myself than to Nevin, 'Enda of Aran apparently knows the location of the Isle of Promise. He has seen it often off Aran's shores.'

'He hasn't been there?' the old monk asked shrewdly.

I shook my head. 'Fionnbar said that he didn't consider himself worthy.'

Nevin's face twisted in the grimace that passed for a smile. 'That would be Enda; it's a pride of a sort,' he said. 'A sinful, twisted pride.' The old man paused, and then asked, 'Why do you not go to Mernoce's Isle and go from there?'

13

I shrugged. 'Fionnbar died before he could tell me where it was. All I have is Enda's name.'

The sun broke through the clouds behind us, sending our shadows dancing across the hard stony earth. The birds seemed to come alive with the sudden light, and their mewling calls sounded like children crying down in the valley below.

Nevin suddenly stopped. 'Do you want to leave all this? Clonfert; it is yours, formed and founded by you. It's immortality of a sort. You're not a young man now – another voyage, especially a long one, might just kill you.'

I looked over the low stone monastery, with its small rounded cells and the almost finished oratory, and I remembered it as it had been when Geoffrey, Nevin . . . and Fionnbar and I had first come here. There had been nothing here then, except the bleak and barren ground, useless for aught but growing moss and lichens. Even the local folk shunned it, saying it had once been a great battle ground where two ancient armies had fought, and the blood of the dead had withered the soil. I did nothing to discourage their pagan superstitions, since it kept them away, ensuring its privacy and leaving it as a place without distractions, a place where a man might be close to God. Fionnbar and I had built a single round hut here, many years ago. The rest of the monastery had grown up around that poor cell. I looked at Nevin, and found him still waiting for an answer. I shook my head slowly. 'No, I don't want to leave it; but I have to go and look for the islands.'

'If I can't stop you . . .' Nevin shrugged.

'You can't.'

'How many brothers will you take with you this time?' He looked away from me, perhaps realizing how much he had emphasized the last two words.

I shrugged. 'I took sixty with me then – and it was too many. A smaller, more skilled crew this time. How many would you suggest?'

Nevin looked up into the pale blue-grey skies and squinted, his face dissolving into a mass of wrinkles. 'You'll need enough men to crew a boat, and yet not enough to make supplies a problem. Twelve men . . . no, say fourteen, and you; fifteen men in all. But no more.'

I nodded. My own estimate had been twelve men.

'Have you given any thought to the brothers who will accompany you? Many will want to, but humility or perhaps even fear will keep some from asking.'

'I know,' I sighed. 'After the last time, I cannot order, or even ask any of them to come with me – possibly to their deaths.'

'But they would be laying down their lives for the Lord,' Nevin said with his grimace of a smile. 'Or so they would tell themselves. No,' he shook his head, 'I don't think you'll have any difficulty finding a crew.'

'Aye,' I said, not fully convinced. 'If the choice were yours, whom would you take?'

'Geoffrey,' he said without hesitation. 'His judgement and counsel are good, and he has the ability to reason with others.' Something in my expression stopped him. 'And that is not to disparage your own abilities as a leader, Brendan; but you are the abbot, and that places you a little apart from the rest of the brothers. For the rest,' he hurried on, 'you need strong young men. I would advise that none of them should be well known to you, lest those not taken think you guilty of favouritism.'

I nodded. His words made sense. 'Go on . . .'

'Let me see . . .' He walked on, and then stopped, turning to look at the walls of the monastery. 'None of the stonemasons, obviously – we need them here. I would prefer it if you didn't take Molua or Moenniu – their knowledge of the soil and seeds is too valuable to lose. Take young Ruarai – he thinks himself a farmer, but he only irritates the older men with his notions for new methods of sowing and irrigation.' He paused and then added, with a sly grin, 'And Fiachra; take him with you. A few months at sea will tame his impetuousness and arrogance.'

'I'm not setting sail with a crew of misfits!'

'No, no, of course not,' he said with a toothless grin. 'There's Niall – strong as an ox and a fine fisherman also. There's Tadgh and Ultan – both capable men, and sure to be steady in a crisis. Take Barran – his faith is rigid and narrow, and he would benefit from experiencing a little more of the world. Dunan and Liber grew up on the coast, so that the sea will hold no terrors for them . . .' he hesitated.

'Martyn?' I suggested.

'Aye, Martyn would be a good choice,' he nodded. 'He has some of the druidic herb lore, and would be useful if anyone took ill. And Mernoc is a tough mountain man, who can light a fire or skin an animal faster than anyone I've ever seen. Now, personally, I'd add Conn or Ronan.'

It took a moment for me to recognize the names. 'But they're only boys!'

The old man nodded. 'But they're strong and devout, and the older men will feel obliged to look after them – and that will be a helpful distraction on what I would imagine is going to be a long and irksome voyage. Have we got your crew yet?' he asked, his eyes sparkling.

I counted through the names: twelve. But including me that made it thirteen. Some superstitious streak in me made me want to reach the number Nevin had originally proposed. 'One more.'

Nevin pondered for a moment, then said, 'Crosan!'

'Crosan!' I said, surprised.

'He may seem like an odd choice at first glance, for he lacks youth and strength, and has not been one of us for very long. But he is cheerful and has a good nature, and he has a marvellous collection of stories from the time he entertained at court. His tales will help to fill the empty hours at sea.'

'I'm not sure we need . . .'

Nevin rested his fingers lightly on my arm. 'Brendan,' he said earnestly, 'once you sail from Erin's shores, there will be no turning back, either for you or any of your crew; and you will all have lost the finest luxury all men enjoy – privacy. Twelve men thrown together on a small cramped boat will need something to relieve the tedium of the journey.'

'We had no problems of that sort on the last voyage,' I said stiffly.

'You had sixty men with you,' Nevin reminded me gently. 'Perhaps it has escaped your notice, but do you not realize that neither Diglach nor Iarlaith have spoken to each other since that voyage because of some slight, real or imagined, which occurred then?'

'I didn't know.' We walked for a few minutes in silence

towards the cells.

'I'll be guided by your advice,' I said suddenly. 'Conn, Ronan and Crosan and the others. So be it,' I said, 'there's my crew – if they are willing,' I added.

'You're decided then – and so suddenly?' Nevin asked.

'It is as good a crew as any,' I said. But I am afraid that by that time my spirit had already left Clonfert; it was with the journey, the sea, and the ultimate goal. Despite Nevin's worries, one crew would be much like another.

Chapter Three

It was close to evening before we came in sight of the largest of the Aran isles. The sun was low in the heavens off our starboard side, and there were already small hard points of light beginning to burn on the land. We had set out with the first tide of the day, taking a south-westerly course and allowing the wind and tide to do most of the work; but even so we were now exhausted, and the isles were a welcome sight.

Stone scraped against the hides of the craft, and the brothers immediately jumped out into the shallows and dragged the light currachs up the rocky beach, before turning them over beneath a low cliff to drain and dry in the air. Some men stretched and worked at stiffened muscles, cramped after a day's inaction, while others sorted through the meagre supplies that we had brought with us, dividing them up into easily portable bundles.

I then had a choice. We could stay where we were or move inland to search for the fires we had seen earlier. But travelling inland over broken and unknown ground could prove dangerous and possibly fatal. Night was falling and the shadows had robbed the sharp edges from everything. Overhead the stars were beginning to shimmer through the evening haze, but there were clouds racing in from the north and east, and fog beginning to roll in on the waves; visibility would be poor.

Suddenly a stone clattered down onto the beach from the rocks above and we turned to see a figure step out from an opening in the cliff.

'So, you have come.'

Even though the light was fading, I knew at once that the speaker could only be Enda, once warrior, now monk. The man was huge, and the loose robe of the order only emphasized his girth. His face was round and fat, his eyes tiny, lost in the folds of flesh, and his mouth was so small as to be almost

18

comical. His bare arms were thickly muscled beneath a layer of fat, and even his fingers were thick and stubby. But for all his grossness, he carried himself erect, and with a curious arrogance, not common in those that have taken holy orders.

'You are Enda?' I asked.

The monk nodded briefly, his bald head glistening slightly in the fog that was beginning to drift in off the sea. 'I am. You are Brendan, abbot of Clonfert.'

It was a statement more than a question, but I bowed and answered him. I then indicated the monks gathered behind me. 'And these are some brothers from the community at Clonfert.'

Enda's huge head shifted in their direction, before turning back to me. Small, dark eyes showed hard and slightly glittering as he blinked slowly, almost deliberately. 'I bid you welcome to this island, in the name of the Lord.' His voice was harsh and slightly rasping, with an odd accent that even I, with my travels, couldn't place.

'You were expecting us?' I asked eventually, when he said no more.

Enda's teeth flashed in a smile in the gloom. 'I was; I knew Fionnbar would bring you here.' The warrior-monk looked over the brothers, and then back to me. 'I thought he would come with you.'

I hesitated a moment too long before replying.

Enda nodded and crossed himself. The huge man suddenly seemed at a loss for words. 'A good man,' he said eventually.

'A good man,' I echoed.

'But this way. You must come this way.' Enda turned away and seemed to disappear into the cliff. I followed him and found that there were a series of crude steps cut into the solid rock, leading up from the beach into the island. The steps were treacherous and slippery with weed and moisture, but by the time I had reached the top Enda was already marching steadily across the rocky fields of Aran, heading towards the twinkling fires.

As we approached the monastery, I could see that the community on Aran was crude even by monastic standards. The cells of the monks were tiny, in some cases mere outcroppings of stone which had been built up with rocks from the beach and roofed over with flat slates and shales. Clonfert was a palace by comparison; and even our new monastery, only half completed, seemed luxurious when compared to this cold austerity.

Enda led us into a rough stone circle in which the walls had been built up to a man's height. 'In time this will be our Oratory,' he said proudly. A fire burned in a small stone-enclosed grate in the centre of this circle, and Enda's followers were seated silently around it. They stood up as we approached.

There were thirty monks on the island. The oldest couldn't have been more than five-and-twenty but their austere life and diet had etched far more years into their faces, and they might easily have been taken for twice their age. It was a long time since I had seen such devotion, and it shocked me. Even in my lifetime, the monk's life has changed, and most men who take the cloth realize that the Lord's work is best carried out if the body is hale and well, and not starved and over-worked.

'Sit . . . sit,' Enda urged. 'We have prepared a meal for you.' As we settled ourselves on the hard earth, a young monk suddenly appeared by my side with a platter of bread and fish.

Enda caught the dismayed looks of some of the younger men who had accompanied me and he smiled, his eyes disappearing behind the rolls of fat into his face. 'Our fare is simple here; we take only what the Lord gives us.'

That might be so, but it did not prevent Enda's followers from ruining even that simple fare. The bread had been burned on the outside and yet remained uncooked in the middle and the fish had been boiled – and I've yet to find men who will admit to liking boiled fish. However, the day had been long and we had not eaten since we had broken our fast just before dawn, and so we ate. Enda's followers seemed to follow the precept that there was a time for eating and one for speech, and for them the meal was a quick, silent affair.

My own brothers sat a little apart from the others, talking quietly amongst themselves, and then in a lull in conversation, I heard someone – Ruarai, I think – say, 'Do you think they always eat so much?'

Immediately, a high boyish voice snapped back. 'Surely they

must? Will you look at the size of your man there.'

I prayed that Enda didn't hear the muffled laughter.

The brothers retired after their meal, and I nodded to my own brethren to move away, leaving Enda and me alone before the dying fire. For a while we sat silently, not yet feeling the need for conversation, merely allowing the night silence to settle into our bones and ease away the day's toil. At last Enda heaved his huge bulk forward and threw a handful of dried seaweed onto the fire. It sparked for a few moments, and then began to smoulder and burn, tainting the salt air with a heavy, pungent odour.

'Fionnbar said that you would come,' he said quietly, in his strange accent.

'He knew more than I did, then,' I said. 'I'm not sure I would have if he hadn't . . . if he hadn't died,' I finished quickly. Fionnbar's death was too recent to be without hurt.

'Perhaps not immediately, but eventually you would have come,' Enda said, leaning back against the rough wall, most of his face in shadow, and only two red spots from the fire reflecting into his eyes.

'Perhaps,' I said. 'Tell me what you know of the Isle of Promise,' I asked. 'Tell me what you told Fionnbar, and Mernoce before him.'

'There is little enough to tell.'

'Please?'

Enda sighed. 'If I tell you will you go in search of Mernoce's community?'

'Yes,' I said simply.

'Mernoce went; I saw him go out as a young man, hale and well. Perhaps he was too keen, but sane, he was sane when he left here.' Enda leaned forward and the glowing fire touched his face with strange shadows. 'He came back aged and mad! Truly mad, too; dangerously so.' He hesitated and then leaned back. 'Fionnbar visited him and went on to this Isle of Promise. Now he too is dead, and you might say it killed him. Have you considered that this island, this gateway to the Promised Land, might not be all it seems? Could it not be but an illusion, or even a gateway to . . . some darker place?'

'I would still like to know what you told them.'

21

Enda shrugged. When he spoke his voice sounded almost angry. 'I won't tell you what I told them because I believed then that they had a choice, and so I had first Mernoce and later Fionnbar sail to an island to the south and east of here. From there I knew they would be able to see the floating isle, and then if they wished to follow it . . . well, that was their choice.' He looked at me, his hard eyes glittering. 'But you, you're different, your decision is already made; and so I'll tell you where I first sighted this isle.

'I was a mercenary before I took this path. I've little regrets for that life – after all, it led me to this. But I've travelled far, and seen much and heard even more, and perhaps that's why such things as your floating isles don't have the same attraction for me as they seem to do for you and your kind.

'I had heard about such things in my travels; most lands have tales about floating islands, or disappearing mountains, or phantom villages, but I had to come to Erin before I encountered one for myself. I was in the far south when I saw it first. I had been hired by one of the minor kings to train his troops, and make them into something approaching an army. However,' Enda waved a huge white hand, 'it was evening – a bright, clear summer's eve, with the sun low in the horizon, and no clouds in the sky – the sort of evening which seems to linger for far longer than it should. I was walking along the beach, waiting for the evening meal to be prepared, when I saw something moving out in the water. I knew, of course, that there were no islands off the coast – after all, hadn't I walked the self-same beach every day for the past two months?

'But there was an island there. A broad, green-hilled, golden-beached, black-cliffed island. And it was floating through the sea like some craft, but it was smooth, very smooth and it barely caused a ripple in the water.' Enda's voice had become soft and reflective, as he remembered his first encounter with the magical isle. 'The island floated past me, not more than three lengths offshore. I saw creatures on it, creatures I had never seen before, creatures I had never heard of before save in myths and fireside tales. There were birds in the air above it that had never flown over this world; and once, just once, I thought I saw a building, a tall, white-walled building, through the trees.

'And then it was gone, sailing serenely up the coast. I followed it for a while, hurrying after it down the beach, and so I judged its speed to be something just slightly faster than that of a running man. I lost it when it rounded the headland and drifted further out into the sunset.

'That must be close to eight, perhaps ten, years ago. In the years that followed, I heard the Word of God and grew disillusioned with my life as a hireling warrior. I cast my armour and weapons away and became a follower of Christ.

'I came here, seeking peace and solitude. And so it was for a few years; but the fisherfolk began to talk of the "Hermit of Aran", and then the others came, at first singly, then in small groups. Most, like me, came seeking solitude and peace. Others were looking for a leader, someone to shape and order their day. Some left, most stayed.

'About the time the first one arrived, I saw the island again. I was standing on one of the south-facing beaches and I spotted it in the distance, moving steadily northwards. It swung around this island, and then curved off into the ocean. I've seen it many times since, and it always follows the same pattern.' Enda shrugged. 'That's all I know. Mernoce's community lies to the south, and from a hilltop there you can see the isle much more clearly, because it's closer to shore at that point.'

'The island always comes from the same direction and takes the same course?' I asked.

Enda nodded. 'Always, without variation.'

'It's following a course,' I said in excitement.

'It's like a ship with a locked rudder. Forced to sail around and around on the same course.'

'Have you ever tried to work out how long between sightings?' I asked.

Enda smiled, his teeth flashing fiercely in the light of the last glowing embers. 'Of course. There are six months, almost to the day, between sightings; it passes here sometime roughly around midsummer and midwinter.'

'And where does it go then?' I wondered.

'When it sails past here,' Enda continued on in a more

23

serious voice, 'the isle moves out into the Western Ocean, where, apparently, it comes close to a series of islands. Then, however, it swings back south and east along a path that will bring it in off Erin's southern coasts; and thus it begins again.'

'I want to visit that island,' I murmured.

'I would advise against it.'

'I have no choice.'

'Do you want to visit the island or the lands that lie beyond it?' Enda asked.

'The lands beyond,' I said, thinking about it.

Enda nodded. 'The island is a lie, a promise that is never fulfilled; but the lands it passes close to are another prospect altogether.' The huge man paused and considered. 'In all probability they might be the Lands of Paradise.' I could see his dark red-pointed eyes in the light from the embers of the fire as he looked across at me, and then he suddenly stood up. 'If you go there following my directions and you meet with your death – does that make me responsible for that death?' he mused. 'I will pray for guidance, and answer your question either way in the morning.'

And with that he was gone, moving surprisingly quietly for such a large man, and leaving me alone with the now dead fire. I sat back against the rough stone wall and stared up into the heavens. The cloud cover had broken some time earlier and the hard points of stars shone with that peculiar brilliance that is only visible when one is at sea, or at least close to its shores. Jarlath had named those stars for me, and told me their tales. He had pointed those which moved and those which stayed still; those which sparkled and shimmered and those which burned with a hard, solid light. It was he who first taught me how to use those stars as a guide, a chart. Time and many travels had made them familiar and welcome companions.

Far out to sea, one described a thin arc across the heavens and disappeared below the horizon, off the edge of the world. Was it another soul lost to Satan, or the death of an unbaptized child; or, as some of the ancients believed, an omen of ill and foreboding?

I shivered; the night had grown chill and damp. I closed my eyes and bent my head in prayer. Warnings and whispers of doom disrupted my devotions, but I decided, before sleep finally took me, that I would voyage to the west, with or without Enda's help.

Chapter Four

The following morning dawned sharp and clear; but already there was a hint of warmth in the air, and even on this bleak island a promise of midsummer fruitfulness. Looking out over the calm sea and cloudless sky, it was difficult to believe in Enda's mist-shrouded tales.

In the distance I could just about make out the thin green line of the mainland, and my thoughts turned back to Clonfert. Morning prayers would be long finished and the brothers would be out working the thin soil, throwing away the stones and pulling up the weeds, turning wasteland into useful ground. It was simple, hard and repetitive, but such work was a pleasure on a day like this.

And I should be with them.

Did I truly know what I was doing? With scarcely a single day past, I was already sick with longing for the monastery I had built myself – my home. I was no longer young, and although still strong, my strength was not that of a young man. I could end my days with honour and piety amongst my brethren, instead of leading thirteen of them to possible death and damnation in pursuit of a . . . a what?

Footsteps sounded behind me, and I felt Enda's huge hand on my shoulder.

'You know the mountain of Didache?' he began without preamble.

I nodded. It was one of the highest mountains in the south, some said in the whole of Erin.

'At its foot, there is a bay with a fine, long sandy beach. At the head of the bay you will find seven ancient pine trees growing on the cliffs. They are alike – so alike, and their positioning so regular, they they might have been planted there. But they were here before the sons of the Gael came to this land; they are said to be the Seven Guardians of the Land.'

26

I nodded. Every secluded bay and valley had a similar tale attached to it.

'There, on midsummer's eve,' Enda continued, 'the floating island is at its nearest point to the land of Erin. Chase it if you will.'

For a moment I seemed to hear my old master, Jarlath, echoing the warrior-monk's words. 'Chase it if you will.' And suddenly I knew that the open seas and uncharted isles were my true destiny – not piles of stone and tilled fields.

'Thank you Enda, and bless you. We'll set out on the next tide,' I said.

'Nay, stay with us another evening, and tell us how it goes at Clonfert and on the mainland. Even we who have left the world sometimes find pleasure in hearing of those we left behind, and especially of those who are doing the Lord's work in their own way.'

'But it will be midsummer's eve in fourteen days' time,' I protested.

'Yes, but you need not be in quite such a hurry to meet your doom.' He grinned and I caught a glimpse of the fierce old warrior now buried beneath the muscles run to fat. 'Come now, I have given you what you wanted. A night's conversation round the fire is a small price to pay. Had I bargained my information with you for it, you would have agreed. Pay it now for friendship's sake . . . for I do not think we will meet again in this world.'

The words chilled me, and I shivered in the sunlight. Enda spoke with such quiet authority, almost resignation, that I wondered again about this strange once-warrior. He had a quality of natural leadership, a blend of forcefulness and insight, that men respond to and follow without question. He might have gone far in the world, I realized.

As if reading my thoughts, he mused, 'It is strange the things men want. There was a time when I wanted nothing more than glory and coin. You should have seen me then, Brendan, I was a hero, demon, a beserk – a legend.

'But the battles went on and on, and then there came a time when each one began to seem more bloody and less glorious. I lost the joy of killing. I slew and butchered automatically; and

27

that is a terrible thing, and terrifying when you realize it. Even my own brothers in arms grew wary of me – I took more and more risks, almost inviting death, daring it to strike me down. And I suppose secretly wishing it.

'My nights were broken by ghastly dreams, my days invaded by doubts; and doubts are as dangerous to a warrior as to a monk, for they can stay his hand for a fatal moment.

'You've never walked a battlefield, Brendan; and I pray you never will. They stink – they stink of blood and bile, of human waste and vomit, of fear . . . they stink of death. And they are surprisingly peaceful places.

'There was one I remember clearly. The skirmish had been small but particularly bloody, desperate men fighting with the savagery of beasts. I sat down on a low knoll and looked around me. There had been perhaps three score warriors on the field, including my own group of ten professional mercenaries. Now there were only six men living, my own men, and two of those gravely wounded. Not far from me was a head – no body, you understand – just a head. On impulse I reached out with my sword and turned it, and found that it was that of a boy – young, fair-haired, down on his cheeks, a bit like that lad of yours who thinks I eat too much.

'I looked into those dead eyes . . . and found I couldn't even remember what we were being paid to fight for. I asked myself why I should fight for others, when I could use my sword to win lands and wealth and power for myself.

'And then I realized that one day there would be another Enda, another warrior with a bloody sword and a greedy purse. Once I thought things through, it all seemed terribly simple. I took off my sword and shield, and left them beside the boy's severed head. And I walked away.'

'You gave up the sword?' I asked.

He nodded. 'I walked away, because at that moment my life ended, there was nothing I wanted, nothing I needed. Yet it wasn't despair I felt, but the beginnings of peace. And into the void that remained came Christ and the Word of God. This island followed – almost naturally it seemed – and then my brethren.' He shrugged, his face flushed, looking vaguely uncomfortable, as if he had said too much. 'I did learn one truth though, Brendan.' He glanced sidelong at me. 'Desire for something, even holy desire, can trap a man as surely as a snare traps a rabbit.'

I nodded, without saying anything, unwilling to admit the truth in what he said. 'We'll stay with you tonight,' I said eventually, 'but I will fast through your meal, so that I may pray for guidance afterwards.'

'Good enough – and besides,' he added with a sly grin, 'what better place to abstain from food than here? Our fare is unlikely to test you beyond your strength.'

I had resolved to spend that night awake in meditation and prayer, but despite my best efforts, I soon fell into a sound sleep. My dreams were troubled and just before waking I dreamt of an island such as I had never seen, where all the plants bore flowers and all the trees were laden with fruit. The pebbles on the shore were rubies and diamonds and emeralds and other precious stones, and beyond . . . but I could see nothing beyond the beach save a formless shadow.

I awoke with the sun full in my face. Images of the isle danced behind my eyes, and I turned away from the sunlight, trying to recapture the image of the island in my dream. But it was too late; the shadowland had gone, and only the familiar world remained. But it had surely been a sign. I knew then that it was God's will that I find the isle.

I resolved to say nothing to the others. Sometimes it is useful to speak of portents and dreams; but this was too personal, too fragile to be shared. It would keep awhile; and later, if the journey proved so long or fraught with dangers that the men began to lose heart, I would tell them of it. Instead, I shared Enda's information with them, and it was all they needed.

We set off at first tide, and luck seemed to be with us. The weather was holding fair for our return to the mainland, and we made the journey to the mountain of Didache with unusual ease and with the minimum of delays. Even Enda's secluded bay with its seven guardian pines proved less difficult to find than I had anticipated.

I had been half expecting to spend several days in search of the single bay in that land of so many bays and inlets; but the third person we enquired of – a shepherd who was wont to range far with his small flock – recognized my description of the seven ancient trees and gave us clear directions, adding that it would be a fine thing to have some Christian monks settle in the area as the Old Religion was still strong in these isolated parts. He himself had been baptized in the name of Christ, he claimed, but there were few enough like him to be found locally. Not that he had anything against those who followed other ways, he added quickly, glancing all around. Some of those in the Old Religion had wonderful cures, and their prophecies could be uncannily accurate, though seldom of use or interest to simple folk like himself.

As we left the shepherd, I mused at how closely his views mirrored the unspoken attitude of so many people, even those amongst my own brethren. Officially the Druids and their lore – indeed, anything that harked back to the pagan faith – were interdict. But I knew that in practice most people – the brothers included – tended to be less than vigilant. Even the shepherd, for all his loudly proclaimed belief in Christianity, had been careful to lower his voice when he spoke of the old ways, and I noticed how he had kept his left hand out of sight behind his back – no doubt making the ancient Sign of Horns, with fore and little fingers, to ward off evil.

It was at times like these that I wondered, would we ever fully have this land of Erin for Christ? Sometimes it seemed as if we were not uprooting the old beliefs, but merely driving them into seclusion. There were holy wells that I knew had got their saint's name long after they had got their reputation for magical properties. There were images carved on our own high crosses that one would not wish to have examined by one versed in Holy Scripture. I had even heard it whispered that our own Saint Bridget was not in fact baptized in the faith of Christ, but followed a far older and wilder god.

As for cures, well, Jarlath, my teacher and master, had studied the herbal lore with a village woman versed in the old ways, and yet I knew of no man closer to God. Prophecy I believed to be another and far more dangerous matter. Perhaps it was because cures could be effected by the utilization of God's own herbs and plants; but surely if God wished us a glimpse into the future, He would reveal himself to those who sought His guidance in humility and prayer and not through ungodly signs in pagan sacrifices.

At several points as our band marched on, following the shepherd's directions, I had the sensation of being watched, perhaps even followed; but perhaps, I decided, it was just the vague sense of unease I always felt when I thought about the old pagan ways. Christianity was a formal religion, the stuff of Order; the Old Faith was the product of Chaos.

However, when we reached the bay, I forgot about it in the effort and confusion of setting up some crude temporary shelter and gathering wood for our fire. My eyes were drawn compulsively towards the sea, though I knew it was not yet time for the Floating Isle to appear.

Towards evening, however, on my last foray into the surrounding wood, my feelings of unease surfaced again, and once I thought I saw movement. Pretending not to be aware of the vague shape that lurked in the bushes off and to my left, I continued gathering the dead wood, moving closer to the figure all the time. When I was about level with the shadow shape, which had seemed to withdraw into the depths of the bushes as I approached, I pounced. Moving with a swiftness that even surprised myself, I burst through the bushes and grabbed the dim figure. To my amazement, I felt my hands close about cloth that was unmistakably the same as my own habit. Anger – or perhaps fear – lent me strength and I pulled back the deep hood from the figure's head.

'Dermot!' I cried. It was one of the younger members of the order from Clonfert. I knew him only vaguely. He had joined us three years before and had always seemed unusually reticent. 'What in God's Holy Name are you doing here?'

'I – that is, we – followed you,' he said softly, his face downcast with some emotion that I could not recognize.

'We?'

With his head still bent downwards, he put two fingers in his mouth and gave a sharp high whistle that made me wince with its shrillness. There was further noise of movement behind him and two more figures came out from the undergrowth. Dermot looked back at me. 'Eoin, Padraigh and I followed you from the monastery. We knew where you were bound, and we

31

wanted to go with you – but you did not choose us.' He said this almost accusingly.

'This is a serious matter, quite apart from the breach of discipline on your part,' I said harshly. 'I chose my men for many reasons, but mainly because of their talents. If you were not chosen, then perhaps your talents were not suitable for this voyage. I have picked my thirteen men, I need no more – nor will I risk any more lives than are necessary. You will return to Clonfert and, if you wish to aid us, then perhaps you might pray for our safe return.' There was a shout from the beach, a voice calling my name. 'Since now you are here, however, you will share our meal with us. In the morning you will return to Clonfert – and you will say nothing about this place for the moment. Is that understood?' I waited while they each nodded silently in turn.

We returned to the beach, where I explained to my brethren what had occurred. If anything, their anger was even greater than mine; these were men who had given their lives totally to God, and who obeyed the Abbot without hesitation or question. However, the odours of food were fresh on the air, and anger is hard to sustain on rumbling bellies, so we sat down to our meal. All but the three brothers, who shook their heads and remained standing.

'Come, eat,' Niall, the best fisherman amongst us, said. The half score of fine sea-bass now roasting on the spit had been freshly caught by him. 'The food is good and wholesome and you three look as if it has been a few days since you last ate.'

The young men's faces were set with a grim stubbornness, although Eoin's eyes glanced longingly for a moment on the fish. It was Dermot who finally spoke. 'If you will not let us join you, we have resolved to fast . . .'

Niall, whose bulk betrayed his fondness for food, laughed rudely and shook his head.

Dermot glanced at him. 'We have resolved to fast – even unto death. Our one desire is to accompany you in your search for the Blessed Isles, and we will allow nothing to deter us.' The sharp-faced young man looked directly at me. 'If it is your will that we die here on this strand, then so be it; but we will not leave.'

32

I recognized the threat. The brothers fell silent, waiting for my reactions; and suddenly the wind seemed colder, leeching even the heat from the fire. Perhaps if I had been accustomed to reading omens in every event, I might have considered this to be an evil one. I looked at the three men in turn. Dermot was young, and I knew almost nothing of him. Eoin had always seemed a pleasant, rather simple fellow, a hard-working son of poor parents in a small coastal village to the north. Padraigh I had grave reservations about. He was clever, and had been trained as a scribe in another monastery to the east, an abbey grander than Clonfert. I had never fully believed his reasons for abandoning his precious skills to join us in our rough life and work. Although he had been a model community member, diligent and uncomplaining, I always sensed hidden things in him and, God forgive me, I could never manage to like or to trust him. If there had been an instigator amongst these three, it must surely have been him.

'There is one other thing,' Eoin said hesitantly. 'My parents were fisherfolk. Brother Niall knows how to catch a fish with his line from the shore or the banks of the river; but I grew up going out to sea with my father. I know the ways of the sea, and particularly these western waters, and I also know the ways of building a currach and repairing it.' He hesitated a moment and then added diffidently, 'None of you has my skills there.'

The brothers began to talk softly amongst themselves, and I saw heads nodding. I had to admit Eoin could make a persuasive case for remaining amongst us. Geoffrey, the most senior monk next to me, said softly, 'There is worth in what he says. A man with his skills would be an asset, one that we should have considered before we set out. It is an opportunity – a God-given opportunity – to include him in our crew. As for the other two, well, I would sooner not have had their companionship forced upon us in this manner, but I would not care to set sail with their deaths on our conscience, however unwilled that might be.' He glanced at the rest of the men. 'I think the others would be of a similar mind.'

What Geoffrey said was true, but that didn't mean I had to like it. I turned to the three newcomers, and told them they might join our company. I spoke at length to them of the possible dangers and hardships, trying to dissuade them; but I knew as I spoke that they were resolved on their course. I spoke also to the original group who had come with me, saying that as we now had more men that we had planned for, any who had doubts or any change of mind might leave us now without weakening the company or losing face amongst us. Everyone listened with polite attentiveness; but I sensed it was only for form's sake; no one was going to turn back now.

The following morning we set to work constructing the currach. We had brought a plentiful supply of wood, wicker and leather with us, and under Eoin's guidance the shell of the craft was soon assembled. Before we started I had discussed the shape with him, and we had decided that it must be longer than the usual currach, high both fore and aft and with an enclosed space for storing dried provisions and fresh water. It must also be big enough to hold fourteen men – seventeen now – and yet it couldn't be too big.

Once the shell had been assembled, it was covered with supple oak-tanned ox-hides, pinned so that they overlapped, and helped form a waterproof seal. The joints were then sealed with holly resin and on top of this we put another sheathing of leathern hides, and then a third! Then the entire covering was coated with tar to seal any cracks. With God's aid and my will, this craft would be unsinkable.

We worked in shifts through the day and on into the night, racing against time to have the craft completed before the Floating Isle appeared around the headland. Finally, we were ready to test the craft; and none too soon, I thought, for tomorrow would be midsummer's eve. No arms strained more eagerly than mine as we heaved the currach into the shallows. Eight of us scrambled in, while the rest gave a mighty push to launch us from the sharply sloping beach.

All my senses felt sharpened. Even on land, the smell of salt air from the sea was the finest scent in the world to me. Here, with the large craft at last on the water, the breeze was elixir. The choppy swell from the shoreline caused the boat to pitch and roll. Some find this motion upsets their stomachs, but I have always found it as comforting as a babe finds its mother's rocking. The empty horizon was like a lodestar and I wished that we might continue outwards, instead of circling in the shelter of the bay. Such feelings are private to a man, and cannot be readily communicated; but I thought that Eoin beside me was experiencing something similar, for his eyes, like mine, were drawn constantly to the horizon. Thus it was not he, but Conn who cried out, 'We're taking on water.'

At once Eoin left my side and moved aft in the boat. He peered down at the starboard side. I thought I heard him mutter something that I would not have expected a man of God to say, but then he was a man of the world before he took holy orders. In any case, I could not rebuke him, for my own thoughts would not stand too close an examination as I saw the steady trickle of sea water seeping through a seam that should have withstood the pounding water.

Eoin wasted no more time in examination or imprecation. 'Turn back,' he said sharply, 'we'll have to strip this section and re-seal it.'

I groaned. Three layers of hide and still a leak; and so little time.

Eoin glanced across at me. 'It happens often enough,' he said curtly, 'that's why we were testing her today. Would you rather we had discovered this later, with all the men and supplies on board, and perhaps a little further from land? Would you have us swimming after the Floating Island?'

I knew he would not have spoken to me thus had his disappointment not equalled my own. But I could not help pressing him. 'Will it be repaired in time? We must be ready to sail from mid-day onwards tomorrow.'

'If everyone lends a hand, and with God's help, we'll be ready.'

I nodded; if we missed the Isle tomorrow it would be a long wait for it to come around again. And I wondered how I'd feel in half a year or a year's time.

When the craft was beached, and the inner layer of hide peeled back, we saw the problem. A small wooden spar must have splintered earlier on when the craft was under construction and cut through two layers of the stiffened hide; but it wasn't until we had been at sea that it finally punctured the outer skin.

We worked as men possessed. By sunset, as the light became too poor for further labour, Eoin at last pronounced himself satisfied. 'But it will have to be tested on water again in the morning,' he said to me, as we watched the brothers daub another coating of tar on the repaired section.

'Impossible,' I said. 'We'll need the morning for loading provisions and seeing to the sails. If we have to test it, we'll have to do it now.'

'In this light? You'd see nothing until your feet were bathing in water,' he said.

'Then we must trust in God's will that the craft is safe,' I pronounced in a tone that brooked no challenge. 'We cannot sit here for six months if we miss our chance.'

And, oddly enough, there was no sign of discontent at my decision. The men were keyed up, longing for adventure and the unknown, and weary of the tedious preparations which attend such matters.

The change in the weather began as we finished our belated supper. Since we had left Enda on the Arans, it had been fair and mild, with bright moonlight taking over from the long days. Now clouds were sweeping in from the west, obscuring the moon and stars, and carrying with them the promise of rain.

In the morning the sea had changed from blue to a murky grey-green colour, and a mist that was not quite a fog hovered over it. The air felt tart and almost charged, and I sensed in my bones that the time was drawing nigh, and urged on all those with me. Fiachra and Ruarai practically ran back and forth with flasks to a fresh-water stream, half a league distant, while Tadgh and Ultan wrapped dried stores in skins to protect them from the salt spray. I helped see to the sails, checking the cloth one final time to ensure there were no tears or flaws.

All was nearly in readiness, with three more piles of stores to be loaded when Geoffrey cried out in a voice that had something of terror in it. 'Look – there!'

Something was moving massively in the mists to the right of our beach, coming slowly around the headland. It could only be the Floating Isle. From what I could see through the mist, it was larger than I had thought from Enda's description and moving more rapidly than I had expected. 'Everyone, hurry! On board . . . on board now!'

'But the rest of the stores,' one of the men shouted. 'It will take but a moment – and we must have them.'

'Hurry,' I groaned, 'hurry.'

The brothers ran with the remaining stores – the dried fish, the grain, the spare hides and the single cooking cauldron – and thrust them into the currach. Now we attempted to move the boat far enough into the water to float. But with her cargo loaded, she was far heavier than before and precious time was lost as we struggled and pushed. At last a wave caught her and almost ripped her from our grasp. Seventeen of us scrambled in, wet and falling about in our haste, and the currach rolled ominously, threatening to capsize. The men scrambled rapidly into their allotted places, balancing the craft.

As we hoisted the sails, the breeze died, leaving them slack against their ropes. The Floating Isle was moving away from us, in a stately and relentless fashion. I called out for all hands to man the oars, but even as I spoke, the island slipped into the mists and disappeared.

Chapter Five

'Row!' I cried, 'After it!'

We rowed strongly for the rest of the morning, but we did not glimpse the Floating Isle again. The mist had solidified into an opaque wall, and we were now battling against both tide and treacherous cross-currents. Despite the chill of the day, we were clammy with sweat and it was taking all our effort simply to maintain a westward course. I knew that unless a wind blew up, the brothers would soon be exhausted and then the tide would push us back onto the ragged shore. Our voyage would end there and then, even as my original voyage had!

Thoughts slipped unbidden into my head, and for a single instant, I saw the bloodied shambles of my first attempt to seek the Isle of Paradise dance behind my eyes.

I prayed then – old familiar phrases, comforting, reassuring – and the leathern sails creaked. I spun around and wetted a finger, holding it up to confirm what I thought I had felt across the small hairs at the base of my neck. It was a breeze – not strong – but a breeze nonetheless, and one which, if nothing else, would help us maintain our course. 'Hoist the sails!' I shouted.

The brothers pulled on the ropes and stays, hoisting the supple leather squares, and no sight was more welcome than their first tentative cracklings. They flapped; and then, like a man taking a deep breath, the sails billowed out. We tautened the ropes and stays, and only then did the men rest on their oars.

We were on our way.

For fifteen days the wind held fair, and we sailed on, always westerly, working and resting in shifts. Although I had lost hope of seeing the Floating Isle again, everything I had heard or pieced together from remnants of legends told me that our ultimate goal must lie in the west, though it might be further than man had ever sailed before . . . to the very edge of the world, if need be. This didn't frighten me. I have always felt most at peace on the open water, and its vastness never seemed empty or lonely. Looking around at the men I guessed that roughly half of them were of the same temperament; but some of the others were obviously frightened, and in the evenings they spoke of the World's Edge.

One day Conn, our youngest brother, and who hailed from Erin's wild northern mountains, finally gave voice to the imaginings of some of the less experienced sailors. It was about noon and, although the sun was high overhead, the air was still opaque with the ever present mist. Brother Eoin had just passed out the mid-day rations and I was about to give the blessing, when Conn spoke.

'Father Abbot, how far west can we sail before we come to the edge of the world? And if we reach it, will we be able to stop ourselves falling off? What of the huge whirlpool that sucks everything over the edge? And what about the monsters that swim the sea. . .?' His voice was becoming high; but Eoin gripped his trembling shoulders, and his hard fingers bit into the younger man's muscles. I saw Conn's face tighten in pain and shock, but his frantic questions stopped.

Some of the brothers laughed, but there was a touch too much of nervousness in their smiles for my liking. I've seen fear sweep through even a sea-hardened crew, reducing them to blubbering wrecks in a matter of days. And all it needed was for Conn's questions to stand unanswered, or for the slightest hesitation on my part.

'I don't believe there is an edge to the world,' I said quietly, but firmly. 'No one, not even the fierce warrior-sailors from the northern icelands, have yet reached the edge of the world, and they have sailed further than any other men. Even if we had the strength and provisions to venture in search of it – which we do not – God would not allow us to stray so far from our true goal . . .'

'How do we know that God watches over these waters?' one of the men asked.

This time I allowed some of my own frustration and anger to

come to the surface. 'Because this is God's world, and we are the followers of God. He watches us!'

In the silence that followed, Conn said, very softly, almost to himself, 'But the sea just goes on and on and on . . .'

I sat down on the deck beside him and looked into his dark, stone-coloured eyes. 'Have you never stood on the shore and watched the sea-birds come winging in when evening falls? And have you ever wondered where they have come from? There is land out there; there are many lands and islands between us and the world's end.'

'But are you really certain of that?' Conn asked anxiously.

I nodded. 'I am certain of it. I would not have undertaken this voyage if I was not sure.'

'But no one has ever come from the west.'

'The Tuatha De Danann came from lands to the west of Erin,' I said, remembering some of my lore.

'Aye, and they were demon-folk.'

'But they came from a land,' I persisted. 'There are islands there, and one of them is the Isle of Paradise. Don't worry about going too far, but rather that we shall not go far enough.' I looked up, and saw the men nodding, and I knew that I had succeeded – this time. 'And now, let's row; that wind seems to be dropping.'

And even as I spoke the wind died, leaving us becalmed on a flat, leaden sea, beneath a hidden sky.

So they rowed steadily and evenly for the remainder of the day, with either Eoin or myself dictating the beat. It was impossible to guess if we made any headway in the shifting fog, but it kept the men occupied. The beat was enough to tire them out, and the evening meal was a quiet, contemplative affair, with each man eating his hard bread and salted meat and keeping to himself. I had them sleep in shifts, so as not to drift off course and lose whatever bit of forward progress we had made during the day.

And so it continued.

But after a week of this, the regimen was taking its toll, particularly on some of the youngest monks, who were not accustomed to the rigours of the open sea. More seriously, the increased physical effort was making for increased appetite, and our stores were beginning to dwindle at an alarming rate. We rowed and we starved, or we hoisted the sails and ate for a few more days. Such was my choice. As the days wore on, the choice became harder – and it was even more imperative that it be made.

Eventually, after a half-night's vigil, I commanded the brothers to rest on their oars, and ordered the sails raised, although there was barely enough breeze to ruffle them.

'But Brendan,' Eoin protested, 'what's the point? There's little enough wind as it is; we shall drift.'

'Then drift we must, for we cannot go on as we are. Trust in God's will. He shall set our course for us, and carry us safely to our destination if we abandon ourself to His divine mercy and judgement.'

If any thought me foolish or mad, they did not say. Perhaps they were too weary. More likely it was a phenomenon I have seen before at sea. The endless horizon, empty even of sea-birds after one has moved far from land, exerts a strange influence of its own. Human perceptions and preoccupations become diminished and a curious resignation and acceptance of the discomfort sets in. The world shrinks, diminishes, until it is nothing more than the boat, and one's body becomes attuned to every slight motion of it. On a calm sea, as this was, the boat is like a giant rocking cradle, lulling one into a submissive peace. I am never surprised when a sailor abandons the world for a life of contemplation in some remote area, nor by how easily they are often won to the Word of Christ. The lives of a monk and a mariner are often similar in their loneliness.

So we continued on until we were forty days from the bay of Didache by my reckoning. We had drifted far too much for me to have any certain notion of our course; but by the stars I knew that we had made some northerly and westerly progress. Unfortunately our stores, which had taken so long to load and which had – as is always the case – looked so inexhaustible, had now almost run out. Following this evening's meal I judged there would be neither food nor fresh water left.

I had not made a point of telling the brothers; but nor had I hidden it from them, and their worried expressions as they watched Eoin doling the rations out told me that they knew. The meals of the past few days had gradually been getting smaller, as I had attempted to preserve what little we had for as long as possible. I saw the men eating slowly and carefully, making every crumb of hard bread last, and methodically chewing their salt meat until their jaws must ache.

I dozed fitfully around mid-day, trying to concentrate on less worldly matters than the aching void in the pit of my stomach. I had fasted before – often for extended periods of time – but perhaps the realization that there was food for me when I had finished my fast made it more acceptable. This time, I knew there was nothing.

I had been staring out to sea in this state for a time before I finally recognized what I was seeing. That smudge on the horizon, that strange too-solid cloud, looked like . . .

An island!

Common sense took over then, and I forced myself to sit still, counting the ever increasing beats of my heart while the shape of the horizon grew nearer and larger. At last I knew it was no shadow-shape, and I bowed my head and gave silent thanks.

I nudged Martyn, who was sitting on my right-hand side, and Tadgh, who was just behind me, tying intricate knots in a length of hempen rope in the idle way that men at sea have. Silently I nodded towards the island to determine if they too could see it. Tadgh looked back at me in a puzzled fashion, as if he could not comprehend what he was seeing; but Martyn tensed with excitement and blurted aloud, 'Land!'

For a moment there was only silence as Martyn's words sunk in, and then there were muffled cheers and murmurs of thanksgiving. The men scrambled to the oars; and then, as if summoned, a light breeze sprang up, half-filling our sails and pushing us towards the island.

However, as the time passed and we neared the island, our joy became muted as it drifted out of the mist and the details came clearer. This was no welcoming green land with sheltering bays and coves; at closer range it looked awesome and terrible, a wall of rock rising from the sea. High cliffs, pounded ceaselessly by the waves, led the eyes upwards to dizzy heights. Even the towering Cliffs of Moher in our own land would be dwarfed by these tremendous walls of rock.

I was standing in the prow, staring up at the menacing black cliffs, when I felt someone beside me. 'We'll find no harbour here,' Eoin said quietly, his experienced eyes taking in the shoreline.

I nodded. 'And yet we have to land.'

The young monk pointed off to our starboard bow. 'There's a current there; it sweeps around that headland. If we manoeuvre ourselves into it, it will carry us around the island.'

I nodded again. We had no other choice.

However, no sooner had we settled into the shoreline current than the mist came down again and our first circumnavigation had to be abandoned for fear of ripping the hull from our craft on a submerged rock or reef. So we dropped anchor and, with rumbling bellies and muttered prayers, we vainly tried to settle ourselves for sleep.

The following morning brought us nothing but renewed pangs of gnawing hunger; and now thirst was becoming a problem. The fog was still with us, although it had lifted somewhat. More to keep the crew occupied than anything else, I had Eoin call a half beat and, with two of the brothers probing the way ahead of us with oars, we crept around the island.

I guessed we were about halfway around the isle, when I thought I could make out a small cove on what I judged to be the south-east side. I ordered the anchor dropped; but the current, now pushing our craft outward from the shore, was far stronger than the light wind blowing landward. The brothers struggled as best they could, but they were weakened by the meagre rations. Slowly but surely, we lost headway and were swept back out to sea.

'What now, Brendan?' Ultan asked me.

I thought for a moment. The island was perhaps three or four miles long and half again as wide. And we knew now that at least in one spot on its ragged shore there was a place where a currach could land, given a fair wind and a calm sea. In any case, we had nowhere else to go; we would land on this forbidding piece of rock or die in the waters surrounding it. However, seeing Ultan's broad face creased with worry, I decided it would be better to voice my thoughts in more positive terms.

'We must circle the island for three days without eating and drinking, and only then shall we find an entry. Only the pure can land on this isle,' I announced with more conviction than I felt. Yet not all of my assurance was for the others' sake. The time span had sprung unbidden into my mind, as had the realization that something – perhaps within ourselves – was preventing us from landing.

Nor did my belief grow less, though our hunger and thirst increased hourly during the next two days. As we grew weaker, so too did the mist thin and the sea grew calmer. We could circle the island more closely now, and with the almost clear sky we began to make out every detail of those immense cliffs.

But the brothers became restless. On the night of the second day, with the sky clear enough to make out the hard points of the stars, I heard a soft movement behind me and, turning my head slightly, I saw Fiachra, one of the younger monks, reaching over the side of the craft with something in his hand. With a speed that surprised me, my hand shot out, striking him across the side of the head. He threw up his hands to defend himself – and a small leather flask fell into the boat. Sea water trickled into the bottom of the boat, and pooled about our feet.

'Do you want to kill yourself before we land tomorrow?' I asked quietly, hoping not to waken the others, although I could sense that there were very few of us sleeping that night. 'The water will only serve to madden your thirst, so that what you feel now will be as nothing in comparison to what you will feel after. When you have vomited whatever remains in your stomach, your throat will begin to burn, and your tongue will swell. You will need more water . . .' I took a deep breath, attempting to calm myself. 'I have seen sea water kill too many men that way, and it is not a pleasant death. If you have no faith in my words, then at least keep your faith in God, who will guide you safely to shore in the morning.'

Fiachra only looked at me with his deep dark eyes, and then he turned away without saying anything.

I did not sleep again that night, for fear of what might

happen. I knew from experience that what one might do so might another. But the remainder of the short night passed without incident, and I was never so glad to see the sky paling towards the dawn.

The day dawned bright and clear. Now the mist had almost totally dissipated, with only the barest covering drifting across the oily waters. The brothers took to their oars with something almost approaching eagerness and once again we made to circle the island. Despite my sleepless night, I was not tired and I kept my gaze fixed firmly on the cliffs as I called a single beat and the oars rose and dipped and rose again.

We struck an inshore current almost immediately, and it swept us around the isle onto the sunlit eastward side. Then, suddenly, I saw a cleft ahead in the cliff face and a narrow strip of rocky beach.

'Bring her into the island,' I called back to Eoin, who had the rudder-oar. 'See, there,' I shouted to the brothers, 'a landing, even as I promised you.'

Before us was a narrow inlet, and within it a small rough beach. The channel was narrow, and it would need great care; but the water was calm and we had a fair wind behind us. We dropped one of the sails, and then another, as we slipped further and further into the inlet. As the cliffs closed on us we shipped the oars, and now the single remaining sail stretched taut in the breeze. Slowly, cautiously, Eoin steered us along the inlet, until we were in a narrow and shallow channel. The cliffs now rose sharply on either side of us, so high as to shade us from the morning sun. I shivered in the chill. Suddenly I felt the bottom of the currach scrape against a submerged rock, but our slow speed and shallow keel allowed her to pass on without it tearing through the stiffened hides . . . There was another terrifying – but mercifully harmless – scrape, and we ground to a halt.

We piled into the water and dragged the currach onto the beach. Those of us who had only recently found their sea legs, now found that they were weak and uncertain again. This was the first time we had stood on dry – or almost dry – land for over forty days. Once our craft was safe the brothers fell to their knees in the sand and I led them in a short prayer of thanks.

I was even more thankful when I saw a rough path leading from the sea cliffs, suggesting that the island was inhabited. I'd had no doubt of finding a fresh-water stream inland, but food was another matter. Under normal conditions, we could fish by day and perhaps snare rabbits by night, but the length of the voyage, the short rations and finally the enforced fast had taken their toll of our strength. In any case, this strange sea did not seem to have any fish life in it; so perhaps we would not find any animals living on the isle.

I was about to move forward and begin the ascent up the rocky beach, when a gigantic wolf-hound appeared at the head of the track. It paused for a single moment, almost as if it were surprised to see someone on the island, and then it bounded towards us at great speed. It stopped abruptly some ten paces away from me, with bristling fur and exposed fangs.

Beside me, Fiachra bent down and picked up a rock from the beach. He raised his arm to throw it, but I ordered him to drop it. The huge grey beast before us would not be deterred by a single stone; indeed I doubted it would be deterred if all of us hurled stones and rocks at it at the same time.

With a silent prayer I took a step forward. The wolf-hound moved a pace towards me. Then we took another pace forward, the dog and I in turn. Then another, until his fierce golden brown eyes met mine. I realized then just how large the dog was; indeed, I had seen smaller horses. It took all my self-control to stand still while he sniffed tentatively at my sodden and salty robes. Then, with a curious low noise at the back of his throat he lay down in front of me. I felt something warm, wet and rasping across my instep and realized that the dog was licking my foot. I bent down and ran my fingers through the animal's coarse hair, scratching behind his pointed, twitching ears. 'This animal looks better fed then we are,' I said over my shoulder. 'I don't think he wants Christians for his supper.'

There was a murmur of relieved laughter behind me, and the thought struck me that it had been forty and more days since I had last heard laughter. The dog rose once again, and began to move up the beach along the worn track. He stopped every ten paces or so and looked back at me.

The message was clear. We were to follow. I shrugged; there was little else to do in any case, so I set off after the huge dog. Had anyone been watching, we would have made a curious sight: a giant wolf-hound in the lead with seventeen tired, hungry and bedraggled monks trailing along behind in single file.

The journey up the beach seemed endless; but by the sun's reckoning it was no more than an hour before we came upon an immense stone building set in a slight hollow in the centre of the isle. The building was smooth and round, and its stones had been smoothed, polished and fitted together with an extraordinary degree of skill. There seemed to be no windows and only one entrance, and this was gaping wide. The dog sat down by the side of the open door, which was twice a man's height and half again as wide. The doors had been carved from a strange, pale-gold wood, and adorned with intricate carving in patterns and symbols that were almost familiar, although I could not place them.

I paused by the door before stepping inside. Before me was a vast hall, seemingly empty. A huge log fire burned at the far end, although we had seen no trees on the isle and there was no one in sight who might have laid it. More puzzling still was the long table that ran the length of the hall, which was set with places to the exact number of our company. Large tureens of steaming soup, platters of bread still smoking hot from the oven and plates of fish were ranged down the centre. There were bowls set out for us down either side, and these were not rough wooden ones, but smooth and carefully worked silver metal inset with precious and semi-precious stones. Along the side of the room was a trough of water for washing; and fresh linen had been set at each place at the table, rolled up and neatly held by silver rings. Each ring was decorated with tracery similar to that which adorned the door, and which I dimly remembered having seen on some of the ancient Celtic standing stones and dolmens.

'Is all this meant for us?' The voice had risen to a high-pitched whisper. It was Conn, his eyes huge as he stared at the table.

'It is set for our numbers; I think it must be – the food and drink, I mean. The precious stones and metal which surround it are not for men who have taken the vow of poverty.' I fell silent, abruptly realizing how foolish I sounded.

We washed our hands and feet, then assembled at the table. I stood at one end and gave the blessing. But before I sat down, I added. 'Eat and drink your fill, but do not take anything that is not given. We landed on this isle in a state of purity; we must do nothing to sully that.' The brothers nodded and looked so solemn that I had to laugh. 'Let's eat!'

No food had ever tasted so good to me as did that first meal in the great hall of the island we would eventually call the Isle of Purity. Yet my mind was troubled. For now that my belly was full and my eyes had adjusted to the dimmer light within the place, I could see evidence of great wealth and artistry all about. Ornaments hung on the walls, as did beautifully wrought vessels, bridles made of silver, carved hunting horns and other objects I could not easily identify. The workmanship was magnificent; the style, barbaric. And there was no evidence anywhere of Christian symbolism.

'That's the best meal I've had since I left my mother's table,' young Conn said, sitting back, and folding his hands across his stomach in contentment.

'I'll pass on your remarks to Brother Donal when we return to Clonfert,' Geoffrey said drily.

Conn blushed. 'I didn't mean it that way. The food at Clonfert is fine; it's just that . . well . . .'

Padraigh came to his rescue. 'I think I ate too quickly to taste the food before it went down, I was so hungry.' His long thin hands indicated the hall. 'What fascinates me is the craftsmanship here. Not just the stonework and wall ornaments – look at these rings for napery; see how delicate the lines are.' He looked from Geoffrey to me. 'I wonder if there's any sort of library or even a scriptorium here? The hand that produced this tracery could as readily grace a manuscript.'

'Why go looking for treasures when you're surrounded by them?' Dermot interrupted him bluntly.

I looked around again. There was indeed a king's ransom here. No monk should lust for material possessions, and by and large there is little to tempt him. His life and needs are simple. But here were riches such as few of us would have seen or would be ever likely to see again. We were monks, but we were men first, and I knew that, without vigilance, greed might enter someone's heart. When all had finished their meal I once again cautioned against taking anything except that which was obviously offered freely to us.

Having said this, I went through a doorway to the right of the fireplace. It was as if the Lord were guiding me, for there I found a chamber set with beds for each of us, soft and inviting. I chose one at random, saw the rest settle into some of the others and fell into a deep and dreamless sleep.

The next morning I decided that as we had spent three days sailing around the island, we would spend three days on it. Apart from satisfying an odd instinct within me, it would give us time to rest and recover our strength before the next leg of the journey. There were minor repairs we could do to the currach, and it would give us time to lay in a store of whatever food this strange isle afforded. I did not question what strange persons or powers moved unseen to provide us with food and shelter, nor did I want to question it. I have lived too long and seen too much not to realize that once you start questioning something like that, the answers may not be all that you wish for.

On the third and final night in the great house, my sleep was troubled by strange and terrible dreams. The dream was unnaturally sharp and detailed and in it, one of my brethren – I could not see his face – lay prostrate before me, dying. As I gave him the Last Rites, his robe began to ripple and shift as something unseen moved beneath it. There was a sudden rending sound, and then a demon burst forth from his chest, and the stench of corruption was everywhere. The hideous dog-like creature turned to look at me, and it was familiar . . . I woke up sweating and afraid, with the foul odour seeming to linger in my nostrils.

As we performed our morning office and partook of a breakfast of fine white bread and honey, everything seemed in order. My companions were by now eager to set sail again – proper sleep and full stomachs are an aid to an adventurous spirit, I have learned.

We made ready to leave after tidying as best we could the rooms where we had rested and dined. I waited by the entrance and stopped each man as he stepped out into the pale morning sunlight. Watching their reactions carefully, I warned them for a third – and final – time that they must leave with what they came in with.

'Each of you must ensure that you are not leaving with anything belonging to this place. Whoever dwells here has given freely to us, and we must not dishonour that hospitality by theft or even by carelessness.'

One by one they passed before me, and with each one I breathed a sign of relief. Soon, only one remained, and that was Dermot, who had been so resolved to join the voyage. He smiled briefly at me, said, 'I've taken nothing, Father,' and stepped out into the morning. And it was as if he had stepped into a wall. He stopped and blood burst from his ears, nose and mouth. He fell to the ground gagging and clutching his chest.

'What have you done?' I cried.

Although he was writhing in agony, he held out his hand and there on his thumb was one of the silver rings which had held the linen cloths at our places at table. He stretched his hand towards me, but even as I watched, I saw the flesh darken about the silver ring, and then it smoked and began to burn from within. I saw the pale bone appear, and then it too darkened as it burnt. The ring fell to the ground and shattered into two irregular pieces.

The dying monk raised his head, and his eyes – now shot through with red – caught and held mine. 'It was so beautiful,' he whispered hoarsely. And then he slumped back onto the ground.

I knelt over him, and bent to catch his words.

'The craftsmanship . . . so beautiful . . . in all my life . . . couldn't leave it behind . . . forgive me, Brendan.'

I could no longer understand him as he tried to force a few more words out, but I hoped they were murmurings of contrition and repentance. I prayed that it was only my dream-laden imagining that saw a faint wisp of black smoke drifting up from his mouth and nostrils as he died. Certainly no one else noticed it, and we gave him a Christian burial on that nameless isle.

It was a sombre group of men who followed the large dog down the sea-cliffs to the beach. As we approached the currach, we saw a youth standing beside it.

I motioned the others back and approached the youth alone. He was young and slender, almost unnaturally so. His pale hair was a strange, gleaming grey colour, and his complexion seemed to have a silvery hue. His features were sharp and angular, with eyes that were slightly uptilted and a chin which came to a definite point. When he smiled I noticed that his teeth were overly long. His clothes were made from soft fine fabric such as I have never seen, and when he spoke, his voice was light and musical. The accent was unknown to me.

'These are for your journey,' he said, handing me a parcel of bread and a large flagon of water. 'Take care that you leave a bit of the loaf and a few drops of liquid after each meal, and you shall never run out of food or drink again.'

He smiled distantly, bowed and then uttered a low call to the wolf-hound, and I watched as the boy and his dog disappeared up the pathway.

And so we returned to the sea.

Chapter Six

We sailed on into the west and, although we were only forty and more days from Erin's rocky coast, everything had changed.

Physically, we were stronger. Uncounted hours of rowing had strengthened our shoulders and arms beyond recognition. Although we had been used to hard physical work, and our hands had borne the scars and weals of that work, no gardener – however diligent – could boast layers of callouses such as our palms displayed from rope burn and salt water.

But despite the strength we had gained in our arms, our legs, through cramp and lack of exercise, now seemed almost pitifully weak. I knew that unless we managed to exercise regularly, we might have serious problems when we reached land again. Eoin and I therefore worked out a system whereby the men changed places frequently in the craft, and moved about as much as the crowded conditions and the motion of the sea permitted.

There were also certain other advantages to this system. Monks are accounted holy by the laity, but it is as well to remember that renouncing the world does not convey automatic sainthood. I had been less than honest with Nevin back at Clonfert when we had been choosing the crew. Perhaps I had resented his opinions and decisions, especially since he had seen nothing but tilled fields and stone buildings since he had entered the monastery. Or perhaps I really had forgotten the pressures that a long voyage inevitably brings. Now I was forced to face them again. Gather together any group of men in too confined a space for too long a time and both friendships and enmities will be exaggerated out of all reason. It is a slow and insidious process, which comes to a head and then may erupt in violent and even bloody quarrels. I've seen it destroy a good crew more surely than a storm. By the time we had reached the rocky isle, three of my brethren were almost openly hostile to each other, while Dunan and Liber were developing a disturbing intimacy. One becomes accustomed to such things on board ship; but such passions breed anger and resentment, and that I couldn't allow.

So I set the men to working, at simple repetitive tasks; and, although not entirely useful, it kept them occupied. As the time passed, they began to take a certain pride in their work; and this, in a certain curious way, seemed to draw them together again, so that they were at once more united as a group and yet more separate and at peace in themselves. As the evenings drew in and grew grey and chill, I prompted Crosan to tell us stories. Some were light fables or riddles, such as he must have told when he entertained at court. Others were eerie, even dark tales from times lost to us, in that age before the Word of Christ came to Erin, when the Tuatha De Danann sailed in their ships of metal from their cities of stone in the wild Western Ocean to walk the land that they would call Banba.

As the atmosphere eased, I found myself more often drawn into conversations with my brethren. I suspect too that I seemed more approachable to the younger monks, and this, in turn, was giving me the opportunity to get to know them better. I had forgotten at Clonfert how remote, even awesome, an elderly abbot can seem to the newly professed. And I resolved then that if God spared me and allowed me to found another monastery – perhaps close to the spot where we had set off on this voyage – I would ensure that the abbot would set aside a certain part of the day to spend with the novices.

I was standing in the prow of the craft when this thought struck me, and I smiled; there were far too many 'ifs' for an old man.

'What's so funny?' Eoin asked, coming up behind me. The days spent at sea had agreed well with the young monk, bleaching his hair and darkening his already tanned skin.

I shook my head slowly. 'Nothing, just dreaming.'

'Have you any idea where we're bound now?' he asked then, lowering his voice.

'West-south-west,' I replied.

Eoin grinned. 'I thought you'd say that. But I can look at the sun and hold a wet finger to the wind as easily as you. You know what I mean; have you any knowledge beyond our immediate course?'

'No.' I pitched my voice lower, for Eoin's ears alone. 'But for four days the wind has held strong in the same direction. I don't think it will be long before we make landfall again.'

He grunted agreement. There was no real pressure on us now except our own longings. As warned, we were careful to leave something of the food and drink given to us by the silver-skinned youth and, as promised, the loaves were always whole in the morning and the flasks full. There must have been some herbal or health-giving property in our rations as well, for our gums no longer bled as they had after every meal towards the end of our initial voyaging.

'So what do we do?' he asked finally.

'We sail on.'

The next morning, shortly after dawn, we saw a small island on the horizon. This time there was no need to man the oars, for the wind was taking us dead on course towards it. As we sailed closer I could see no sign of building or habitation of any sort on the rocky land; but, curiously, the top of the island's only hill seemed to be covered in white. Snow at the end of summer? I looked even closer and saw that the snow seemed to be shifting. I was going to say nothing to my less far-sighted companions, lest they think that my age was taking its toll on my mind; but, one by one, the monks remarked on it.

As we moved to within perhaps a quarter-mile offshore, the wind gently subsided. But the tide had us now, and before us was a wide strand which offered one of the simplest beachings I have ever chanced upon. There was even no need to use the oars, and the tide pushed us up into the shallows.

Our spirits rose as we dragged the currach ashore, for we could now see that what I had first taken to be snow was no more than a dense flock of sheep; and where there were sheep there needs must be a shepherd. An islandman would certainly have some information regarding our present position and perhaps a night's shelter.

As I trudged up the beach, with the brothers behind me, I

heard Conn murmur, 'Roast mutton' in a hopeful manner to Barran.

'It's a Friday,' Barran said shortly. 'A fast day.'

'We've had a year's worth of fast days already,' Conn said with a grin.

We continued up the gently sloping beach. Low sand dunes rose up before us, and beyond these was an irregular grassy plain dotted with stones. We were still moving cautiously, adjusting once again to having land underfoot, when there was a sudden movement off to one side, and an elderly man with a shepherd's staff rose up from behind a boulder and approached us.

My first impression was of age – great age – although I could not say why. Certainly it was not evident in his erect bearing, nor in his hair, which, though white, was thick upon his head, while his face was curiously unlined. Perhaps it was his eyes; they were an intense, unclouded blue against his tanned skin, and seemed incredibly knowing. Whatever the reason, I knew that he was old, far older than I.

'Welcome, strangers to my island.' His voice was firm but slow paced, as if he were unused to speech.

I bowed slightly and was about to speak when Dunan burst out discourteously, 'Where are we?'

'Is it not obvious?' the old man asked. 'This is the Isle of Sheep. I am Erc, and I tend the flock.'

'You tend them well,' I commented, looking around. A few sheep had wandered down the hill towards us, and I thought that I had never seen any so large or so obviously healthy. 'Are there any other men living on this island?'

Erc shook his head slowly. 'Not now. Once in a while a boat chances upon here, like yourselves. What manner of voyagers are you, if I may ask, and where are you bound?'

'We are Christian monks from the abbey of Clonfert in the land of Erin,' I replied formally, 'and we are sailing in search of the Isle of Paradise.'

'I was a sailor once myself, though not such a holy one.' He smiled. 'Our boat met with a fierce storm and capsized near here. Those of us who could swam to shore. But come, you must hunger and thirst after such a long voyage; I will take you

55

to my dwelling. It is too small to contain all of you, but there are cheeses and milk there, and we may eat together outside. It has been a long time since I have had anyone to talk to; you can tell me more of yourselves and I will tell you something of myself and my island.'

Erc's hut was cunningly built from stones similar to those that were scattered in the surrounding fields, with a low sprawling shape that would blend into the terrain to a distant eye. Though not spacious enough for our company, it was large enough for a solitary man, and one entire chamber to the back of the building was given over to stores of cheeses and dried seaweeds and other herbs I could not identify. He bustled about, gathering up huge wheels of cheese, and although my crew and I were no longer accustomed to food at mid-day, to refuse his hospitality would have been churlish.

So we sat in the sun, with our backs to the warm stones, eating his ripe, pungent cheeses, and smelling the tart odours of burning seaweed mingling with the salt of the sea. For the first time in many days, I felt the tight muscles across my shoulders and back loosen and relax. As we ate, I told him of our journey and experiences, leaving out only the sorry tale of Dermot's death. Finally, I enquired if he knew the sea and islands hereabout, and could perhaps direct us.

'No, not really,' he answered finally. 'But the shepherd who was here before me told of an island called the Bird's Paradise which is some three days' sailing to the west of here. I think it must be on your course, and perhaps you might find directions onwards from there.'

I looked into the sky, gauging the time and tide; but Erc caught my look and continued, 'If you will stay the night with me, I will point you on your way with the morning tide.'

I nodded; it would be pleasant to spend a little time on dry land again. I looked around. Some three hundred yards away from Erc's rude dwelling, I saw a strongly built and obviously ancient stone well and asked if we might draw some fresh water to drink and bathe with.

'No,' Erc said sharply. 'I will take you to a stream of pure fresh water, where you may drink and bathe to your heart's content. But do not touch the water from the well.'

'Is it poisoned?' Fiachra asked, twisting around and looked across at the well. 'Why do you not board it over?'

But Erc stood up without answering, and motioned for us to follow him. As promised, he led us to a lovely, rippling fresh-water stream that bubbled up from the earth and ran, twisting and curling along the ground, for a short distance before sinking back into the earth again. Without ceremony, I sat down at the edge, removed my sandals and let the water run over my salt-encrusted toes. The sun was warm on my back and the stream cool on my feet – it felt good to be alive, and the others were not long in following my rather undignified example.

After we had disported ourselves in a manner not wholly suited to monks, paddling like children, we washed ourselves, wiping away the second skin of irritating encrusted salt, then made our way back to the shepherd's dwelling. This time I noted that amongst the rough stones randomly distributed in a field to the rear of the hut there was a small cleared area with a larger stone at one end. I walked over and examined it more closely. It was obviously a grave marker. Less obvious was a shallowly cut cross in the stone.

Erc came over beside me. 'The shepherd that tended the flock before me lies here. I buried him myself, and this was the best I could do for a tomb.'

'You are a Christian, then?' I asked curiously.

'I am now. The old shepherd converted me. When I arrived, I and my fellow sailors were all pagans. He read to us from the Gospels and told us of everlasting life through Christ, but I was the only one to heed him. The others were all too interested in the well and all that it offered.'

'And just what properties does this well have?' I asked, looking over at it. 'We have some in our own land whose waters are said to remove warts or heal disorders of the chest or stomach,' I added.

Erc strolled off towards a few sheep, as if he had not heard me. Perhaps there was a touch of the storyteller in him and he wanted to save the most interesting tale for last, I decided. In any case, I was sure that he would reveal no more than he wished to at any time, so I turned my thoughts from the mystery of the well and looked with interest at his sheep instead.

What a difference lush green grass for which neither man or other animals competed had made in his flock. Our poor sheep at Clonfert, constantly moving, constantly vying for food, would be as lambs compared to these huge specimens. Each would yield twice as much wool or meat as two or three of ours. Yet there was something odd about the flock which seemed to be tugging at the back of my mind. Experimentally, I approached a ram who stood placidly chewing his cud. He did not shy away as sheep almost invariably do, nor did he challenge me as rams occasionally will. I reached out and thrust my fingers into his thick fleece, and then scratched him behind the ears, as if he were a dog.

'They're very docile and tame animals you have,' I said to Erc.

'Aye, they are now. But then they know there's nothing can harm them.'

'Except you.'

'Not even I. They provide me with milk and fleece in season, but I do not eat their flesh,' Erc said shortly.

I was startled. How, I wondered did he keep the sheep from multiplying at a rate that would at last exhaust the island's meagre resources? I looked around, something glimmering at the back of my mind . . . and then I realized what it was that had seemed strange to me: wherever I looked, there were only fully grown animals. I would not have expected lambs this late in the summer, but there should have been half-weaned hoggets near the ewes.

'How many sheep do you have?' I asked.

'One hundred and twenty-nine.'

'How many did you have last year?' I persisted.

'One hundred and twenty-nine.'

'Is this some property of the water from your well?' I asked, trying to keep the disgust from my voice. Suddenly his sheep ceased to look large and handsome, but fat and sterile instead.

Erc smiled strangely. 'In a way you might say it is; but do not rush to judge matters you do not yet understand. Let us return; the night will soon be drawing in. We will eat and I will answer your questions as far as I can.'

In the clearing before his dwelling, Erc joined the monks, who were busy assembling a fire. The evenings had turned cool now, and even if Eoin and Ultan failed in their efforts to catch fish to cook on it, it would be pleasant to sleep around a blazing fire once again.

I stood back and watched the men, and looked at Erc moving amongst them; and I found myself wondering what sort of threat he presented. One part of my mind seemed to whisper, 'Leave, leave at once, there is danger here . . .', while the reasoning part told me that we were sixteen in number and Erc was but one. Moreover, I wanted his directions and the right tide to press on to the Isle of the Bird's Paradise.

My companions, by contrast, seemed well content. Some of them must have harboured secret fears that we would spend another period as long as the first on the open sea; to have made land again so easily and so soon was a comfort, and something to make the most of.

As it turned out the fishermen were unlucky, and once again we had Erc's cheeses to supplement our bread, and also an unfamiliar but pleasantly fermented brew provided by him, of which I was careful to partake but lightly.

In the end, it was not I, but Dunan, who broke into the general conversation to ask, 'Now, tell us, Erc, is the well poisoned?'

'It is just the opposite,' he answered in his slow way. 'Those who drink from it can never die. Its gift – or its curse – is immortality.'

In the silence that followed, Fiachra's voice sounded very loud. 'How can you call that a curse?' he asked. 'What man has not hoped in his heart that he would live forever?'

'Before I came here, when I too was a sailor, I met a man – a Greek, I think – and a pagan of course, but a wise man in his way. He told me a saying of his people, that when the gods are very angry with us, they answer our prayers. I remembered his words when the shepherd who was here before me told me of the well.' He paused and looked broodingly into the fire. None of us dared interrupt his thoughts, and finally he continued, 'You are Christians, and you know that when mortal life ends,

59

then there is eternal life through the True Religion. For us, such a thing as the well is an abomination.' He paused and added, 'Fifteen of us were shipwrecked on this island, and I was the only one who did not drink from the well.'

'And the others?' Dunan asked. 'Did they really become immortal?'

'Yes.'

'But how do you know? Where are they now? They are gone from you. They could all be dead and it could just be a story the old shepherd told you,' Fiachra said.

'Afterwards,' Erc said heavily, 'I saw one try to kill himself, in wild regret at what he had done. It was impossible. You see that ledge up there on the hill?'

In the dying light we could just make out a shelf of rock protruding from near the top of the hill on its steeper side. It was perhaps three hundred feet above a rocky stretch of the beach.

Erc continued. 'Twice I saw him climb up and hurl himself from the ledge onto the rocks below. Neither time was he injured in any way.'

After this we sat silent, some of us in meditative prayer, some of us perhaps brooding on the terrors that never being able to die might hold. At last, by some unspoken common consent, we stretched out on the soft ground and slept.

In the morning light, Erc's tale seemed more difficult to credit; but I noticed that my brothers tended to give the well a wide berth as they carried our few possessions back to the currach. We quickly finished our ablutions and the boat was soon loaded. My brethren stood about on the beach, while I took note of Erc's course for the Bird's Paradise.

We were about to launch the boat when Liber cried, 'Where's Dunan? Dunan's not here!'

I quickly counted the men: fifteen, including myself. 'He must have wandered off for some reason,' I said angrily, 'not realizing that we would be leaving so early. We're going to miss the tide . . .'

Erc put his hand on my arm, motioning me aside. 'There is something you should know . . .' His face, that had been so expressionless before, was now a mask of pain. He pointed to a fine-looking ram that was moving down the strand in an odd, bewildered fashion. 'You are now fifteen in company, and my flock now numbers one hundred and thirty. I will tend the new one well, as I tend the others. Now you know the secret of the well, and the price that must be paid for immortality.'

'Why didn't you tell us everything?' I demanded harshly, my mind struggling to comprehend what he was saying.

'I am not permitted to. The right choice must always be made freely. Fifteen of you were not tempted. One failed the test. He might have failed you later, and perhaps with dire consequences for the others . . .'

I could speak no more, and left him.

Chapter Seven

I'm not sure how I felt as the island, with its hideous secret, slipped below the horizon. I tried to tell myself that I was not responsible for Dermot's death earlier, or Dunan's – what to call it? – Dunan's unholy transformation, if indeed it really had been that. But I felt responsible. It's true that once a man has heard and accepted the teachings of the True Faith, he is responsible for his own soul and makes his own choices for good or evil; and while I could guide other men, there was no possible way I could force them to resist temptation.

And yet, and yet . . .

I was making excuses. Had I stayed within the confines of life at Clonfert, Dermot and Dunan could have lived out their allotted spans in useful service and piety. But it was I who had led them into spiritual peril, even as I was leading the others into mortal danger, and possibly worse. There would be times of testing in the future, perhaps harder – and I wondered how many more amongst my brethren might be found wanting.

But a leader, I reminded myself, cannot wallow in self doubt. At the very least I was guilty of too much absorption in my own goals. I should have studied my companions more closely, tried to learn their weaknesses as well as their strengths. I could not undo what was done, but I could – and would – wrest my mind now from dreams of Paradise and my joy in the sea itself to those around me.

I turned, leaning back against the tall prow and looked down the length of the craft at my crew.

First, there was Geoffrey, whom I had known for many years. A short broad, bulky man, whose years as a missionary across the continent had etched themselves into his seamed face. He was a practical man, not a dreamer, and his organizational abilities and experience were excellent. At first by chance, and later by design, he had taken charge of the winter stores at Clonfert, and had managed to provide for us so well that we now usually had a surplus that we expended in charity.

We had been friends for a long time, and when I had gone in search of the Isle of Paradise all those years ago he had been the first I had asked to accompany me. Although he was perhaps eight or nine years younger than me, he appeared older. I tended to think of him as a contemporary and I trusted his judgement second only to my own. He had confirmed Nevin's choice of the men for this voyage, and had discreetly approached most of them, at my behest, back at Clonfert. Our temperaments were very different, but I could imagine no better man to have by my side in a crisis. Above all his faith was as solid and as practical as himself; neither doubts nor unlawful desires would torture him.

Eoin, I felt similarly confident of, though I had scarcely taken heed of him before this journey. He was less than half my age, and yet I knew that our instincts on the deeper levels were very similar. It was not simply that he shared my love of the open sea, nor even his eagerness to push on, to head further into these strange unknown waters, but a quality harder to define. I can best explain it by saying that while most men fear the unknown, and many will come to terms with this fear, it is only a very few who long for the untrodden paths and uncharted ways. Eoin and I were such men. He listened intently, obeyed immediately and questioned occasionally – but always with good reason.

There were differences – but perhaps that only helped to emphasize the similarities. Eoin was tall and well muscled, and his hands were huge. His features were smooth and rounded, almost tending to fat, but his eyes were a clear, deep piercing blue. Our backgrounds were completely dissimilar: my parents were prosperous, wealthy landowners, while his were poor fisherfolk; and yet, looking down the currach at him, with the salt sea wind in his hair, I sometimes seemed to see my younger self.

If Eoin's temperament was instantly recognizable, Brother Martyn's was unusually difficult to fathom. He was a short, slightly built, sharp-featured man of perhaps eight-and-twenty, dark-eyed and dark-complected. Despite his small stature, he was surprisingly strong, and all his movements had the deft economy and neatness of the natural athlete. I don't think he had ever set foot off dry land before our voyage, and yet within ten days his handling of the ropes and stays was second only to Eoin's.

I knew little about his background. At Clonfert it was known that he had been reared by the Druids, and had trained in the Old Faith – indeed, it was said he had been destined to become a priest of the ancient belief. There were rumours that he possessed strange powers, and that he only studied the way of Christ to aid him in his pagan practices. I knew only that he came to Christ from a pagan background. And as for the rumours, well, I disregarded them, for he had always seemed devout.

Converts generally fall into two types: those who enjoy talking about the wicked, lustful or simply godless ways they left; or those who prefer to forget the past utterly and are absorbed in their new life. Martyn was certainly the second type. He never spoke of his boyhood. Indeed, he rarely spoke of anything unless directly questioned; but I noticed that his eyes often seemed to turn inwards and, at such times, he radiated an almost frightening strangeness.

One brother whose background we all knew much of was Crosan, for his earlier life had been very public indeed, as a court jester in Tara. When I first heard that he was joining our community in Clonfert, I had worried that a professional merrymaker would disrupt our necessarily stern and serious life there.

I need not have feared. Back at Clonfert Crosan had been nearly as silent as Martyn, albeit in a different manner; his was a gentle quietness that had nothing secretive about it. Once when I commented on it privately to him, he said, 'All the time when I was making others laugh, I felt as if I were crying inside myself. Now that I have no jokes or rhymes or pranks to play, I find that I have learned to smile.' The habit of pleasing others is a persistent one, however, and Crosan was probably quicker than I to sense a need for diversion; and although he was neither strong nor quick, his talent made him invaluable.

Crosan was short, almost dwarfish in stature, with one shoulder standing slightly higher than the other, and his left elbow had an odd twist to it. His features were plain and smooth, but handsome enough in their fashion, and his eyes were huge and luminous. He came from sea folk to the west of Erin and, although he was perhaps not wholly suited to such a long voyage, his skill with the needle and gut was quite extraordinary, and he was far from weak. My only worry with Crosan was his health. Even allowing for our limited diet, his stomach had begun to trouble him unduly, and though he did not complain overmuch, I sensed that he was often in pain.

A sudden scraping sound beneath my feet interrupted my musings. I looked over the side of the boat, and saw that we had fetched up on a large sandbar or small island that seemed to have sprung up from nowhere. I swore briefly. While I had been day dreaming, I had ignored the mist about us, which had changed almost imperceptibly into fog.

I turned around, about to give the order to bring the mainsail down, but Eoin had anticipated me and was already working at the stays. Martyn was beside him and, with Fiachra and Niall also rendering assistance, I could see that I wasn't needed.

I turned around and looked down at the small isle, and announced the obvious. 'We've run aground.'

I was going to suggest that we might be able to push ourselves free with the oars, but, surveying the thickening fog and the weary faces of the brothers, I changed my mind. 'We might as well take advantage of this islet. We can stretch our legs and have our mid-day meal, by which time the fog may have lifted.'

Fiachra made his way up the craft and stood beside me, peering into the fog. 'Do you want me to look around and see if I can find some brushwood for a fire?'

I nodded, adding a warning to take care. God – or the Devil – only knew what this place held. I watched the young man lower himself over the side and drop into the shallows. He walked up the dark slope, turned and waved, and then vanished almost immediately into the mist. I hesitated a moment, almost expecting him to return.

Fiachra. There are always a few brothers in every community who are totally unsuited to the monastic life, and he was one of these. He had been the cherished eldest son of wealthy parents, and in his youth he had wanted for nothing and never known hardship. But God had called him and, with a great amount of courage, Fiachra had answered that call. His parents had not been pleased at his decision to take the vows, but they had relented enough to bestow a rich endowment on the chapel. At Clonfert I had thought him physically soft, indeed, almost lazy, although somewhat rash. The rashness remained, but the softness had gone. Still, what did I really know of him except that he was young, willing and sometimes over-eager to question, to explore? For that matter, what did I know of Barran, Ruarai, Mernoc, Niall, Ultan and Tadgh? A third of the men who had set sail with me, and they were still little more than names and faces to me, I realized bitterly. It is foolhardy – but all too easy – for an abbot to remain remote from his men, even in the safe confines of his abbey; but on a voyage such as this, my ignorance was inexcusable, and potentially lethal. Well, the situation was already changing and would continue to change.

In the meantime, I clambered over the side of the boat to have a look at how badly aground we had fetched. I knelt in the chill lapping water and looked at the damage. We had been lucky – this time. The outer layer of skin was cracked, and the inner layer had been badly skinned nearly through to the third layer. Now it was a weak spot and would have to be repaired and quickly. Fortunately the wood-and-wicker framework was unharmed.

We now had two choices: we could hope that time and tide would float us off, but, failing that, all we could do would be to push the currach off ourselves – and that I didn't relish.

I walked up along the isle and looked around. The surface of the islet was a curious one: dark grey, neither sandy nor stony, and with no hint of vegetation. It had an odd, slightly springy texture underfoot, like bog or marshland, and seemed completely devoid of all life, except for scores of limpets stuck fast to the ground, and long strands of seaweed. I wasn't surprised when Fiachra loomed up out of the mist, a little while later, empty-handed.

'Did you get any idea of how large this island is?' I asked him.

'It's not wide,' he answered. 'Barely two ship-lengths across, and perhaps five ship-lengths or a little more long.' He shrugged. 'I'm not sure, I couldn't see much in this fog. There's nothing growing here, and I could find no sign of any running water, no animal tracks or runs – nothing.'

A huge barren rock rising from the sea, I thought. We had been lucky that whatever curious substance it was that covered the surface had cushioned us when we ran aground. Unexpected land is every mariner's nightmare. A seaworthy boat will ride out all but the most violent storm, but it takes only a small hidden rock to tear a fatal hole in the bottom of a craft.

Geoffrey heaved himself over the side of the boat to join us. He stared at the ground beneath us and then peered into the mist for a few moments. 'Well,' he said finally, 'there doesn't seem to be anything here for us, and there I was hoping for a nice warm fire to take the damp from me. On the other hand, where there's one rock, there's likely to be another, and who knows what we might run foul of next in this weather?'

I nodded. 'We'll wait until the weather clears. And you can have your fire, Geoffrey.' I looked around for Fiachra, who had wandered back down along the shoreline. 'Take some of the stored wood and light a fire here – it will do us all good to feel some real warmth in our bones.'

'You don't want the boat unloaded?' Geoffrey asked.

'I don't think there's much point in mooring properly or unloading. We'll just peg in one mooring rope to steady us against a sudden change in the tide. In fact, it's probably best that most of the men stay in the currach – we've no idea how the tides run around here, and for all we know this islet may be submerged at high-water mark – it might account for all the limpets everywhere. Will you organize the men into groups of four or six, so that they can take it in turns to come ashore to stretch their legs?'

Geoffrey nodded and made his way back to the craft, where he was helped aboard by Eoin and Martyn, who had just disembarked. Eoin was holding a line and Martyn had a small metal stake and hammer. They were followed ashore by Ruarai and Fiachra, who were carrying a bundle of dried and slightly oiled firewood.

There was a sudden rumbling, grumbling sound, and then the ground trembled beneath my feet, shuddering, then subsiding. I looked around, but could see nothing except Eoin bending to tie a rope to the stake which Martyn had finished driving into the hard-packed grey soil.

'Did you feel that?' Fiachra demanded. He and Ruarai had just stacked up the firewood, only to have it shaken apart by the shuddering. 'What was it?'

'Just an earth tremor,' I answered, with more confidence than I felt. 'Such things are common in some parts, I believe.'

'Not where I come from, thank God,' Ruarai exclaimed, straightening up and walking towards me. Behind him, Fiachra struck sparks from flint and blew gently on slivers of dried wood.

'And where might that be?' I asked curiously, motioning the wiry, red-haired youth closer to me. Ruarai was an arbitrary choice of Nevin's; all I knew of him was that he was an excellent carpenter.

'My people come from around Muritheme, where there are low hills and rich fields, and the sound of the sea is mercifully absent,' he replied with more spirit than I had yet heard from him.

'Then what on earth made you volunteer to accompany me on the open sea?' I wondered.

Ruarai cast his eyes downward and the easy flow of words died from him. 'Oh, well . . . you know . . .'

'No, I don't know,' I snapped. 'I may be an abbot, but I cannot see into men's minds to know what drives them to do something they obviously hate.'

'I know it sounds proud and selfish,' the young man said slowly, colour rising to his cheeks, 'but I wanted – I've always wanted – to do something for God. I wanted to test myself, my faith. I've always hated and feared the sea. I can't swim – if you dropped me in the water, I'd sink like a stone. When you spoke to me of this voyage my heart seemed to contract, but I knew at once that this was my chance to prove my devotion –

not to you, not perhaps to God, but to myself. I knew that I had to come with you.'

For a moment I was angry, thinking that an unskilled and unhappy sailor was the last thing we needed. Then I suddenly felt humbled by the young man's determination to face that which he feared most . . .

I had never spoken of it, but I have a strange, almost uncontrollable hatred of dark, enclosed spaces. Would I have gone under the earth and settled in a cave for many months just to test my own faith? Even the thought of it made my palms and face sweat.

'I will try to take special care of you,' I said gently, 'and you must stay by Eoin or Martyn when I am not there, since only the fish seem more at home with the sea than they.'

There was a sudden crackling sound as the oiled sticks burst into flame, and scores of tiny sparks spiralled upwards. Fiachra sat back from the blaze, red-faced and gasping. 'I thought I'd never get it . . .'

The ground abruptly trembled again, this time more violently. Then it rolled slightly from side to side.

'I don't like this Brendan,' Martyn said urgently. It was rare for him to address me familiarly, and never by name before. 'We must return to the boat – there is something terribly wrong about this place.'

I nodded. The ground trembled again, and this time I actually saw a tremor ripple beneath the surface of the earth. Fiachra's carefully built fire collapsed in a jumble of crackling sticks. 'Pull up the mooring peg,' I ordered.

Once again the ground heaved, and then, incredibly, there was water about our ankles. The island was sinking – no tide I had ever known moved this rapidly.

'Get on board!' I shouted. Fiachra and Eoin raced for the craft. I grabbed Ruarai's arm – he seemed petrified with fear – and pulled. 'Move!'

But he stood still, his eyes wide and staring, but seeing nothing. The sea was at our waists, and then the ground disappeared entirely from under us.

I was beneath the water for perhaps a heartbeat or two, and although I learned to swim almost before I could walk, in those few heartbeats I suddenly felt as if I were going to drown. Then my head broke the surface, and I shook the salt water from my nose and eyes. It took another terrifying heartbeat before I orientated on the currach, and then I remembered Ruarai. I thrashed around, but then Martyn's voice came from behind me. 'It's all right, I've got him. You get aboard, Abbot.'

A few strokes brought me alongside the stern, and two of the brothers hauled me in. Moments later, I saw them pull first Ruarai and then Martyn up out of the water.

'Whither now?' Geoffrey asked.

Before I could answer, Martyn pointed directly away from where the island had been. 'That way, and with all speed.'

I moved to the stern, staring through the thinning mists at the open water where minutes before there had been land.

And then, further away still, the island reappeared, and rose, higher and higher. A geyser of water shot up from one end. It moved further from us and then it arched into the air – and I saw the tail of a fish.

Despite the frantic rowing, several other brothers had looked behind them and had seen the same thing. 'What is it?' someone whispered.

'A whale,' I answered in awe. 'I've never seen anything like it before though. Look at its size! Surely it can only be the largest whale in the world . . .'

In the silence that followed, Eoin murmured a name. 'Jasconius!'

Chapter Eight

There was complete silence as the huge beast flowed past: rippled grey skin, dotted with scores of limpets and long strands of seaweed. We briefly glimpsed a monstrous fluke, and then the creature disappeared with a clap of water that rocked the currach.

'Jasconius,' Eoin whispered. 'That I should see Jasconius and live to tell of it!'

The huge creature had frightened me, and the younger man's murmured amazement didn't help my temper. 'Who, or rather, what, is Jasconius?' I asked with some asperity.

Before Eoin could answer me, Martyn said, 'Why, he is the King Whale of legend, the oldest and surely the largest living creature on earth. Every race tells of the Godfish. Even those who live by hunting his kind fear him, for he is said to swallow boats as easily as we would swallow a sardine.' He seemed faintly surprised at my ignorance.

I glanced out across the still-rippling waves, the full realization of just how lucky we had been beginning to sink in. I crossed myself.

'He is not supposed to be a real whale,' Martyn continued, 'but rather one of the ancient sea-gods of this world, which time and the sea's natural magic have transformed into that form.'

'It looks like a whale to me,' Eoin said firmly. 'Bigger than any other, but still a whale, one of God's creatures.'

'When I was training in the Mysteries,' Martyn said softly, 'I learned that Jasconius was the last of a breed of ancient sea monsters that once swam in all the waters of our own world.'

'Everyone knows that the druids love to invent mysteries, even where none exist,' Barran snapped.

Whatever it was – ancient sea-god or ancient monster-fish – it was utterly terrifying, and visions of being swallowed in that

71

vast maw flashed vividly through my mind – and through the minds of the others also, judging by their faces. 'God has spared us,' I said loudly. 'Let us pray to God for our salvation.'

The next two days and nights were mercifully uneventful, with the sea flat and grey beneath a sky of metal. There was enough of a breeze to make rowing unnecessary, but I had Geoffrey set the brothers to the oars at regular intervals to keep them occupied.

However, on the morning of the third day following the sighting of the huge whale, I noted a pair of sea-birds flying low and steady over our heads. Land must be near, and, with God's grace, we might be heading towards it.

Around mid-morning the wind freshened somewhat, enough to fill the sails but not enough to make the sea choppy. I walked the length of the currach, sure that this, coupled with the sighting of the birds earlier, was a certain indication of land. When I reached the stern, I found Martyn sitting alone with his back against some cords of wood, idly carving a scrap of wood with a bone-handled short-bladed knife. I squatted down beside him and looked at his workmanship; it was a chessman, a bishop.

'May I?'

The young man smiled and handed me the piece, a carving of a monk. It was a marvellous piece of workmanship. Martyn had used the grain of the wood to suggest the monk's robes, and every line of his carving suggested suppressed tension and force. I held the figure up, tilting it so the sunlight could fall upon the miniature features. They showed a man in later years, with a long, slightly gaunt face, high cheekbones and sunken eyes. With a start, I realized the features were my own! As I turned the figure over and over in my hands, something gnawed at the back of my mind; but it refused to surface, and eventually I handed the piece back to Martyn.

He held it between finger and thumb and smiled. 'I'll have a full set before we return to Erin,' he said, with absolute certainty.

'Can you see, then, what is to come?' I asked, half seriously.

72

Martyn laughed. 'Not I; that is a gift – or curse – that is bestowed on few men nowadays.'

'I would have thought everyone would like to be able to see the future,' I said.

'Men often think they would,' he said, adding a line to the chesspiece. 'But I suspect they lack imagination. They fail to see how destructive it might become if they could know the consequence of their every action. Even the various pagan faiths and systems of belief warn of the danger of too much knowledge – they only differ in their definition of how much is too much.'

'I wonder if we all don't have momentary glimpses of what might be?'

Martyn considered my words, then nodded. 'That is true, I suppose; and yet there were some of my people who could genuinely perceive something of the future's shape and course. And all those who don the white robe of the Mysteries must have some of the sight. As a boy I used to pray to other gods that I would be so gifted – my people make much of such matters, as you know. But I never developed the Sight to any marked degree, and yet . . .'

'What?' I prompted.

'And yet in the back of my mind I have always thought that this voyage is part of my destiny – my doom mayhap.'

'Perhaps your salvation,' I said, and smiled.

He nodded. 'And even now, though I feel wonderfully at peace, I wonder if fate is nipping at my heels.'

'That's just some pagan fancy from the dark druidic ways of your boyhood,' I mocked him gently. 'You're with good Christians now, and this voyage will bring you to Paradise – and not your doom.'

'I expect you're right, Father Abbot,' Martyn said good-humouredly. He stared out across the sea and then glanced back to me. 'You said we all get glimpses of the future . . .?' I nodded. 'Well, at this moment, I feel confident in predicting land ahead.' I was about to ask how, when he added, 'In fact, if you turn around, you won't even need a druid's powers.'

I rose slowly, pressing my hands to my stiffened back and found that Eoin and Geoffrey were already correcting our course towards the dark smudge of an island that lay almost dead ahead. For once, I was content to let them get on with it, while I continued to relax. There would be a time for decisions when we were nearer to the island. I glanced over at Martyn, now engrossed again in his carving. Would I want to see the future, I wondered? What would it be like to know . . .? Without doubt, uncertainty, and even danger, where would be the adventure?

When I next looked towards the bow of the currach, I could make out a distant pattern of lush greenness on the island ahead – sure signs of fertile soil and fresh water. I shaded my eyes, looking for the telltale signs of tilled fields or smoke, but there seemed to be neither. Still, I thought hopefully, the absence of farmland only meant an absence of farmers – there might yet be folk living there. There was a flapping overhead and I looked up as a half-dozen birds flew by. Against the sun-washed noonday light, their plumage was startling – these were not the black, white or grey creatures that generally lived by the sea. One of their number swooped low, hovering over our craft on wings that were almost invisible, regarding us with small black eyes, before darting away.

'What was that?' I asked, without turning around. 'I've never seen any bird like it before.' No one answered, but I turned around to find Martyn staring after them in a puzzled fashion.

The wind picked up and the tide caught us then, and the island rose up out of the sea like . . . like a whale, I thought wryly. I muttered a quick prayer for a safe landing, and God heeded my call, for the beach we sailed up to was of fine white sand, perfectly situated, with deep water followed by a shallow bar. The currach drifted into the silt and sand with barely a shudder. While the brothers eased the craft free, and pulled her up onto the long, low rocky shore, Geoffrey and I continued on up to the beach.

Dried seaweed and shells crunched and cracked underfoot as we made our way towards the low rolling sand dunes that enclosed this section of the shoreline. We saw evidence aplenty of bird life – droppings, cracked shells, streaked stones and feathers. Some were recognizable as belonging to the sea- and shore-birds we knew, but some of the others were completely unknown. There were feathers everywhere, singly and in bundles . . .

Geoffrey suddenly stopped and his fingers bit into the flesh of my arm. He pointed.

At first it seemed that a jumble of feathers was moving towards us in short, quick, nervous runs. It stopped, barely a score of paces away, and every feather in the pile – which was about chest high – began to quiver and tremble.

Then I spotted an eye. A hard, black, unblinking eye set amongst the tangle of coloured plumage. The eye moved, the feathers twitched and then I suddenly distinguished a human head.

It was the face of a woman – a crone, her face sunken and withered like a fruit left to rot. Age had taken away all but four snaggled teeth in the front, and these, coupled with her hard, unblinking eyes, accentuated her birdlike appearance. She raised a sticklike hand and pushed back the hood of her feathered cloak. There were slivers of yellow and scarlet feathers jabbed any which way into her straggling hair, and more hanging from her ears. There was no pattern of colour, nor was there a shape to her garb, but on either side her shoulders were decorated with black ravens' wings, and the clothing glimpsed beneath her cloak seemed to be feathered.

The crone was surrounded by birds; they swarmed all around her, sometimes landing briefly on her head, or on her arms, which were outstretched towards us in a gesture of greeting.

'Welcome, Brendan,' she said, looking directly at me. Her voice was harsh, and the lisping accent was one I did not recognize, or perhaps it was the lack of teeth.

'You know my name?' I asked cautiously.

'Who does not know of Brendan, called the Navigator.' Her voice fell to a sibilant hiss. 'My pretties told me of your coming; didn't you?' She reached out with surprising speed and snatched one of the birds from the air, and brought it close to her face. 'My pretties, they knew you were coming; they learned of it from the others who are of their kind, but not of

75

their kind – if you take my meaning.'

'I don't,' I said, looking back at Geoffrey. He shook his head slightly, and mouthed a single word. Mad.

'Look,' she cackled, thrusting the bird in her hand into my face. 'My pretty pretties.'

I stepped back; there was a strange, musty odour coming from the bird – or the woman. 'What is this island called?' I asked. 'Does anyone else live here?'

'Of humankind, there is only me,' she replied. 'Morag, I was called in your language. Morag, yes, Morag; but it's a name I have not been called for many years now. Morag. You can call me Morag. I am not alone here . . . not alone, never alone. There are others, in a manner of speaking. Yes, there are others. Aren't there?' She brought the trapped bird close to her face and stared into its tiny eyes; and then she cackled softly to herself, and for all the world it looked as if some message had passed between her and the creature. She looked back at me, and then to the bird again. 'Shall we tell him what this place is called, shall we, my pretty?' The old woman smiled slyly. 'This is the Isle of Paradise.'

I heard Geoffrey gasp behind, and I was aware that my heart had started to pound. 'If this is so, then we have achieved our hearts' desire,' I said humbly. 'For more days than I care to count, we have been sailing in search of Paradise.'

Morag simmered with some vast, private amusement. 'I think not, Brendan, unless your paradise be filled with birds. Paradise means different things to different beings and creatures, and this is not the paradise of the followers of the White Christ.' She spread her arms wide. 'This is my kingdom. This is the Bird's Paradise.'

Even as she spoke, two enormous creatures with curled talons, parti-coloured bodies and savage-looking beaks flew in and landed on the lower branch of a tree some ten paces from Morag. Their cawing was so harsh as to make Morag's rough hiss sound musical by comparison.

She glanced over her shoulder at them, and then turned back to us. 'You intend to stay . . .?'

I nodded. 'If we may, a day or two to rest . . .'

'Have you any weapons?' she asked urgently. 'Spears,

knives, swords?'

'What use have men of God for weapons?' I demanded. 'We have nothing with us that could harm any living creature, except a few fishing lines, and a bow to hunt small game, should we chance upon it.'

The old crone nodded. 'Weapons. Bladed or pointed, they are all weapons.' She smiled then, and hissed, 'My pretties do not like weapons. Leave them in the boat if you intend to come ashore – and live.'

I looked over the old woman at the birds sitting in the tree. The hideous creatures seemed to glare back at me, and one flapped his wings, stretching them out to a span that was twice a man's height. The other opened his mouth, revealing an odd alignment of jagged edging inside his beak; and I found I didn't want to dwell on what these birds ate.

'Can we find a night's food and shelter here on your island?' Geoffrey asked Morag.

'Aye, you can, if you mean no harm. There's fruit and nuts and vegetables aplenty, more than we can eat, and my pretties will make you snug, dry nests to sleep in.'

'Surely, you don't expect us to sleep in trees?' Geoffrey protested.

Morag cackled. 'No one expects you to learn to fly and roost, old man. Your beds will be of fine, firm heather – though they may seem oddly fashioned to you.'

We waited for some of the brothers to join us, and then we followed the old woman up along a sandy path that led into luxuriant woods. We followed a worn track until we finally reached a grassy orchard. Every tree we passed seemed to be alive with birds, some of which were fantastic creatures that none of us had ever seen. I was grateful for the familiar sight of several apple trees in the clearing, even if a medium-sized bird with scarlet, yellow and blue feathers and a tall crested mane was sitting in one of them.

'Morag's a hag, Morag's a hag,' it called.

'It speaks,' Eoin gasped.

'Oh yes,' Morag said matter-of-factly. 'It speaks. But it doesn't have much to say for itself.'

She picked up a handful of stones from the ground and

hurled them towards the creature in a playful manner. 'I'll teach you who's a hag,' she added.

'Morag's a hag, Morag's a hag,' it screeched again, flying higher into the branches.

The old woman ignored it and walked over to one of the trees, where she reached up and picked a shiny green fruit from amongst the many that hung on it. 'Try this, and see if it eases your hunger. You must peel it – but the skin comes away easily.' Her clawlike fingers bit into the hard pebbled skin and pulled it away in strips.

Morag then tossed one to me, and I tore away half the green outer layer, to reveal a sweet-smelling juicy orange-coloured flesh. Experimentally, I tasted a small bite. It was delicious, with a refreshing tartness underneath the scented sweet succulence. Seeing my pleasure in it, Morag picked more, tossing them like balls to the rest of the company. We sat down on the grass to eat them, Morag joining us.

A small, plain, dove-shaped bird flew in and perched on her shoulder, chirping away into her ear, and taking pecks of the fruit she held out to it. She shook her head, and the bird chirped again, more insistently this time; and suddenly the old woman's eyes filled with tears.

'What is it?' I asked, concerned that we had in some way caused some offence.

'He says that one of you here will be his doom.'

I looked at the bird, unable to decide whether the creature had actually spoken to her, or if she were indeed just mad. However, judging from our previous experiences on this voyage, I decided it may very well have spoken to her. 'Tell him we intend no harm to any creature that lives here,' I said firmly.

But Morag continued to cry silently as the bird chirped, rocking to and fro on her heels. I moved over to her and said gently, 'We will return to the boat, if our presence here distresses you.'

She shook her head again. 'Too late. This little one is a Corr. He sees what has been, what is and what will be. But I think I love him the best, because he is so gentle and plain-coloured.'

She stood up abruptly and wandered off into the woods with

the small grey bird still chirping noisily into her ear. I took the opportunity to address the brothers privately.

'Now look, whatever this island is and however strange Morag is, we must be careful to accept her ways, and above all, to kill nothing, even by accident. God alone only knows what powers she possesses,' I added, remembering the two monstrous creatures we had seen earlier.

The temperature and air on this island were different to any I had ever known. It was always warm, as warm as the hottest day I could remember in our own misty land, and yet the air was laden with moisture. I could feel the dampness in the air, I could taste it with every breath I took, and yet, looking at the sky, I could find no trace of a cloud, let alone rain. Moreover, the weather must often be like this, for how else to account for the lush green growth which surrounded us on all sides? Was there ever a winter in the Bird's Paradise? Not in any sense I knew, I reckoned, for the fruits which grew so abundantly would never have survived the harsh winds and frosts of Erin. It was not the true Paradise I sought, but it was paradise of a sort, I thought, stretching out in a half reclining position on my side, the soft grassy ground beneath me.

Martyn moved over and sat down, drawing his knees up to his chest and circling them with clasped hands. 'This is not a natural place,' he said abruptly, staring across the clearing towards a huge flock of tiny yellow-coloured birds that swooped and darted through the trees.

My eyes had closed against the bright sun, but I half-opened them and squinted up at him. 'I may be old, but I am not yet feeble-witted. I can recognize a touch of magic as easily as the next man, but there is nothing of sorcery or evil here. I would feel it.'

'These birds,' Martyn persisted. 'I've never seen them before, but I know of some of them. They are creatures from legend, not from life. I've recognized chamrochs, lumerpa, ercine and gryphons and . . . and the grey bird, the Corr.'

He was silent, but it was a silence that begged to be broken. I would have preferred to keep to my own thoughts and enjoy the sun's warmth, but I reminded myself that I had practical and spiritual responsibilities – always. So, I prompted him. 'The Corr? What's so special about that bird, Martyn?'

'If it is the bird the elders of my people spoke of, it is a creature of time; it can see into the future,' he said slowly.

'Morag said it knew what was, what is and what will be,' I said and added, 'but I've never heard of it.'

'None live in our land – and perhaps it is a good thing. In any case,' Martyn added, 'it will only speak to one person, and that person is chosen by the Corr. And it only chooses those who are pure of all worldly desire – so that those who seek its knowledge rarely gain it . . .'

'. . . And those who have access to its knowledge have very little use for it,' I said, with a smile. Often it has struck me that while the wonders of our own True Faith are straightforward, these pagan mysteries always seem to have a catch, a twist, a sting in the tail. There is a promise of wealth or power or knowledge, and yet, no matter what is given for it, it must be paid for, either in blood, body or soul, and at the end there is only fairy gold – illusion. I said as much to Martyn. Here we saw it again – a fabulous bird who could foretell the future – yet would confide it only to those who had no interest in knowing it.

'That is true, Father Abbot,' he said slowly. 'And often have I seen men make a bad bargain, even losing their souls for that which is not what it seems. But surely some things are worth the gamble, the risk?' he asked pensively, looking quickly from me and then back to the trees.

'Like the Corr?' I asked.

He nodded. 'Like the Corr.'

'But you said it will only speak to those who are free of all worldly desires. And I've yet to meet a man who cares nothing for this world.'

'There is a way to learn what the Corr sees, or so I was told . . .'

'How?' I wondered.

Martyn looked sidelong at me. 'Its heart must be torn from its living body and eaten raw.'

I thought of the tame, soft grey bird and shuddered. 'That's disgusting.'

The young monk nodded slowly, his eyes on my face. 'So it is; but men are often forced to consume flesh and blood to assume godhood, or to take on the attributes of a god.' He nodded to me and stood up, moving away before I could say anything.

The implications of what he had said had not escaped me, and even in the sun's warmth, I felt chilled. I must have dozed then, because when I again became aware of my surroundings, the sun had slipped lower in the sky, and the shadows had lengthened perceptibly. I heard voices behind me, and I rolled over. In the distance, Martyn, Eoin, Geoffrey and Ruarai were sharing a joke together, and my earlier forebodings about the young druid-trained monk slipped from my mind.

As the evening drew in, Morag returned, still with a bird on one shoulder, but this time a small blue-feathered creature which sang softly to itself all the time. The old woman, too, seemed in better spirits, and drew a bag from inside her cloak of feathers. 'Here are some nuts for you and your men, Brendan,' she said. 'Though they are small, they will fill and nourish you more than you would think.'

She was correct. The shells cracked easily between our fingers, and the white flesh within was dense and satisfying. When we had finished, she gathered more fruits for us and joined us in our repast.

I asked if we might light a fire – more for cheer than anything else, since the night was mild.

Morag shook her head and her manner and speech suddenly changed, becoming harsher, more brittle. 'No, my pretties don't like the flames. Oh no, they don't. Fire frightens them; they know what humankind does to the feathered folk with fire.' Her voice dropped to a whisper. 'Humankind eat the feathered folk, and so there is no fire here. When you eat, you must take your food raw here. Fire uses wood, and the trees are sacred to my pretties. So, if you want fire, you must burn your boat, not our lovely trees.'

Perhaps it was as well. There's something about a fire that encourages talk long into the night, and it was prayer and sleep that we needed now. Morag gestured into the shadows, and there we found rough beds of heather, leaves and pine needles, woven together for all the world like beds. I yawned hugely; the constant damp heat was enervating and I sank down onto one of the beds and fell effortlessly and deeply asleep.

The morning dawned moist and warm as the day before; but my body had become more accustomed to it and my brain seemed clearer. Peaceful and magical as this island was, there was nothing that we sought on it, and it was time to continue on our quest. I asked Morag if we might have some of the fruits to take with us for a change of diet when we were again at sea.

'Take what you want – as much as you can carry,' she said. 'You can take anything you want – except my pretties.'

I thanked her. Although the food we had been gifted with by the magical youth earlier in our voyage was filling and sustaining, it was bland and almost tasteless, and the fruits and nuts would be a blessing.

I stood with Geoffrey beside the currach as the brothers loaded her up with what seemed like armfuls of brightly coloured fruits and small, dark nuts; and then I suddenly noticed that I had seen neither Martyn nor Conn since sunrise. I asked Geoffrey, but he hadn't seen them either, and now, with the memory of the Isle of Sheep still bitter in our memories, we went in search of them.

We found Conn some little distance from the beach. He had found one of the trees which produced the delicious nuts that we had enjoyed the night before, and was busy stuffing the front of his robe with them. He looked up guiltily as I appeared and swallowed hard. There were scores of broken shells around his feet. Boys are always hungry, I thought a little wistfully, but the years steal away both appetite and taste.

Although I hadn't it in my heart to chastise him, I still demanded sternly, 'Have you forgotten that gluttony is one of the deadly sins?'

'They're not just for me. I'm going to share them with all. We'll be glad of them, Abbot . . .' His voice trailed off. 'I'm sorry, Father. I'll return at once.'

Martyn was more elusive. Geoffrey and I called out and searched through the groves systematically; but even so it took us most of the morning before we spotted Martyn, on the far side of a glade, crouched under a tree. There was something in his frozen stillness that suggested more a forest animal than a man. His face was averted.

'Don't come any closer,' he cried, as we approached.

'Martyn, what's wrong?' Geoffrey asked, concern and alarm in his voice.

'Go away; return to the currach. I'll be with you soon, I swear, but don't come any closer. Don't look at me!'

Geoffrey stopped, but I walked over to the man. I stood above him, feeling something cold and chill and sickening settle into the pit of my stomach. 'Look at me,' I whispered.

He shook his head. I gripped his shoulder with one hand and reached around and caught his chin with the other. I twisted his face up towards mine. And his face was that of an animal. Blood dribbled from the corner of his mouth, and was smeared on his chin and hands, and there were feathers and tiny white bones stuck in his robe. At his feet lay the torn, pathetic body of the Corr.

'I told you not to look,' he whispered.

Chapter Nine

Martyn had killed and eaten the Corr.

I won't say I didn't think of leaving him on the island. I did. The sight of his bloodied face disgusted me, but it wasn't just that that sickened my stomach and heart. Martyn had killed one of God's creatures – not for food, and not because it was threatening him, but for gain, for knowledge, for power. I turned my back on him and walked away, trying to quieten the pounding in my chest and head. Geoffrey came up to me and put a hand on my shoulder. 'Whatever Martyn has done, Brendan . . .' he began, when I interrupted him.

'He has taken an innocent creature's life,' I snapped.

'But it is still not so long since he saved a man's life,' Geoffrey reminded me gently.

'Had he drowned, at least Ruarai would have died in a state of grace,' I said bitterly.

'So may we all, I hope, but not, please God, just yet,' Geoffrey said. Then he added. 'Martyn's soul is in great peril. It is our duty to help him. And, already he regrets what he has done. Look at him!'

I turned and forced myself to face Martyn again, and immediately wished I had not. Martyn's pale face was now bone white, against which his bloodied lips and mouth stood out in startling contrast. His eyes were dull and flat and seemed to stare inwards into something dark and unfathomable. Never before have I seen such agony on a human face – I hope never to again.

But I was still bitterly angry. 'Well, was it worth it?' I demanded. 'You have slaughtered a gentle, defenceless creature that was dear to another because of your lust for knowledge. Have you got what you wanted? Can you see what you wanted to see?'

The young man looked up at me with his flat expressionless

eyes, and I immediately crossed myself – they were the eyes of a dead man. 'I don't know. I don't know what I am now.' The words were slightly slurred, wrenched from his throat.

And suddenly the anger seemed to drain away, and I felt incredibly weary and saddened. 'You had best come with us, now,' I said, deciding. 'I don't know if you want to stay with us, but there's certainly nothing for you here. We'll stop by the stream, and you can clean yourself up as best you can. I don't want the others to see you looking like a wolf that has come in fresh from the kill. I don't want them to know what you've done. You will say nothing, and Geoffrey and I will keep our own counsel on this.' His eyes were still flat and dead, and the expression on his face remained distant and withdrawn. 'Do you understand me?' I asked, crouching down beside him. It took a score of heartbeats for my words to sink in, but eventually he nodded. 'Come on then,' I said softly.

Martyn followed us obediently, stopping when we stopped, moving when we moved, his movements jerky and uncoordinated. At the stream which ran near the clearing where we had rested, he washed his hands and face, in the same mechanical manner. He seemed to find his own reflection fascinating, and also took a long time scrubbing his long-fingered hands together. Seeing that Martyn was going to ignore the drops of blood that spattered the front of his robe, Geoffrey stooped beside him and rubbed at them with the hem of his own robe, which he had dipped in the water. He looked oddly like a mother tending a small child.

I had half-expected the old woman to be waiting for us on the beach, but it was deserted, with not even the usual sea-birds wheeling in the air or bobbing in the choppy waters. The rest of the brothers were already in the currach waiting for us. Martyn climbed in and sat down passively, letting Eoin and Barran hoist the sails instead of helping in his accustomed manner. Once we were out of the bay and at sea again, he immediately lapsed into a deep, exhausted sleep.

'What's the matter with Martyn?' Ruarai asked me after a while. 'Is he ill?'

I nodded. 'I think something he ate on the Bird's Paradise didn't agree with him.'

Geoffrey looked up, startled, and I could seen the pain of betrayal in his eyes. He obviously thought I was going to tell the crew, but I smiled and shook my head slightly. Before I could say anything, Crosan interjected, 'I know just how he feels. All that fruit, and nothing you could put a name to. I've been doubled over with cramps since yester-eve.' The small sad man smiled bravely. 'Give me good plain bread, fit for Christians, any day – and you can keep your fancy fruit!'

'Well, I thought it was lovely,' Conn said. 'It made a change from that muck we've been eating for the past few weeks. When we get home from this voyage, I'm going to work in the garden and raise herbs and fresh vegetables, and I'm never going to look at another fish again!'

'You won't say that when I start to breed fat golden carp in the fish pool I'm going to build next to your kitchen garden,' Geoffrey said with a smile.

'Oh, yes I will. I'm not even going to watch them swim in it,' Conn insisted, laughing.

They all sounded so natural, so normal to me, in their good-humoured bickering. Here they were, sailing on an enchanted sea in search of the fabled Isle of Paradise, and yet they could find the time to laugh and joke and plan for their eventual return to Erin. For an instant, all around me seemed strangely unreal, as if they were shadows or dream-wraiths. How could they remain unaffected by what we had seen? I sat back and looked at my crew, and then I slowly realized that their very naturalness, their very acceptance of the islands and the voyage so far, was, in itself, unnatural. And then I realized that that unnatural acceptance might well be what was keeping them sane; perhaps if they were to dwell too long on what they had seen they might suddenly lose their reason. But what about me? If I was the exception – as I seemed to be – did that mean that I was now slipping towards madness?

Martyn was awake for our evening meal. He spoke to no one, but ate his food in a quiet, rapid fashion, his chin tucked down onto his chest, his shoulders hunched. I could not bring myself to speak to him yet, but Geoffrey went and sat beside him. 'Feeling better?' he asked softly, kindly.

'No,' he said hoarsely, shaking his head; and then he turned his head and looked at me with his flat, dead eyes. 'Father Abbot, I am in need of a confessor.'

I could not refuse. Nor can I, of course, repeat what was said. I can, however, say that there was no doubt as to the sincerity of Martyn's contrition, and I learned more about the druid-trained monk in those few moments than I had in the years he had been at Clonfert. The usual penances seemed wholly inappropriate and, ultimately, I could only tell him to trust in the infinite mercy of his Saviour.

His confession also, in some strange way, eased my own mind. I think that perhaps, deep down, I blamed myself for not realizing what the young man had been hinting at during our conversation earlier that day. But now I felt easier about the whole affair, and I suppose I preferred to forget about it. So I put it from my mind, until two days later, when Martyn, who was standing beside me in the bow, said, in an abstracted fashion, 'Perhaps we had best cast out some lines for fish. It will be a long time before we see land again.'

And so it was to be. We passed a jagged spur of rock later that day, as the shadows were lengthening towards evening, and that was the last piece of land we saw for . . . well, for a long time. Geoffrey marked the days, but I preferred to lose track of them, so that I cannot for certain say for how long we sailed the endless sea, except that the moon was twice full before we saw an island once again on the horizon.

I can't describe the excitement, first at the sight of landfall, and then, as we neared the shore, at the extraordinary sight of buildings not dissimilar to our own at Clonfert. The closer we came to the island, the more evidences of civilization we saw. What was even more startling were the growing suggestions of a monastic settlement. Indeed, there was no need to haul the currach up on sand or stony shingle. For the first time since we had set out, we found a sheltered deep-water harbour on the leeward side of the island, and a primitive, though sturdy, docking wall. Small, crudely constructed bollards were ranged along it, and Martyn and Eoin leapt nimbly onto the dock and secured our stays to them in what might have been record time.

I stood up in the rocking currach and Martyn leaned over the dock and reached out his hand. I hesitated a moment, long enough for rejection, for me to see the hurt in his eyes, and then I gripped it around the wrist. 'Welcome ashore, Father,' he said in a curiously formal manner.

I stood up, swaying slightly, still with the feel of the sea in my legs, and looked around. The quayside led directly onto the beach, which was smooth, with an undulating line of seaweed and stones showing how high the water rose on the island. Beyond the beach, low dunes rose into equally low, white stone cliffs, which were dotted with caves of various shapes and sizes. Tiny purple-headed flowers were growing in abundance from the cliff-face, and there were birds darting into some of the smaller holes; indeed, it was so natural, and so normal, that I felt a sudden wave of homesickness.

I was just about to turn back to the currach when something flickered at the corner of my eye. I turned back to the cliffs and shaded my eyes from the glare . . . For a single moment I thought my old eyes were playing tricks on me, but then Eoin's iron-hard fingers bit painfully into my arm. 'Look,' he breathed.

On the top of the cliff a figure had appeared. A figure wearing the robes of a monastic order. It was unbelievable: surely this couldn't be a community of monks? How would they have got here? Then logic provided the answer: just as we had. For a moment, along with my joy, I felt an unworthy stab of disappointment that others of my kind had reached where I had thought to be the first.

The figure on the cliff disappeared, only to reappear a moment later on a thin winding track that led down the cliff and onto the beach. At closer range, my first impressions were of height and thinness and I could see that his long hair was snowy white. His skin had the thin, bleached, parchment-like texture and colour of great age; against his face his eyes seemed huge. And yet, for all his years, his back was straight, and his stride had the swift assurance of a much younger man.

He stopped a few paces from us, his hands folded into the sleeves of his white robe, and bowed slightly. I inclined my head in greeting. 'I am Brendan, abbot of Clonfert, in Erin.

We have been sailing these many months in search of the Isle of Paradise. We would very much like to rest for a few days on your isle . . .?' I paused. The man seemed to understand my words, but he didn't speak, nor did he make any effort to speak. 'May I ask where we are, and your name, good father . . .?'

To my surprise, he shook his head, then held one finger against his lips in the universal language of silence and shook his head, smiling slightly. He looked around, and then walked over to a patch of sand and picked up a small piece of driftwood. With the wood, he traced strange twisting shapes in the sand. He looked up at me with his dark, unblinking eyes, but all I could do was to shake my head. I didn't know what he wanted. The man rubbed his bare foot across the marks, and I noticed that his toes seemed extraordinarily long and slender. Bending over he began to scratch more shapes into the sand. He tried several designs and patterns of lines and twisting curls, and then suddenly he was scraping familiar Latin letters in the sand. They read 'Ailbe'.

The man or the island, I wondered. I pointed at him. 'You are Ailbe?'

He tapped himself on the chest and nodded, and then gestured for us to follow him. He was obviously an educated man, almost certainly a Christian monk; and we had no hesitation in following him. He led us up the beach and along the track he had taken down from the cliffs. When we topped these, we found that the island opened out into a lush valley. Nestling in the centre of this valley, surrounding an almost perfectly circular lake, was the grouping of stone buildings I had seen from the boat. There was a recognizable refectory, with small sleeping chambers ranged off it, facing a central courtyard with two wells. At the other end was a building obviously designed as a chapel.

More robed men emerged, and viewed us with evident curiosity as our guide led us down into the valley. None spoke, except in gestures, and even then these seemed to be kept to a minimum. Without doubt, I realized, we had found a community of monks, but they appeared to be a silent order. It was a strange feeling. While I have known men in my own land who have chosen this austere form of devotion to God, this was the first time I had personally encountered an entire silent community. By my reckoning, no religious life is harsher or more devout than the silent orders, save that of an anchorite. These would be worthy men, of course; but my heart sank at the prospect of the cold cheer we should enjoy here after all the long days and nights at sea. A silent order would certainly not give much thought to the pleasures of the flesh – and they probably included eating and sleeping as luxuries.

As if he were reading my thoughts, Ailbe pointed towards the refectory, and moved his hand to urge us within.

And then I got my second surprise. Silent and isolated this order might be, but its members were not without their creature comforts. We sat down to a table laden with the finest, whitest loaves of bread imaginable, and though there were only fleshy roots, unfamiliar vegetables and goblets of water to accompany it, the roots and vegetables were sweet and filling, and the water had a cool, sparkling quality more often associated with wine. All of us ate with gusto, and though Ailbe's men did not join us, they stood around replenishing our plates and goblets at every opportunity.

When we had eaten and drunk our fill, Ailbe, who had vanished for most of our meal, appeared in the arched doorway and once more indicated that we should follow him. Not surprisingly, he led us to their chapel, to join them for vespers.

Their place of worship was breathtaking from the inside – indeed, almost indecently so. The walls were whitewashed, with a thin blue-green band running close to the floor, and the arched stone ceiling also had this delicate colouring. The floor was smooth, hard-packed earth covered with mats of woven reeds. Here there was no rough stone altar, but one of elaborately carved and worked crystal, inset with green and blue gems. Surprisingly, while there was a cross inset in the altar, there was no representation of the Christ or the Virgin, although I did make out what looked like crystal statues glimmering in the shadowy alcoves on either side, set behind and back from the altar.

Nor was the service what I – after a lifetime of service to my God – was used to. Ailbe took his place at the altar, while we and his monks knelt on the floor, with heads bowed. What can I say of their service? No one spoke throughout, though Ailbe's monks all fell to their knees as one man at intervals. The silent ritual obviously followed some pattern; but I certainly couldn't make out what it was, and there was no guidance or signals from Ailbe, who remained motionless behind the crystal altar. We followed suit as best we could, saying our devotions in silence to ourselves, so that we might not defile the rules of their order with our voices. I cannot say I found it a particularly satisfying experience, but I consoled myself that God could hear our thoughts as easily as our spoken words. If the truth be told, I was very tired, and saw signs of great fatigue on the faces of my brothers. It is difficult, if not impossible, to sleep properly at sea – and we had been long asea.

Ailbe must have seen it also when the service ended, for he took us back to the courtyard. Night had almost fallen now and blankets and rough bedding were spread out for us, near the wells. We were destined to sleep outside, obviously, and without a fire; but that seemed no great hardship in the mild air. At least there was solid ground beneath us.

Ailbe then showed me over to the wells. One, he mimed with a cup, was for drinking, and indeed within it I could see the clear sparkling water we had enjoyed earlier. The other well held murkier, but unusually warm water. This, he indicated with scrubbing motions, was for washing. The strange silent man then bowed slightly, smiled and faded back into the dusk. I turned back to the low stone wells and decided to wash. It would be good to scrape the salt from my skin. I was pulling my robe over my head, when I heard someone come up and stop beside me. It was Martyn and I can't, in all honesty, say I was pleased to see him.

'What do you make of this place, Abbot?' he asked quietly.

'Their ways are not ours,' I said shortly. 'But they are certainly very holy men.'

'Holy men, aye, but which religion?'

'The one true religion,' I snapped. Martyn's heretical tendencies were too much for me to stomach in my exhaustion. 'These are monks, Christian monks – you saw the cross worked into their altar; what further proof do you want?'

'I wonder,' he mused, as if to himself. Then he said, 'The cross was a symbol of devotion with some before there was a Christ, you know. There is something strange at work here, I sense. No, Abbot, do not turn away from me. It is not foreknowledge or any forbidden thing I use; it is only my own observations, coupled with a little of what I learned as a young man with the White-Robed Teachers. Have a care not to sleep too soundly tonight.'

So saying, he left me. I tried to put his words from my mind; but it was impossible and, although my body ached in every muscle and felt leaden, my mind refused to relax. I lay down and closed my eyes; but I knew that the slightest noise or footfall would rouse me. The dangers of long nights at sea have taught me to doze lightly when there is none to keep watch.

And yet sleep I did, because, although I can almost swear that no one crept past me through the courtyard, late in the night I awakened to the sound of chanting in the distance. It was faint, but rhythmic and insistent, and throbbed through the still, heavy air. I rubbed my eyes and looked about. My crew lay all around me, wrapped in the thin blankets, huddled or sprawled, but all unquestionably asleep – all save one, who sat up with his back propped against the well.

Moving as quietly as possible, I scrambled across to him and was not surprised to find it was Martyn there, bright-eyed and awake.

'You hear it?' I asked softly.

'Yes. Do you wish me to rouse the others?'

'No, we'll go and investigate for ourselves.' I took it for granted that he would come with me. Prudence, however, made me add, 'I'll wake Geoffrey and tell him that we're going, and that if we do not return within the hour, he and the others can come after us.'

'Good idea,' Martyn said. 'I grew up and was trained in the forests of our own land. My night vision and hearing are better than most. I think I can guide us, if you will let me take the lead.'

I nodded. 'Stay here while I speak to Geoffrey.'

At first Geoffrey wished to accompany us; but I pointed out

that if any mishap befell us, he would be needed to organize and lead a rescue party.

So Martyn and I set off, skirting the lakeshore and moving deeper into the dark forest that surrounded it. The chanting gradually became louder and louder. We made our way through the forest, using Martyn's extraordinary night-sight and then, when the trees thinned out and the ground began to slope upwards, Martyn cautioned me to proceed with the utmost quietness.

Once through the trees, we made our way up a definite slope, beyond which we could hear the pounding of the sea. We crested a small rise, and then dropped flat to the ground, staring down at the strange sight below. We could make out a sheltered horseshoe-shaped cove, bordered on two sides by tall black cliffs and on the third by a beach of luminescent whiteness. Ailbe and his men were gathered in a semi-circle on the beach, facing the open water. They were naked and their hands were raised to the heavens, palms outwards, fingers splayed. Their chanting was in perfect unison, and in a language I had never heard. It was high, thin and sibilant; but one word seemed to be repeated over and over, 'Manannan, Manannan, Manannan . . .'

'Go no further, Brendan,' Martyn whispered, one hand on my arm.

I'm not sure I had any intention of going anywhere. 'What is this?' I whispered back, into his ear.

'They are summoning Manannan, Lord of the Sea. He is one of the People of the Goddess Danu, the Tuatha De Danann.'

Even as he spoke the sea began to change, to resonate in time and in keeping with the chanting. Both the surf and chanting grew stronger. Whitecaps fell upon one another, and the water swirled as if in a storm, though there was not a trace of wind and no clouds obscured the night sky. I blinked as something darted before my eyes, something long and thin and green. It moved again and again, and it took me a few moments to realize that long lines of emerald fire were twisting and darting beneath the waves, coming ashore with the surf. The beach began to glow with an unholy phosphorescent greenness.

'We must leave,' I hissed to Martyn.

He nodded, and then, in the reflected green light, I saw the expression on his face change. 'Too late,' he whispered. 'Too late.'

Suddenly I felt a pain in my head, a piercing dagger that drove deep behind my eyes. Then a voice seemed to speak within my head. 'Stay where you are, Brendan of Clonfert. You have always been a curious man, and now that curiosity will be your doom. You had the choice of staying with us and leaving in peace, but this you did not take; you should have left us alone. Now you know we worship the Lord of the Sea, I'm sure you would wish to join us, for you, of all people, will not wish to anger Manannan.'

I looked down at the single figure of Ailbe standing alone, with the silver-white water foaming around his ankles. 'How is it that you speak to me thus?'

'We have the gift of speaking mind to mind. We do not use our voices, except to summon our God. For the rest, we have as little use for spoken words as we have for your feeble church and Saviour.' Although I couldn't hear the words, the tone of the reply was proud and scornful. All around Ailbe, the others continued their chant. 'Perhaps the small one beside you would make a fitting gift for Manannan. For behold, the Lord of the Sea comes . . .'

Now the chanting was only the single frenzied word 'Manannanmannannnnnnn' repeated over and over again. My will seemed to have deserted me and I could only lie frozen on the hard ground watching the seething water in the bay begin to twist and revolve. It spun, gathering speed into a terrifying whirlpool – and then the water erupted upwards into a single tall spout. But it didn't come crashing back into the waves again. It froze, solidified, resolved itself into a manlike shape, a huge, terrifying, horrific creature from the depths of every mariner's nightmare. Its hair and beard were composed of seaweed, long, filthy and matted. It was hard to define the skin – mercifully – but it seemed to be scaled, and there were long questing tendrils set at regular intervals along the creature's naked body. The eyes were nothing more than pools of water – constantly shifting, twisting, turning. To look into those eyes was to drown. Arms outstretched, the creature reached toward

94

Ailbe and his men – in blessing, or for something else? Ailbe turned towards us, and his men's eyes followed. I saw his arm rise and point . . . and then something cold and utterly unhuman seemed to slide and slither behind my eyes.

From somewhere deep inside myself I found a last vestige of strength. I pressed Martyn's head down into the rough grass. 'Don't look,' I commanded him. 'Ignore it, ignore everything – just pray.'

I prayed then: prayers from my childhood, learned by rote, the formal ritual prayers of my faith, the prayers I had originated in Clonfert and finally just the simple prayers of a man to his God. I do not know how long Martyn and I prayed together while the presence of the sea-god attempted to engulf us. I only know that it seemed a small eternity before I could hear only silence and then, faintly, the start of the dawn chorus of birds. Fearfully, I opened my eyes a fraction. But the beach below was empty, the sea calm and unruffled. Light was just streaking across the bottom of the horizon, though the sun itself had not appeared, and the stars overhead were still hard and sharp.

Stiff and weary, I rose, rousing Martyn who had fallen into an uneasy sleep sometime during the long night. He woke with a scream, and then looked from the beach and back to me. 'You have saved us from the Lord of the Sea, Father Abbot.'

'There is only one Lord,' I said wearily. 'He saved you.'

He stood up and looked down to the beach again. 'No one has ever escaped the Sea-God's appetite. But you defeated him,' he said in wonder.

'Your faith saved you,' I said firmly. 'Now we must check that the others are all right. I'm worried that Geoffrey did not follow.'

But when we returned to the courtyard by the wells, the brothers, including Geoffrey, were still fast asleep. With a sense of betrayal, I shook Geoffrey's huddled form. 'Why didn't you come looking for us?'

'What . . . Brendan, what is it?' he asked drowsily.

'Last night, you were to follow Martyn and myself if we had not returned after an hour,' I said firmly.

'What are you talking about? Follow you – where?' he asked

95

in a troubled manner. 'You didn't say you were going anywhere. Have you been dreaming, Brendan?'

I looked at him for a few moments, and I knew there would be little point in telling him. 'Perhaps,' I said; and perhaps it had all been a dream. But even as I spoke, I looked at my grass- and dew-stained robes, and at my ankles, where the forest branches had scratched them, and I knew it had been no dream.

Geoffrey, now fully awake, sat up and looked around at the buildings which, in the sharp morning light, looked long deserted. 'I wonder what happened to the men who lived here. Were they Christian monks, do you think?'

I looked around at the buildings, which would have been familiar to almost every monk in Erin. Martyn had said that the cross was an ancient symbol before Our Lord was crucified on it; did it then follow that the places of worship should be also familiar? And what of the strange, silent 'monks' – what had happened to them? I could have sworn that they had been real and substantial, yester-eve. But Geoffrey seemed to have no memory of them and, looking around, I could see that the rest of the brothers seemed unperturbed by the absence of the white-robed ones. 'I wonder what happened to the monks,' I said aloud.

'Perhaps the community just died out, with no contact from the mainland,' Geoffrey said quietly. 'It's so isolated here, and I imagine it would be very easy to be forgotten. I wouldn't fancy it myself; and I'm not sure that it would be a very good place for a community of any sort.'

I stared at him and said finally, 'What a very sensible man you are, Geoffrey!'

He looked puzzled, but pleased at the compliment.

I nodded. 'Perhaps.'

Chapter Ten

Eoin, who had been leaning over the prow of the currach, sat up and scraped long tendrils of slime from his fingers. 'This sea looks unwholesome and has the smell of death about it.'

He did not bother to lower his voice – and why should he? Anyone who looked could see the murky, weed-choked water that surrounded us. Foam that was more like scum floated on the rainbow-hued surface, and in places filthy weeds had woven together to form floating mats that were home to scores of long-snouted rats, which darted into the currach at every opportunity. The air was thick with insects, which rose in clouds and settled on our skins, attracted by our sweat and leaving us with tiny red pinpoints which quickly rose into ugly blisters.

This verminous sea had come upon us overnight and, at the back of my mind, I wondered, was it some sending of Ailbe – or, even of the sea-god Manannan? Indeed, I wasn't even sure we were still on the same sea we had left the previous night. The sky was a pale, washed colour and the sun was just a copper disk behind a gauzy covering of thin high cloud.

Small islets abounded in this sea of weeds, but our progress was too slow and badly hampered by the clinging, sticky mass to encourage exploring them. Now we seemed to measure our journey in paces rather than lengths, and every oar-stroke was a concerted effort by the men, as if we were rowing through liquid mud.

A day slipped away, and then another. Soon, our diet was once again reduced to the bread and water which we had been gifted . . . how long ago now?

Nerves frayed quickly. Ruarai and Barran began arguing about their homelands, an interminable quarrel which seemed to centre on which area produced the finest grass and wheat.

Fiachra suddenly became obsessed about a little milk cow that had been in his charge at Clonfert. Martyn whittled on a piece of wood, carving fantastical faces into it that were truly demonic. Even calm, solid Geoffrey snapped at Padraigh when his rowing stroke fell behind the others. And, to be truthful, I felt rather miserable myself, and it took all my inner resources to maintain a cheerful and decisive outward manner. Inwardly, I simply prayed for a favourable breeze to push us from these parts.

After seven interminable days and restless nights, I knew we could stand no more, and I began to be convinced that we were simply going around in circles. The small islands and knolls of rock which we passed all had a dreadful similarity. We would have to land, I decided, and hope for a mountain from which we might be able to plot a course out of this sea. I looked for the largest island on the horizon and gave orders to alter course for it. Both Eoin and Geoffrey looked at me strangely, and I knew what they were thinking – if the sea was so inhospitable, what would the islands be like? But there was nothing for us here, and even less advantage in exhausting our strength further. We had to land.

Hauling the currach onto the beach was heavier work than usual. The thick, scummed water clung to the craft, almost as if it were trying to suck us back. But at last we were on dry land again, and this, in itself, was enough to raise our spirits, although our bodies were wasted by the week's exhausting toil.

The island was similar to many off the coast of Erin: a bleak mixture of stone and sand, with rough scrub grass growing away from the tide's reach. The land was obviously barren of either human or animal life; and yet once this isolated place must have provided home and shelter to someone, for at about a hundred paces from the shore's edge there were the low ruins of a series of rough stone walls. In the centre of the walls was the rounded regular shape of a well. Numbed by the past few nightmare days, we wearily tramped towards it without speaking. Fresh water would be welcome; what we carried in our flasks sustained our lives, but it was flat and stale and there was no pleasure in drinking it, not to mention that our rations of it had been meagre.

Ruarai and Fiachra ran on ahead and reached the well first. When the rest of us arrived, they were already preparing to lower an ancient wooden bucket they'd found lying in the long grass beyond the well, using a length of rope which Ruarai had brought ashore from the currach.

'Almost there, almost to the bottom,' Fiachra said. He was leaning so far over the well's edge that I feared he would fall in. He suddenly pulled himself back and sighed in disappointment. 'There's not enough rope . . .'

Ruarai hauled the empty bucket back up and then untied the cord which held his robe around the waist and spliced it into the rope. 'I'll need a few more,' he said, looking around at the brothers. Several others surrendered their belts, and the lot were knotted together. It tells much of our tiredness that no one was prepared to make the short journey back to our craft for more rope. 'That should be enough, now,' he said, and lowered the bucket over the low lip of the well, with Fiachra once again guiding him.

We all distinctly heard the distant splash. 'That's it!' Fiachra breathed in relief, and then he went to help Ruarai pull the bucket back up.

Eoin and I looked at the water within. It seemed perfectly clear and odourless. 'Someone must fetch a few cups,' I said firmly. 'I'll not see us dipping our heads to a bucket like animals.'

Martyn, who seemed to be less wearied than the others, volunteered, and set off at a steady trot for the beach. Minutes later he returned with half a dozen cups, and as he handed them to me, I noticed the distant, slightly fearful look in his eyes. When he spoke, his voice was low and slow. 'Let no one take more than he requires . . . Do not overindulge . . .' And then he turned and wandered away.

As abbot and as the eldest I was deferred to and the first drink was handed on to me. I sipped at it cautiously. There was none of the brackish flavour one expects from a long-disused well; the water was as cool and sweet as any I had tasted from our own fresh spring at Clonfert. But Martyn's words echoed in my mind, and after the single cupful I gave

99

way to the eager men beside me. A few, like me, took only the single draught; others took two cupfuls and a few – Crosan, Geoffrey and Ultan – took three. I watched the brothers for any signs of ill effects – but there seemed to be none.

I was about to go in search of Martyn when suddenly I felt as tired as I have ever felt in my life. The past week had exhausted me, of course – as it had all my brethren – but this was a sudden leaden tiredness that left me feeling as if I had been struck. I stretched out full length on the ground and attempted to pray, but my tiredness was pressing down on me like a weight. I managed to raise my head and saw that the brothers too were slumping to the ground, yawning hugely. It must have been something in the water . . .

When I awoke, I thought at first that I had dozed only for a few minutes, for the sun was in much the same position as when I had fallen asleep. A few others were stirring, while more lay still soundly in slumber. I sat up slowly, feeling my stiffened muscles crack and ache, and looked around. Martyn was sitting with his back to the well, facing me, whittling one of his strange chesspieces. He held it out between thumb and forefinger for my inspection; it was a pawn in the shape of a monk – and it had his features.

'It's marvellous,' I said shortly, looking at the rest of the brothers. 'I haven't seen you working on that before.'

'I started it when you fell asleep,' he said, with a secretive smile.

He caught my surprised look. Martyn's chesspieces, in all their marvellous, intricate detail, sometimes took days to complete. He laughed shortly. 'Abbot, the sun has set, the moon risen and the sun returned since you were last awake.'

'Impossible; never in health or fever have I slept for so long without pause!' I exclaimed indignantly.

'But never before have you drunk the waters of Lethe.'

'Lethe . . . Lethe,' I murmured. The name was familiar, but vaguely so.

'Lethe is the River of Forgetfulness,' Martyn murmured. 'Luckily you only drank cupfuls of the water. Any more and you would have awoken with the mind of an innocent. Even so, those who took three cupfuls will not stir for another two days,' Martyn added.

I ceased to argue, knowing instinctively that he spoke the truth. Instead, I said with some small anger, 'Why did you not warn us? We can ill afford this delay.'

'The waters of Lethe, drunk in small quantities, have a certain restorative power. You, for example, feel refreshed, ready to continue with the voyage, and you only needed one cupful of the water. The brothers drank according to their need. Crosan is not a well man, and therefore he drank thrice, but he will awaken – like yourself – refreshed. He and the others needed this respite; the past week has been hard on them.'

I stood up, stretching to my full height. What Martyn had said was true – I did feel refreshed and alert. And, if the water did indeed have the same effect on the rest of the brothers, then the delay would indeed have been worthwhile.

As Martyn had said, all were finally awake on the third day. By that time I was almost beside myself with impatience to be gone; but I had to admit that all the brothers, even Crosan, looked wonderfully restored by their rest. We set to sea with the first tide, and the brothers took to the oars without urging, pulling strongly and evenly away from the shore. Strangely, the filthy sea had disappeared as quickly as it had come, and the water had returned to normal. We rowed on into the morning; but I was anxious not to push the brothers to the point of exhaustion, so I ordered the sails hoisted. There was barely a trace of a breeze, but I preferred to trust once again in providence and the current.

As before, we drifted, losing course. Days passed, and all of them without incident. Unlike the previous times, no winds rose to our rescue. Now it was the tide that carried us, while our sails flapped limply. The old fear of sailing around in circles began to grow in me again. It only intensified when, with something approaching despair, I saw in the distance an island that looked remarkably like the Isle of Sheep. Had we slipped back so far? We were losing ground – perhaps even being drawn back to Erin. And then everything, the hardships, the dangers, and the deaths, would have been in vain. I couldn't allow that; it conjured up images of my first disastrous voyage in search of Paradise, all those years ago. And now we were being drawn towards one of those very islands where we had lost a brother to its foul magic. Without explaining why, I at once ordered the brothers to the oars. If we had to lose headway, we had to, but nothing would induce me to revisit that place. I had Eoin call a fast beat, and I didn't let the men rest until I was certain that we were well clear of that accursed island. And, by the grace of God, no sooner had it slipped below the horizon than the sails billowed slightly, the currach lurched and once again we found we were moving westwards.

The breeze picked up, holding steady, and we continued on in this fashion through the remainder of the day and on into the night.

Morning brought colder, sharper weather, a stiffening breeze – and a familiar island. Eoin, who was standing in the prow, shading his eyes, turned to me. 'We are approaching the Bird's Paradise again. Do you want us to land and take on fruit?'

Involuntarily, I glanced at Martyn. His face was grey and sweating. He looked at me, but did not speak. There was nothing in his eyes of fear or desire, only a lonely fatalism. At that moment, I knew he saw something that was to happen – and I pitied him his gift. I turned back to Eoin. 'No, while we have the wind we should use it to move further in our course.'

Both he, and several of the others who had been listening, looked disappointed – I imagined they were thinking of the succulent island fruits.

As we sailed slowly past the length of the island, swarms of birds flew out towards us. They chittered and called out to each other, circling over us, now and then diving lower and nearer to our heads. At first, the men were amused by the sight, but one of the birds' unfortunate habits was making itself noticeable, first on the sails and then, inevitably, on our robes. I saw Eoin brush the top of his head, and then heard him swear. The language was inappropriate from a monk, but I hadn't the heart to reprimand him. Beside him, Conn laughed, then stopped abruptly to feel his own hair.

Abruptly the swarming birds wheeled as one and regrouped

high over our craft before darting back to the island. 'I wonder what that was all about,' Eoin said, scraping muck from his face and beard.

'They might have been just curious . . .' I began, and then I spotted the two massive creatures winging low over the water towards us. They were long and slender-bodied, with an over-large head and beak balanced by an equally large crest or horn, which jutted out from the back of their heads. Their wing-span was huge, and even from a hundred lengths their talons and beaks looked menacing. If ever the embodiment of pure evil could be distilled into a creature of the air, then surely this was it.

'Row,' I shouted. 'As hard and as fast as you can. Row.'

'Which direction?' Geoffrey asked.

'Any way you choose, but get us away from this island.'

The men responded to the alarm in my voice, and the oars moved with strength and precision. Still the great birds were gaining on us, and they were overhead in moments, their hideous shadows darkening our deck. Suddenly one dived down and stabbed at Martyn with its beak as it swooped by. It was so close that I could actually see the tiny coarse feathers that covered its foul-smelling body, and when it opened its mouth and screamed, I saw the hundreds of tiny triangular teeth set in rows all along its jaws.

Blood trickled down Martyn's forehead; but he remained at his oar, rowing steadily. The second creature folded its leathery wings with a clap of sound and swooped at him, claws extended. Martyn looked up, and I saw his eyes glaze over, but whether from terror or his prescient gift, I couldn't tell.

As the creature dropped, Barran, who was sitting behind Martyn, brought up his oar and swiped at it. The sudden movement distracted the bird, sending it careening off to one side, where it struggled with its ungainly wings, attempting to gain height. But now the first bird had returned for a second attempt. It darted in, but once again Barran – and now Fiachra – drove it away with their oars.

More and more of the brothers were lifting their oars from the water, and the currach was beginning to wallow. 'Keep rowing,' I ordered. 'Keep rowing.'

The huge birds continued to hover, but less certainly, seeking advantage. One darted in, but Fiachra caught it a blow on the underside of its black-feathered body. Its shriek was terrible, an almost human-sounding blend of rage and pain as it flapped away, the wingtips actually brushing the surface of the sea as it attempted to climb. The other made a final assay at Martyn's chest, but Barran was too swift for it, and thrust the end of his oar upwards, at its neck. Its long beak closed instinctively over it – and Barran jerked downwards at the same time, pulling the creature into the waves. It screamed again and again and then thick reddish black ichor stained the water all around it, until at last it disappeared in a welter of bloody foam. Its mate watched its death struggle, and then it turned away from our craft, and headed back to its paradise.

Geoffrey moved quickly to Martyn's side, cleansing his wound with water and applying a compress of herbs to heal the cut, which, although it was bleeding profusely, seemed shallow. I moved up to the prow of the craft, indicating to Ruarai that I would take his place beside Eoin. For a while we rowed in silence, then Eoin paused to wipe the sweat from his brow. He said to me, 'What was that all about?'

'The birds did not wish us to return. Or perhaps Morag commanded them to keep us away,' I said evasively.

Eoin was not satisfied, any more than I would have been with such an answer. 'Those creatures would have killed Martyn – perhaps all of us; they really didn't seem too fussy. I'd call that more than a warning. Why did they attack us?'

'I'm your abbot, not some supernatural being who can see into the minds and hearts of all living creatures,' I snapped. 'I have enough trouble understanding myself, let alone the rest of you. I don't know what the bird creatures wanted; perhaps they have a taste for man-flesh.'

'I beg your pardon, Father Abbot,' Eoin said, with stiff formality. 'I did not mean to question your authority.' Again he applied himself to rowing, and every strong stroke, every motion of his powerful arms, rebuked me. I could not bear to hurt him. Eoin had become dear to me. I tried to be a father to all my monks, to love all equally; but I was human, and had my favourites. Some, I considered to be little more than children; others, like Geoffrey, were good and trusted companions. Some, like Martyn and Padraigh, I could never feel at ease with, though for different reasons. But Eoin touched some desiccated place in my heart and made it green again.

'There is a reason the birds attacked,' I said slowly. 'But I am bound, partly by my judgement, and partly by the confessional, not to reveal it. I would not willingly speak of another's sin.'

Eoin turned to me in understanding and quick sympathy. 'Of course, father; your goodness and courage are a lesson to us all. It is not my place to question your wisdom.'

Obscurely, his praise made me feel even more uncomfortable than his earlier withdrawal. It cast me in a heroic mould, even as I sometimes saw myself in more arrogant moments; at the same time, it isolated me from my few companions in a way that promised only loneliness – and disappointment.

There was no time for musings, however, for the storm clouds were gathering. The men's rowing had slowed in response to a sea that grew ever more turbulent. Gusts of wind pushed at the sails, then died. The sky was changing rapidly. There was an ugly, sulphurous-yellow cast to the horizon that betokened foul weather indeed. We were starting to pitch and roll in a growing sea. Crosan, I noted, was vomiting over the side of the currach, the only incidence of seasickness since the first week when we had left the foot of Didache. I went over to him, dipped a cloth in the water and mopped his brow.

'Lean back, close your eyes,' I advised. 'The sails will do most of the work, now.'

'Oh, it's not just the sea. Too much rich food in my unrepentant days at court, Brendan.' He attempted a smile. 'I'd hoped to atone in the hereafter, but it appears my stomach must do penance in this world.'

'You'll be fine,' I murmured. 'When the storm eases, then so will your contrite stomach.'

'Just as you say, Brendan.' He put a hand limply on my arm, drawing me closer. 'If it is more than the storm this time, if I should not be able to complete this voyage with you, I would rather be buried at sea. I don't want to rest till Judgement Day on some unknown island. Leave my remains to the water and the tides, and who knows, maybe they'll be washed up on the shore of my own land?'

'You're not going to die,' I said, with more assurance than I felt. 'It's only the seasickness. Believe me, it can make more seasoned sailors than yourself wish for death.'

His eyes, bright and feverish and far too large in his small face, looked up at me. 'Promise me, Brendan?'

I nodded, suddenly chilled. 'As you wish.'

The currach was now racing along, with wind and current pushing us I knew not where. I moved back up to the prow, my eyes constantly scanning the sea, the horizon, for any sign of land. I did not hope to find shelter. An island now could pose the ultimate danger, for any sort of beach would be impossible. No, I kept fearful watch that we would not be driven towards land before we could make some effort to alter course, our boat smashed against the rocks which would lurk in shallow water. Eoin joined me, and we divided the sea between us; he to watch the port side, and I the starboard. Like me, he knew the other danger signs – sand bars, freak waves.

A bolt of lightning shot across the sky, briefly illuminating the blackish clouds against the ominous yellow background, and then the rain started. It poured on us, soaking us to the skin in minutes. Eoin and I stood firm, though a quick glance behind saw the others huddling miserably in their sodden robes, an instinctive attempt to curl up and present the smallest target to the fierce natural elements.

How long we stood and how far we travelled, I do not know. It felt endless, but I suspect that it was no more than half a day in real time before Eoin shouted, 'Ahead; something! Martyn, Geoffrey, Fiachra, Ruarai, be ready at the sails.'

Through the rain and murky gloom, I too could discern something rising in the sea. A rock perhaps? Certainly it was far too small to be an island. Whatever it was, we did not want to wash up against it. 'Alter course as best you can to port,' I ordered.

We began to tack. The fierce current had eased, but it was slow progress working first with and then without the wind. I knew we were moving away from our former course, yet the rock seemed no further away. Indeed, the next time I looked to measure the distance, it was closer than before and taller. With horrified eyes, I saw it start to change shape, or rather to reveal its shape. It was moving towards us, faster than we could travel away.

'My God, what is it?' Eoin breathed. His strong hands grasped the prow so tightly that his knuckles gleamed white.

'God alone knows,' I replied. 'A sea creature probably, some creature utterly beyond my ken. And only God can help us now, for we cannot outrun it, and our few weapons will not triumph over it.'

As it came closer and I could see more of its form, I felt a terror greater than I had ever known. It was like a squid, those many-limbed tiny creatures that are sometimes washed up on Erin's shore. But this was huge, and there seemed to be too many waving tentacles for a squid. I briefly saw two flat discs above a triangular beak before the creature sank beneath the choppy waves. Around me my brethren began to pray audibly.

A blow hit the side of the currach, causing us to roll so deeply that we shipped water in over the side. We righted, and a long thick tentacle slid along the side of the craft, as if it were caressing it. Then a second blow struck the craft from behind, pitching us forward and up. There was a moment of respite while the monster dived below the surface, and disappeared completely. Then, with a ghastly sucking sound, the entire currach rose beneath our feet, right out of the water. We were suspended for what felt like an age on the monster's back, looking down at the sea on either side; then, as suddenly, we dropped back again, smacking the surface of the water with a force that drove everyone to their knees. It was, I realized, playing with us as a cat will with a mouse – we were prey too small to demand a quick kill. And even as a small animal will go quiet, losing its fear in the certainty of imminent death, so my fear abruptly left me.

It was as if I had stepped aside from my body and could now look at it and judge its actions dispassionately. I took some comfort from the fact that I had tried my best. If my life and this voyage were to end here, like this, then so be it. Perhaps the ancients were right, and our fate is ordained from the moment of our birth. If this were so, then I would meet that fate standing erect, as a man. And I knew then, in that calm stillness while waiting for the creature to attack, that I had come to terms with myself, and what I was.

Though my knees ached from the jarring, I hauled myself to my feet. Eoin did the same.

We waited.

And nothing happened.

The craft continued to pitch and roll, but only with the sea. The monster was no more than twenty lengths away from us; but it, too, was still and poised, as if it too waited. Then, before our eyes, the sea rose up and parted behind the terrible creature. A jet of steam issued forth, and I saw that which I had not thought to see again: Jasconius.

The whale seemed larger than I remembered it, larger than my mind could happily comprehend. The sea monster seemed as mesmerized as we were. Then it shuddered from a blow as great to it as its own had been to our boat. Jasconius struck again, sinking the monster. It resurfaced and attempted to wrap its tentacles around the whale, but Jasconius shook them off almost arrogantly. The creature tried to move away, but the whale was on top of it, its massive flukes and tail battering at the squid-like tentacles and bloated body. The wake from their struggle pushed the currach away from them both. Each time the monster surfaced, Jasconius struck it with his massive body. Jasconius too was moving, a stately, measured movement, in the opposite direction to our craft's slight progress – almost as if he were deliberately leading the creature away from us. Finally, he was in a position to lash out with his great tail. The blow was swift, and unimaginably violent, thrusting the water out into a huge wave which bore down upon us. I tried to turn our prow into the wave, but too late. Instead, it caught us astern and the force of it drove us from the site of the battle.

I don't know how long they struggled, but large waves followed one upon the other, pushing us further and further away; and it was late evening before they at last slackened – a sign that the battle was over. I wondered briefly who had won.

But no fight was left in us. We had ridden with the waves as best we could, but it had been hard, exhausting work. There was nothing from which I could take a bearing, and the cloud cover was now so thick that I doubted even the stars would shine through to guide me by night.

'What now?' Geoffrey asked at last, in a voice weary of every emotion.

'Nothing. We sleep and we drift,' I said.

Chapter Eleven

We drifted, then. After twenty-three days, I stopped counting. The days merged imperceptibly into one another. By day the sky was grey and overcast, with rain-storms following one upon the other. Nor did they let up when night fell; so we were without moon or stars to guide us. If the truth were known, the stars had become little more than a reference – we had long since given up trying to use them as we would the stars off Erin – but I would still have found comfort in those points of light.

And always there was the wind, and the swollen battering sea.

I dozed for a lot of the time, awakening without realizing it, then drifting back into sleep again. Perhaps the elements had got into my old bones and a fever set in, for the days passed like a dream – as perhaps they were. But no, not like a dream, for that suggests something pleasant. Call it a nightmare instead, full of phantasms and fear and an aching tiredness.

At some half-conscious level I was aware of what was happening aboard the currach; but when I felt the boat hurl itself against something solid, it took long, precious moments before full realization of what was happening sank in. I heard Eoin call out, 'Land,' and then someone else shouted, 'We're going to hit,' and I came fully awake as a huge wave caught us astern, lifting us and carrying us perhaps a hundred paces. The wave crested – and then disappeared. There was a momentary impression of hanging in mid-air, and then we smashed down onto a golden-sanded beach. The currach tipped at a crazy angle, its prow partially wedged in the sand. Everything – oars, flasks, provisions and monks – was thrown out onto the beach, leaving us scattered amongst our belongings like so much flotsam and jetsam.

I lay on the warm sands, dazed and sickened, hearing bells and a high-pitched twittering ringing in my head. After a score or more of painful, throbbing heartbeats, the ringing sounds died down; but the other, the giggling sounds, remained. And then I suddenly realized that I was actually hearing someone laughing, in a young, high, girlish voice!

I scrambled to my feet and then stood there, swaying dizzily, and looked around. There was no one in sight; but the woods enclosing the strand on three sides could hide any number of people.

'Who's there?' I called out. Around me my brothers were slowly climbing to their feet.

I heard giggling sounds again, but this time the noise came from several directions. 'Who's there?' I called again, peering into the trees and bushes. But I was still ill and shaken after my slight bout of feverishness and the shock of our landing, and for a few moments they swam before my eyes, assuming strange and sometimes familiar shapes. As I stared towards a gnarled oak-like tree, the broad leaves parted and a small face peered out at me. I shook my head, pressing the heels of my hands into my eyes. But when I looked again, the face remained and bright golden-brown eyes stared merrily into mine.

'What are you?' I demanded; and then fear made me angry. 'Who are you,' I snapped, 'that finds the distress of others so amusing?'

The leaves trembled and then parted to allow a slight figure to drop to the ground. There was a moment's confusion as leaves swirled and eddied, both from the tree and the ground where the figure had dropped; and then I suddenly realized I was looking at another human being. A girl, who appeared to be in the first flush of adolescence, stepped forward.

'I'm sorry,' she began. 'We did not mean to mock you, truly we didn't. But you looked so funny. Those long brown dresses, and your faces, all that hair on them.' Her mouth trembled, and then she put her hand over it to stifle a laugh.

My hand went instinctively to my chin, feeling the heavy growth of beard. It had indeed been a long time since I – or indeed, any of the others – had had the opportunity or thought to shave. I stared at the girl, taking in her appearance fully for the first time. Her skin was dark, deeply tanned, but her hair

111

was the same kind of tawny golden brown as her eyes. Her features were delicate and lovely, in a heart-shaped face that ended in a small, slightly pointed chin. Her gown was the colour of forest leaves in spring, loose-flowing – and . . . I averted my eyes. As she stepped out from beneath the shadow of the tree, I suddenly saw that the fabric was nearly transparent and it was obvious that she was rather older than I had supposed. I felt the blood rush to my cheeks and I was suddenly glad of my beard.

I turned my back on her – and found most of my crew gazing goggle-eyed at her. 'See to the currach and our stores,' I snapped, 'unless you plan to go hungry tonight.'

Turning back to the girl, I chose a spot somewhere over her head and kept my eyes firmly fixed there. I cleared my throat, which had suddenly gone dry. 'How can you criticize the appearance of Christian monks, whose every effort for months has been spent only in surviving?' I demanded in my most authoritative voice. 'What right have you when you yourself are dressed – or should I say nearly dressed – as you are? Have you no decent garments to wear? You are too old to wander around as naked as a small child. Have you no shame?'

I lowered my eyes carefully, as far as her face, but the girl only looked puzzled and not abashed.

In the tone of a parent humouring an unreasonable child, she said, 'If my dress displeases you, I'll remove it.'

'No!' I shouted as she reached down for the hem of her gown. I took a deep breath and asked in a more moderate voice, 'What are you called, and who are your people? Are your parents nearby?'

'I am Gwennan. Some of my sisters are quite close by. I'll call them, if you promise me you mean no harm?' Her voice rose in a question.

'We are holy men,' I said. It might be an exaggeration, but I strongly sense that the word 'Christian' would mean nothing to her. 'We intend no harm here, or anywhere in our travels.'

She smiled, showing small, perfectly even white teeth. 'Oh, good. My sisters are ever so curious to see you close up; but they were afraid. I'll call them.' With that, she put two fingers in her mouth and whistled what sounded like a bird's call.

112

Leaves and branches all around us rustled and quivered and five more girls emerged from behind the trees. They were so alike that they might have been taken for sisters; but as they came closer it became clear that, although they might have been related, they were too close in age to be sisters, as Gwennan had claimed. All, like Gwennan, were short for their apparent years, and slender, moving with quick lithe grace. Some had darker hair, some more fair. Two had golden-brown eyes like Gwennan, three had eyes the colour of the sea. All were pretty, all were smiling, and all were wearing the same sort of unfortunate costume. They were neither a proper sight nor fitting company for any man, and especially men unaccustomed to the society of women in the first place, and who had been so many months at sea in the second.

For the sake of our souls, I decided we must leave this island quickly. But a glance at the currach told me that this would be impossible. Several of the staves had been broken in our hasty beaching and there were at least two holes punched through the triple thickness of hides. Not only must we stay awhile on this isle, but we would probably need help of some sort if we were to get afloat again quickly.

'Can I meet your parents?' I asked Gwennan.

Gwennan frowned, suddenly making her small face seem older. 'Well, you can't meet my father. Even I've never met him – well, at least I don't remember meeting him, though my mother told me he came to see me shortly after I was born. Certainly I can take you to my mother, if you wish.' Her voice became soft and wistful. 'She is very beautiful and very wise, but she speaks so rarely to us these days.'

Ordinarily, this tale of a feckless father and silent mother would rouse my deep sympathy, but the girl herself was without any trace of self-pity, probably because she had come to accept this as normal.

'Come along,' she said, extending a small hand to me.

I looked back at my brothers, who suddenly became very absorbed in studying the damage to the currach. All except Martyn, who was looking at me, and smiling in amusement. I wasn't best pleased with his knowing grin, but at least I could discern no trace of unlawful desire in it. Perhaps the women of his own people had gone about in a similar state of inadequate covering, and he was used to it. In any case, his knowledge might prove useful, and I decided to take him with me.

As if reading my thoughts, he walked over to me. 'If I might be allowed to accompany you?' he asked softly.

I nodded silently and, after a moment's hesitation, I took Gwennan's small, long-fingered hand. Martyn fell into step beside me. As we entered the forest, he leaned over and murmured softly to me, 'Her mother may be rather different to what you expect.'

'I'm absolutely sure she will be,' I muttered half under my breath.

Gwennan led us surefootedly along a winding animal track through the woods until we reached a small circular glade. My first impressions were that this was a holy place. It had that aura of peace and tranquillity that pervades the shrines of the Christian as well as the pagan faiths. The grass was short and tender, with a springtime freshness to it, although autumn was upon us, and there were small clusters of brightly coloured flowers clustered about the base of the trees. In the middle of the glade was a single tall aspen tree. Gwennan ran over and wrapped her arms about its slender trunk. 'Look what I have brought you, Mother,' she murmured. 'The older one wishes to speak to you.'

Suddenly all the exhaustion, the doubts, and the fear welled up in me and almost as quickly dissolved away, leaving me with but one emotion. Anger. I had come too far and endured too much to indulge a young girl's games. But before I could speak, Martyn laid a hand on my arm, his fingers squeezing warningly. 'Listen,' he said shortly, staring at the tree.

I turned to look at him, but he was ignoring me, staring at the tree. I looked back at the tree and listened. The forest was surprisingly quiet, a few birds called to one another in the background, and faintly in the distance I could hear the vague susurration of the sea. Leaves rustled in the faintest of breezes. The delicate branches of the aspen quivered in the slight wind, giving the illusion that they were bending to respond to Gwennan, who was still embracing the slender trunk of the tree. I heard nothing out of the ordinary and was about to say so to Martyn when the leaves of the aspen brushed against one another in an audible, recognizable sound.

'Wel . . . come Brendaaaannnn.'

Martyn's fingers tightened on my arm. 'It's as I thought,' he said in an awed whisper. 'She is a dryad, a child of the tree.'

'And what was her father?' I snapped. 'A pine cone?'

'Oh, her father was possibly a passing sailor, or even one of the lesser sea-gods,' Martyn said casually, taking no note of my sarcasm. 'His identity or nature would not be that important to them.'

'I've never heard of them,' I said, looking at Gwennan and then at the aspen tree.

Martyn turned to look at me in genuine surprise. 'But you must have; every race has some legends of the Tree Folk. Surely you've heard of Woodwives?'

I nodded sourly. 'Aye, I've heard of them. Females from the front, and nothing but a hollow tree when looked at from behind. I've always thought it strange that men only discovered their true nature when they had lain with the tree or woman or whatever it is,' I snapped.

'There are such things as Woodwives,' Martyn said quietly. 'Just as there are dryads. There are two distinct species. There are dryads, who live with and amongst the trees; and hama-dryads, who are the offspring and spirits of a single species of tree. Of course nowadays the names are often confused. Dryads are always lovely to look at and endlessly romantic when young; but, in the long term, they prefer the company of their own kind . . .' Martyn paused, frowning.

'What is it?' I demanded.

His voice changed, becoming more serious. 'I know their ways – they are most keen on conception, Abbot, and I'll wager men of any sort do not come to this island often. They may find our brothers a sore temptation.'

'How?' I asked, puzzled.

Martyn grinned. 'Like most races, the Tree Folk must perpetuate themselves – they may – nay, will, attempt to enlist the brothers for that purpose. They are not immortal; but they live a very long time and, as you can see, they alter greatly. The aspen would once have been very like Gwennan, you know.'

'No, I don't know,' I snapped. 'All I can appreciate at the moment is that we are surrounded by scantily clad, giggling females who you say are somehow related to this . . . this tree. And I also know that we must find some wood to repair the currach's frame and be on our way.'

Martyn chuckled to himself. I'd never seen this sombre soul so light-hearted before. 'Indeed, we must. I like the dryads and understand them a little – I've met one or two in my childhood, though they are fast disappearing from our own land. One thing more,' he added. 'I'd have a care to ask them what wood you may take. They are sensitive on the subject of living trees, even those not of their own kind.'

I nodded shortly; and then we waited while Gwennan chatted softly to the aspen tree – I still couldn't think of it as her 'mother'. When she finally came over and joined us, I asked her if there might be some dead wood about which we could use to replace the broken staves in our craft.

'Mother said we are to render you every assistance,' she said slowly, looking from me to Martyn and smiling slyly.

'Aye,' I nodded uncomfortably, aware of the flush spreading over my face. 'Thank you.'

'We'll go back to the beach and you must show me the wooden shapes you require. Then my sisters and I will find some for you. That way, you will not harm anything by mistake.'

Back at the currach, all was in chaos. There were at least two score of Gwennan's sisters swarming around my brothers, fingering their robes, touching their faces. I even saw one reach up daringly to Geoffrey's beard, but he slapped her hand away – and then drew back his fingers, holding them as if they stung.

'They are Tree Folk,' Martyn reminded me with a smile. 'Thick skinned.'

'You needn't sound so pleased,' I said sourly. 'We're leaving here as soon as possible; and I don't want anyone wandering off on his own.' I quickly counted the brothers. There was one missing. 'Where's Conn?'

The sudden alarm in Martyn's eyes frightened me. 'He could be anywhere on the island,' he said unhappily. 'Wait –

listen, from behind those trees . . .'

Barely a hundred paces to our right, the trees came down almost to the waterline; and the sound of laughter carried from behind them. Martyn and I broke into a run towards the source of the merriment, fearing the worst.

We found Conn in a clearing amongst the trees, surrounded by three of the waif-like girls. They were tossing a brightly coloured disc from one to another, while he ran to and fro attempting to catch it. And while they were all laughing – Conn more than most – I noticed that the eyes of the creatures were cold and calculating.

Conn spun around – and crashed headlong into Martyn. Colour rose to his face. 'It was only a game,' he began, but the look on Martyn's face silenced him.

I wrapped my hand in the rough cloth of his robe and hauled him through the trees, only releasing him when we came in sight of the boat. 'Join your brethren,' I said coldly, nodding to Ruarai and Tadgh.

I hurried over to the currach. I found Eoin deep in the prow, peeling back layers of hide from part of the frame, while one of the dryads peered solemnly at him over the edge of the craft. He looked up at me red-faced. 'Can't you do something about them? Can't you make them go away?' he demanded.

'Yes, yes,' I said impatiently. Easy to say, but how to dispose of the maidens, I wondered. I stood up and looked around, and then something a long way down at the far end of the strand caught my eye. 'Show them the two broken ribs of the boat,' I said, still staring down the beach, 'and tell them to go off and find something similar. Say that Gwennan's mother said they were to do it.'

I looked around my crew. Since Ruarai, Conn, Tadgh and Fiachra seemed less displeased with the female companionship than the others, I told them to come with me. Fiachra put down the cat's cradle of string he'd been demonstrating to one of the fair-haired girls, with some reluctance. 'They're very different to the farmers' daughters I grew up with,' he said wistfully. 'I wonder if all the women on this island are so pretty . . .?'

'They change drastically as they grow older,' I snapped.

I hurried down the strand, with the four brothers trailing almost reluctantly behind. As we neared the object, I began to get a vague idea of what it was. My suspicions quickly became a certainty. I knew now who had won the sea battle.

The squid creature lay sprawled on the beach ahead of us. When we were within ten paces of it, Tadgh restrained me, saying, 'Perhaps it lives still, and is only resting. Have a care how close we get.'

I shook my head. 'It's long dead,' I said. Could he not smell the stench of putrefacation and death? I walked on, knowing that I must face one final time the monster that had brought me to such extremes of terror and that even now haunted my dreams.

Even in death, it was a terrible sight. The grey tentacles – there were a dozen of them – were scattered about, revealing rows of blood-red suckers along their undersides. The beak-like mouth gaped, and inside was a curious arrangement of teeth: three rows lined the upper half and two rows were on the bottom. The outer rows were sharp and pointed, for ripping, while both inner rows were blunt, grinding teeth. The middle row in the upper jaw had odd serrated edges that I realized could saw away at any substance. The brownish-grey hide was tough, even now defined by layers of muscle, but there were huge gaping holes in it, where it had obviously been torn away by Jasconius. There were two bloodied holes on its huge bulbous head, where the eyes must have been, before the sea-birds got to them.

Whatever private demons I had laid to rest, the carcass had an equally sobering effect on my young companions. They ceased to chatter about the dryads' many charms and walked back with me in silence.

When we reached the currach, I found Martyn kneeling beside Crosan. The former jester was clammy with sweat and already seemed to exude something of the smell of death my nostrils had so lately held.

I knelt in the warm sands beside Crosan and he smiled up at me. 'Those nymphs would break many a heart at court, Brendan. Even at my age, I'm tempted to try a few of my old jests on them. It's probably as well my stomach restrains my baser nature.'

'Be quiet, you old reprobate,' Martyn said gently. He eased his head upwards. 'Here, take another draught of this to cool your hot blood.'

Martyn held a flask with herbs infused in it to Crosan's lips. Minutes later Crosan closed his eyes and lay back, resting. Martyn disengaged his arm and we walked a little away from the sleeping man, before standing to stare back at him. In a soft voice, he said, 'I have given him what medicine I have. If nothing else, it will ease his pain. But I think he is dying.'

I nodded. Another death that could be laid at my feet. 'Join the others,' I said finally. 'I will stay here, and pray for him.'

'I'll bring you some food . . .'

'No, I'm not hungry.'

Crosan's condition continued to deteriorate during the remainder of the day. I spent the time by his side and resolved to pass the night with him. I had seen men die before, and I knew it was only a matter of time. Much as I wanted to depart this island, it would be cruel to take a man in his state back to sea. The least I could do would be to allow him to die on firm land.

Much of the time he hardly seemed to know where he was. Then he would have periods of lucidity, when he would speak to me of his life, of how much joining our community had meant to him. My brethren worked quietly on the boat, and almost casually thanked Gwennan and her sisters when they returned a little while later with pieces of seasoned wood. The girls wandered over to look at Crosan; but something about him seemed to frighten them, and they slipped away into the trees and were gone.

Martyn wandered over and handed me a pitcher of cool water. 'Where have they gone?' I asked.

'They are young; they have never seen death,' he said. 'It is outside their experience and they fear it.' He nodded to me and wandered away.

While Crosan slept, I contemplated the dryads. They could not fathom men who found them less than enchanting, and I could not really understand what seemed to be a curious mixture of wantonness and innocence. I knew intuitively that I could lecture them on Christian moral values from now 'till next year without making the slightest impact on their minds or souls. And yet, incomprehensibly, they had nothing of the sordid air of corruption I had always sensed beneath the physical allure of other fallen women I had encountered. Even amongst pagans, I had found some latent sense of sin; but not here. It must be, I finally decided, because they were not fully human.

In the meantime, on the currach, the hides were being carefully restitched round the new ribs, and other small tears were scrutinized minutely. When Barran suggested finding a spring and refilling the water-flasks, I passed the task to Geoffrey and Martyn. Since I could not leave Crosan, I judged them the least susceptible to nubile charms.

By dark, all had been done to the currach that could be done. The brothers had a simple meal, but I was still fasting. I noticed that Gwennan and her sisters were watching us intently from the safety of the trees. Even had Crosan not needed me, I would have stayed awake that night, for a man caught between waking and sleeping is rarely master of himself, and the girls might prove too much of a temptation. And sure enough, as the moon passed behind a cloud, I heard a faint rustle, and a slender, shadowy form stole out from the trees and made its way towards where Fiachra lay. Terror lent me speed. As the dryad bent down towards the sleeping form, I grabbed her from behind, round the waist, and lifted her off her feet.

For one so slender, she was surprisingly heavy, and instead of struggling with her unknown attacker, she seemed to melt against me, her arms wrapping around my neck, her bare legs coiling around my waist.

I was tired and I was angry. Half-carrying and half-pushing her, I stumbled to the water's edge – and dropped her into the icy shallows. 'Don't come back,' I hissed and stalked off. There were no further incidents to break my night's vigil.

Just before dawn Crosan awoke. His speech was so clear that for an instant I allowed myself to hope that he was rallying. But no, it was simply that God had granted him a last respite to make his peace with this world. His confession was slow and painful both for him and me, and towards the end his words became laboured and difficult. At last he looked quizzically at me and said, 'Your promise . . . you remember your promise, Brendan?'

'It shall be as you wish,' I assured him.

The small man nodded, satisfied. Crosan spoke no more, and as the reddish hues of the rising sun were just visible on the horizon, a curious rattle came from his throat and he was gone. He died too young, too soon; but unlike many he had made his peace with himself and his God.

It seemed auspicious to me that he should pass away on a fair dawn with the coming of a new day. From what I knew of the ancient Celtic lore, it was a good time to die. Soon it would be time to leave, but for a little while I wanted to be alone. Scarcely heeding where I was going, I headed down the strand, away from the others, who were still fast asleep.

Soon, I was upon the spot where yesterday the dead squid-like creature had lain. Now there was nothing to be seen but its bare bones – and surprisingly few of them at that. The waves played lightly at their edges, but there were no high tide marks above them to suggest what had happened to strip them so clean of all flesh.

I would not question it. In that cool, red-gold dawn, I preferred to take it as another friendly omen for our voyaging on.

Chapter Twelve

And so we lost another man.

We held a service for Crosan, on the beach close to the spot where he had breathed his last; and I found that his death seemed to have more of an effect on my brethren than our earlier losses. He'd been a good-natured and self-effacing companion, the sort of man who would listen to a man's worries without attempting to unburden himself; he gave advice only rarely, and it was always to the point. Except when he assumed his clown's guise and entertained us, he was a quiet, private man, and one whom we all admired and respected. Sadly, such men are often only fully appreciated when they have gone. While he'd been with us, we'd taken him for granted; but there was genuine grief on most faces as I spoke the words of a simple service over his body.

I gave the final blessing and crossed myself, and then I looked around the still, silent group. 'Our brother had no desire to be buried on these pagan lands,' I began slowly. 'It was his final wish to be buried at sea.' I saw several nodding. 'I'll need someone to prepare him . . .' I added.

Padraigh and Barran stepped forward immediately, and volunteered to wrap his body in a spare blanket, weighting it carefully with some stones so that the corpse would not float back to the surface of the water. When preparations were complete, we set sail quickly, ignoring the small faces of the dryads, which peered inquisitively from the forest. Since Crosan's death they had kept well away from us – almost as if we were diseased – but I realized afterwards that it might have been the first time they had ever seen someone die.

I stood in the prow of the currach, watching the men carefully lower the body of their brother into the waves. There was a brief splash, a few ripples; the brown bundle was visible for a few heartbeats as it sank – then nothing. Crosan had passed from us. Our numbers were once again diminished, and would be more so before our voyage's end. I knew this with a chilling certainty, as if – like Martyn – I too had been gifted with some degree of foresight. I looked at my brethren, wondering which one would go to our Maker next.

I turned back to the island. The current was quick and the tide was with us. Already we were a league and more out to sea, and the isle was little more than a green haze on the horizon. As it vanished completely I wondered just how well I had chosen my crew . . . not too well, to judge by the results so far.

But at the back of my mind, a small voice reminded me that I had passed on that responsibility to Nevin. Had I wished, in some way, to avoid the guilt of their ultimate fates? But all had been eager to come; indeed, three had actually forced themselves upon me. Yet I always came back to the same question: if they truly knew the manner and duration of the voyage they were starting upon, would they have been so eager? Had I told them enough for them to make their decisions?

My reverie was interrupted as Padraigh came and stood beside me, staring back across the waves. And almost as if he had read my thought, he said, 'Would that I had known how long this journey would be, and the fears and sorrows it would bring, on that evening long ago, at the foot of Didache.'

'Would it have made any difference?' I wondered. 'And would you have threatened to fast to death if I didn't take you with me? Would you have come?' I asked curiously.

'I don't think so. I don't know,' Padraigh replied, but softly, as if he were speaking more to himself. 'I was looking for something in Erin, something . . .' He shrugged uncomfortably. 'I'm not even sure what I was looking for; something strange and magical. I've seen wonders enough – but I never realized just how helpless I would feel in the face of them.'

'You have your faith to sustain you,' I advised him.

He glanced quickly at me. 'There are degrees of faith, Abbot, and mine does not give me the power and comfort yours gives you,' he said.

'Faith is faith,' I said impatiently. 'Either you believe or you do not – and if you don't then you are damned.'

123

'Have you never wondered, never questioned?' Padraigh asked, very quietly, with almost a note of pleading in his voice. 'Was there never something which meant more to you than your belief in God?'

'No,' I said quickly, suddenly feeling uncomfortable. 'I've never doubted.' I straightened up and rubbed my hands together, feeling the palms hot and moist. 'We are Christian monks,' I said quickly. 'Our faith is all we have – trust in it, for it gives power and sustenance to us all.'

I moved away and occupied myself with our course. By the position of the sun we were bearing due westward, with a moderate wind and a favourable current. West, our voyage had taken us always into the west, with some little deviations either to the north or south; but in the main our course remained fixed. And we still didn't know where. What I would have given for a chart . . . but I'd never even seen a crude map of the seas so far to the north and west of Erin.

A map! How could I have been so short-sighted, so foolish? All along, I should have been sketching the islands and the waters we had seen, fashioning a record for those who would undoubtedly follow. Was I really so arrogant to believe myself not only the first man to sail this course, but also that I should be the last ever to do so?

But it wasn't too late – although much time had passed since we had commenced our voyage, the islands and differing seas were still as fresh and as vivid in my memory as if they had only happened yesterday. Some things one can never forget. I determined I would try to recall the islands and distances between them as best I could, and note any other points of reference which might be useful. There were any number of scraps of hide in the currach, left over from past repairs or set aside for future use, and Padraigh had some ink and crude pens which he always carried about his person. He lent them reluctantly, I thought, but without comment; and so I sat down in the stern of the currach and set to my task.

I am no draughtsman, nor even very much a man of letters, though I was schooled as well as any. I have for so long been a man of action that any form of writing, let alone drawing, is slow work for me and, as abbot, there was always someone to do my writing for me. I suppose I got out of practice. My brethren were curious, but reluctant to ask directly what I was doing – all except Padraigh, who came and sat by me, peering sidelong at my work. I saw his lips curl and I remembered that he had been a great scribe before he came to Clonfert.

After watching me for a while, Padraigh spoke in a carefully neutral voice. 'I think I could help you, if you wish, Abbot. Most of the work I once did was on manuscripts, but I am tolerably good at charts and plans.'

My first reaction was that I preferred to struggle on in my own way, but then I realized that this was certainly vanity on my part. If God had gifted our brother with skill, then why not let him use that God-gift? I nodded and handed him the hide and pens. 'I am trying to draw a plan of this enchanted sea, noting the isles we have passed or stopped upon, the creatures we've seen – don't forget Jasconius – and the number of days between the islands.'

Padraigh listened attentively, then looked at my crude effort. 'I see what you want,' he said, nodding. With a deft stroke he began to copy and improve on the chart. At one point he queried a detail of the mountain on the Island of Birds, which he remembered differently, and I was forced to admit that his visual memory was more accurate than mine. When the map was almost finished, he wrote in the points of the compass in a neat, elegant script, and then roughly sketched in the western coastline of Erin down the right-hand side of the chart.

'Your skills were wasted at Clonfert,' I said, taking the curling chart from him. 'Why on earth did you leave your own mother abbey?'

The young man shrugged, as if to brush the question aside. For a while he studied the map and his handiwork and then made a minute change. When I had given up hope of an answer, he suddenly said, 'I worked directly under Aengus, whose manuscripts are prized throughout the Christian world for their clarity, simplicity and great beauty. Some thought my skills exceeded his own; I thought so too, at times,' he added with a wry smile. 'Aengus claimed that I spent too much time in illumination, that I was obsessed with the beauty of my craft above the glorification of God, which should have been the only purpose of my work. Perhaps he was right. Perhaps he was jealous. In the end, the abbot asked me to leave; he thought that a less worldly life would improve my soul.'

'That seems harsh,' I said, 'to pass judgement on a man for such a small thing.'

'I think he feared that I was becoming too proud of my work – as work, and not as a bible or gospel.'

'Even so . . .' I began.

'There was more,' Padraigh added. 'I loved books and read as widely as I could. Not all expressed the orthodox views of our faith, but I found much in them to interest me.' Something like animation crept into his voice and features, and for once his face lost that cynical, rather ugly mask, and became almost boyish. 'Did you know that there are substances which can change the very nature of things – which can take base metal and transform it into gold? I have read of unguents that can heal the dying, and tinctures which can keep a man from ageing in the normal way. Do you know that there are some who say that this world is not flat, but round, like a ball? The ancient sages believed so. I have read the formulae which can raise the spirits of the dead . . .' He stopped, seeing the look of horror on my face. 'But no matter. My former abbot passed judgement, and he is accounted a wise and just man.'

'The things you speak of smack of sorcery,' I said uncomfortably.

'Sorcery? Aye, perhaps. But surely sorcery is just another name for the unknown? Or perhaps they are merely things that Mother Church has yet to come to terms with, to incorporate into herself, as she has so much else that might be accounted unchristian.'

'How can there be anything unchristian in Christ's Church?' I demanded.

Padraigh gave me one of his cool, faintly mocking looks – it was that very look of his, I realized, that prevented me from warming to him – then he said, 'Have you ever looked closely at one of our own High Crosses, Abbot? There are figures and symbols carved on them that Rome would never recognize. But those who follow the old gods in our homeland would know them well.'

126

Against my will, I recalled the squat, grinning half-human figures which lurked in the carvings of a great stone cross I had grown up near. As a child they had caused me nightmares. I had put them down to the fancies of an uneducated but skilled craftsman; but in my heart I knew that everything the masons carved had some meaning, and I can still remember the small offerings of bread and milk which would be left beside them on certain nights of the year.

'And what of our own holy Saint Bridget . . .? I think if you look a little into her past and consider that the fire her followers have kept burning for so long now is the same fire that was kept burning in pagan times . . .'

I interrupted him. 'As your temporal and spiritual leader, Padraigh, I warn you that it is dangerous to think too much on such matters. That way leads to temptation, and we know where temptation leads us . . . We have been shown the true path, and it is our duty and our salvation to stay on it.'

Padraigh's hands sketched a gesture of obedience. But his dark eyes remained detached, skeptical . . .

Over the next few days, I spent a lot of time with those amongst my brothers whom I considered to be friends, especially Geoffrey, Eoin and Fiachra. I won't say I was consciously avoiding Padraigh, but he had disturbed me in some way I couldn't quite touch. The other three represented types of monastic fellowship that eased my burden, rather than added to it. At one extreme there was Geoffrey's solidity, contrasting with Fiachra's impulsiveness and carelessness; but they were both good and devout souls always. Eoin stood firmly in the middle; more lively than Geoffrey, more balanced and mature in judgement than Fiachra. They never questioned, never probed, never discussed non-Christian values. They accepted, and in that easy acceptance I found ease with them – in them I could see myself.

And then, on the morning of the fourth day – and in answer to my prayer – the lookout cried, 'Land.' The current was running fast and strong and three small islands, very close to one another, appeared on the horizon almost immediately.

Eoin, who had the tiller that morning, looked to me. 'What should we do, Abbot; come in to shore or pass them by . . .?'

I looked around at the weary faces of the crew. We had been long at sea, and just to walk on dry land again would be a pleasure. 'Bring us in to shore,' I said quietly.

The islands were tall and rugged, although not very big. There was vegetation on the slopes of the mountains, and the early-morning sunlight turned the many streams and rivers of the middle island molten. At a distance, the islands looked as if they were almost touching; and, as we closed with them, we discovered that they were separated by no more than two or three boat-lengths. The mountain range on all three was continuous, as was the pattern of vegetation, and it was obvious that the isles had been one land mass at one time.

And they were all inhabited.

To be truthful, this didn't entirely elate me; the folk we had encountered thus far on our voyage were not what I had hoped for. But perhaps that is just my vanity and selfishness speaking again. In truth, I am not sure what manner of men I had thought to meet on this voyage. I'm not even sure what sort of voyage I imagined I was undertaking, so long ago. A voyage in search of the Isle of Paradise . . . but how long now was it since I last thought of Paradise . . .?

The beaches were lined with still, silent figures. As we closed with the middle island – this being the largest and nearest – we could see that they were all men. All looked strong and healthy, all appeared in the prime of manhood – but there were no women to be seen, even in the background. Nor were there the children one might have expected to be drawn to the arrival of a strange craft. The tide was with us and carried us up onto a smooth sandy beach. A half dozen of the islanders ran forward into the shallows to help us beach the currach, while their companions – their unnatural stillness broken – milled about the strand with a restless energy. In the silence that followed the beaching of the currach, I heard sounds, which I first took to be birdsong, but which I soon realized was singing. The sound was thin and high and constant, but both the air and words were unknown to me.

As my brethren staked the currach to the beach with the aid of the islandmen, one man, whom I took to be the leader or spokesman, approached us. He was tall, fair and unusually handsome, with even features, pale blond hair and eyes of a deep, intense blue. The islandman – like all his companions – was broad and remarkably muscled, with every sinew and cord outlined against deeply tanned skin. He wore a short sleeveless tunic, belted around the waist, and high-thonged sandals, of a type that have not been worn in Erin for many years. The man raised both arms, with his palms facing us, and bowed slightly.

'You are welcome, strangers,' he said, a trace of an accent in an otherwise neutral voice.

'Where are we?' I asked abruptly. The months at sea had taken their toll of my manners.

'This is the Isle of the Men of Strength,' he replied courteously, bowing his head again. 'May I be permitted to ask who you are, and whence you have come?'

'I am Brendan of Clonfert, a Christian monastery in a land far to the east of here called Erin. I am a monk, as are all these with me, and we come in peace, seeking only a night's rest on land, and perhaps some fresh food if you have anything you can spare,' I said, in as civil a tone as I could.

The islander nodded, a brief smile touching his lips; but his eyes remained calm and detached, moving dispassionately around my crew. 'I am called Ulric. You shall have what you wish, and none here will disturb you. It has been a long time since we had visitors.' Ulric continued to look at my brethren, his fingers all the while beating a nervous rhythm against his thigh. 'You are of very different ages, but yet you travel together in the one craft?'

'We are united in our faith,' I replied slowly, wondering at the strange remark.

'Customs differ, I suppose,' Ulric said dubiously.

I nodded, schooling my face into as expressionless a mask as I could. To change the subject, I asked, 'We saw some more islands on either side of this as we sailed in – are they inhabited?'

'The three islands are considered as one – they are all the Isle of the Men of Strength.' Ulric nodded again, and continued, 'Nor are they islands truly; if you would care to come with me, I will show you what I mean.'

'Of course.' I turned around and nodded to Eoin, Barran

and Padraigh to follow me. For some reason I was loath to be left alone with these strange people, although really they seemed the most human and natural we had yet met. Perhaps that itself now seemed unnatural to me. Had I come to expect only magic and monsters?

We walked for perhaps three lengths along a path that ran the length of the island, until we came to a small promontory. From this vantage point we could see quite clearly one of the islets which we had spotted as we had sailed in.

As we walked across the isle, the singing I had noticed when we landed grew louder and clearer; and now from where I was standing I could see its source. The island across from us was inhabited by young men – the oldest no more than eighteen summers – who seemed to be joined in an unceasing song as they moved about their duties. Both in looks and clothing, they were in all respects similar to Ulric and his followers. I stood still for a moment, captivated by the intricate weave of melodies, tones and patterns such as I had never heard before. There was something in the music which touched some deep part of me with a yearning for . . for what?

I suddenly realized that Ulric was speaking to me; but it was with the greatest reluctance that I turned back to him. He was pointing to the channel of water between the islets. It was very shallow, and large rocks, like giant stepping stones, appeared with a regularity that couldn't be accidental. So our earlier assumption had been correct: the islands were one in reality, but time and the changing sea had partially submerged them. 'It is the same on the other side?' I asked.

Ulric nodded. 'As you see, it is easy to pass from one stage to the other, when the time comes.'

I looked at him, but he was already turning away, his long stride taking him quickly away from us . . .

When we rejoined the rest of my companions on the strand, we found them eating large segments of a thick-skinned fruit with great relish. Ulric gestured to one of his own men, who wordlessly ran to a tall tree on the edge of the strand and shinnied up it like a squirrel. We saw a flash of metal, and then something large and solid thumped into the sand below, followed by a second. The islandman slid down the tree trunk and picked up the two head-sized objects. He handed them to Ulric and passed him his knife. 'We call these Goldenfruit,' he said, deftly sliding the point of the flat-bladed knife beneath one of the thick overlapping squares on the fruit's skin, and peeling them back. He then cut them open and divided each into sections, passing them to us. The flesh was thick, soft and yet slightly fibrous. I bit into it cautiously, not sure what to expect. And I'll swear I have never tasted anything quite like it: the fruit itself was sharp and bitter, but yet its juice was sweet and sticky.

As we ate, Ulric and his men excused themselves, saying they would return at dusk. Although the formal courtesy was constant, I could feel in them a suppressed desire to be off on their own affairs. They were friendly, but not, I realized, very interested in us; and I also got the impression that something about us disturbed them – but perhaps that was just a natural wariness of strangers.

In the meantime we had plenty to occupy us, and we used the time to examine the currach thoroughly. We had been at sea now for many months, and our craft had been thoroughly seasoned and tested during that period. Her ribs were swollen, and moulded by the water to the shape they would hold forever, barring disaster or as many months again on dry land. The skeleton was sound; but what of the covering? The sea and wind constantly assaulted the fabric of the currach, and while we found that the hides themselves were strong, the stitches had worn loose in places. As for the sails – I looked at them morosely. They had been patched so often now that soon we would be patching the patches themselves.

Geoffrey and Eoin cleared an area of hard sand, then spread the sails out carefully on it to examine the repairs more closely.

'We need a large piece of strong leather to reinforce this central area,' Geoffrey said a few moments later. 'Otherwise . . .' He shrugged; we all knew what would happen. 'We'll do what we can, but God alone can help us if a strong gust of wind catches us unawares.'

'Is there nothing left in the stores?' I wondered.

They both shook their heads negatively. Martyn had come up by my side, and was staring at the mainsail in a similarly

131

dubious manner. 'I wouldn't trust that,' he said unnecessarily.

'We could ask the islanders,' Eoin suggested. 'The worst they can do is to say no – and they do seem a friendly lot.'

I glanced instinctively at Martyn. He caught my look, and then nodded. 'Eoin is right. Those men mean us no harm, and might well help us, so long as it does not keep them too long from their own pursuits.'

'I'll ask them.'

In the distance, we could hear muffled shouts and what sounded like cheering. It seemed to be coming from the centre of the island. 'Padraigh, Geoffrey and Eoin, you can come with me,' I said. 'But the rest of you should remain with the currach.'

Even had the island been larger, we could have located Ulric and his fellows by the racket they were making. As it was, we walked in towards the centre of the island and quickly came upon a grassy clearing, long and wide, and roughly squared off at the four corners. It was completely surrounded by the islanders – and now, suddenly seeing so many of them together, and noting the similarity between them, I began to feel a little disturbed.

The men acknowledged our presence, but only by brief glances; they seemed wholly absorbed in games which involved running, jumping and, in one corner, wrestling. There was also archery and javelin throwing, and a score or more were fighting, using broad-bladed flat swords. Although we were a little way away from them, the swords looked real enough.

And beneath the din, I could still make out the threnody of song coming from the islet on the southerly side. How could anyone work or think, I wondered, with this constant assault of noise?

When it became apparent that no one was going to interrupt his sport to speak to us, I shouted to Ulric, the only one I knew by name. Reluctantly, he abandoned some sort of relay race, and came over to us. His eyes were evasive and restless. 'How may I help you?' he asked, his courteous manner now visibly strained. Padraigh explained what we needed for our boat; but Ulric shook his head impatiently. 'No, no, we have nothing like that here,' he snapped, shifting his weight from one leg to the other. 'We do not concern ourselves with crafts at our age. We have enough work to do on our bodies. Go to the other side. They can make or mend anything there, and will be glad of something new to work on.'

'Go where?' Padraigh demanded.

'To the northerly isle,' he snapped and with a final, repeated promise that he would see us at dusk with food, he raced back to his fellows.

The four of us trudged to the northerly end of the Isle of the Men of Strength, where, as we had expected, there was another series of stepping stones, leading to the third islet. 'Who wants to go first?' I asked with a smile.

'I'll go.' Padraigh stepped out onto the first stone, which surprised me. I had not thought of him as a particularly adventurous or brave type.

The stones were not that easy to negotiate. Waves lapped over them, making them treacherous and slippery, and the spacing was such that only the long stride of a fit man would match it. If the sea were at all rough, they would have been impassable, and I wondered how often during the course of a year these three islands – so close together – were cut off from one another.

Still, we managed nimbly enough, and made the crossing without mishap. This island was very different to that which we had just left. The first isle was predominantly rock and stone, and what growth there was – aside from the playing field – Ulric and his men had left to itself, with no attempt to impose order on it. But here, immediately, was evidence of man's hand, for a glistening path led from the water's edge. Countless tiny, coloured stones formed mosaic patterns, which led the eye upwards along the path, while both sides of it were edged in what looked like silver. I paused, not wishing to walk on anything so beautiful, but Padraigh strode ahead in an oddly confident manner. The pathway led towards a thicket of trees which were symmetrically pollarded on either side of the path. As we neared it a score or more of figures emerged from amidst the trees. Like Ulric, they were tall well-formed men with straight backs and pale hair. Unlike Ulric and the islanders, they were all past their prime, though I would not have called

133

them aged.

When we reached them, they looked at Geoffrey and me, almost ignoring Padraigh and Eoin. 'I am Brendan . . .' I began.

One raised his hand. 'We know of you; but what do you want from the elderly?' His manner to me was as brusque as mine had been with Ulric.

Eoin explained our needs. 'We need leather for our sail,' he said simply.

'Bring us the sail,' one elder said, still deliberately looking at me. 'We will have it mended for you by morning.'

'But you haven't even seen it!' Eoin exclaimed.

The man smiled in a patronizing manner, almost as if our queries amused him. 'We are craftsmen. We create and we mend and we give shape and form to things. Nothing is beyond us.'

Once again I realized that I could hear sound. But this time it was not the sound of men, of singing and chanting, but of chisel against stone, hammer against wood, the hum of a loom – sounds of craftsmen at work. 'Thank you,' I said abruptly. 'We'll return directly with our sail, if we may.'

The old man bowed. 'You may.'

Back at the currach, we folded the sail as carefully as we could, rolling it up into a tall tube, which was the best we could manage without causing further damage to the fabric. Even so, it would be an awkward bundle to manoeuvre across the treacherous stones. Eoin and Padraigh offered to carry it back across to the island.

When I protested, Padraigh said, with his pleased, almost secretive smile, 'There's no need for all of us to risk wet robes or twisted ankles.'

Despite vague misgivings, I knew he was right. Geoffrey and I were unusually fit for our age; but the younger men would be more sure-footed, and the sail was quite a weight. We walked with them as far as the bridge of stones, then watched them carefully make their way across. When they disappeared up the mosaic path and into the trees, Geoffrey and I turned back to the currach.

The mid-afternoon sun was lowering in the sky when Eoin returned. His eyes were bright and shining, and he was stuttering with excitement. 'B-B-Brendan . . . I mean, Abbot, they are making us a new sail! What–what Sorn told us is true – they can make or mend anything, and their work is finer than anything you've ever imagined. I wish you had seen the cloth they weave, and the sculptures and – even the fire-pit is a work of–of–of art. I'd take you back with me, but they say that many of their ways are secret except to apprentices of their crafts, and they don't want outsiders watching them work. They've let Padraigh stay, so that he can show them exactly how we want our new sail. I wish I had been allowed to stay,' he finished, wistfully.

At dusk Padraigh had still not returned; so I assumed he would spend the night where he was – he'd be foolish to chance the stones in the poor light. In the meantime, Ulric and half a dozen others had returned to us, with platters of the same fruit they had given us earlier. In return we offered them some of our meagre supplies from the boat; but they refused politely.

'Our diet is not so light as it appears. The Goldenfruit will sustain even the strongest man and keep him in perfect health, so we have no need to take from your supplies. We will leave you with some whole ones, which will keep fresh for several days, to take with you on your voyage tomorrow.'

It was more than a hint – it was an order. Something about us made him uneasy; something which we did or said, or how we acted made them want to be rid of us. Eventually I said, 'I have the feeling that you are unaccustomed to strangers such as ourselves?'

Ulric's natural courtesy seemed at war with a desire to answer. Haltingly he said, 'We are unused to men of vastly differing ages living together, travelling together. To us it is unnatural – against our customs and our ways. We do not wish to foster such desires in our people. Here, as you see, the ages are separate; the young develop their mental powers and memories, their voices, hearing and sight. We – men in the prime – develop our bodies; and the old men develop the many crafts. Considered as a whole, we form the complete man, a man strong in mind and body and ability.' He bowed quickly, a quick bobbing of his head. 'Perhaps you will excuse us if we leave you now? We will be back to help you launch your craft in the morning.'

That night I slept more soundly than I had for months; Ulric's strange explanation having in some curious way calmed my fears and doubts.

The morning was sharp and bright, with just enough of a chill bite in the air to make me think about winter. I rose and washed quickly, and experienced the usual pangs about the morning ritual of a monk which had slipped away during our voyage – these days we didn't pray half as much as we had in Erin. But perhaps this entire voyage was a prayer in itself. I was walking down the beach to the water's edge when I heard footsteps and voices behind me. I turned and found it was Eoin and Padraigh returning with the long tube of our new sail between them. I opened my mouth to say something when I noticed both Eoin's troubled face and Padraigh's withdrawn expression.

'Is the sail all right?' I demanded anxiously.

'It is splendid,' Eoin replied, without enthusiasm. 'It's not leather, but it's a lighter, stronger material such as I have never seen before.'

'What's wrong, then?'

'I am staying here,' Padraigh said, looking me directly in the eye for the first time I could recall. 'I will have to spend some little time with Ulric, working on my physical development,' he said quickly, 'and then I will join the craftsmen – to study and to create, eventually.'

'But your faith, Padraigh,' I said quietly. 'These men are pagans.'

'I am a Christian, Brendan,' Padraigh said slowly. 'But art is my true faith. I've known it in my heart, but I've always denied it. I've fought what I knew was truly meant for me for too long now; but now I don't think I can give up this God-given opportunity . . .'

'You'll be leaving everything you have known – your companions, your home, your life . . .'

'This is my home, Brendan,' Padraigh said with a terrible finality. 'This is my life, my destiny. Sail on, Brendan, in search of your Paradise. I have found mine.'

Chapter Thirteen

There were times when our voyage became unreal, taking on an almost dream-like quality. Days slipped easily into one another and, with the unchanging sea, time became meaningless. I often felt numb, close to despair, knowing that we would never reach the Isle, knowing that we were doomed to wander this haunted sea, knowing . . . and then – almost miraculously – my mood would change and I was filled with a boundless optimism, and then God seemed very near, so near that I could sense Him watching over us, guiding me.

It was one of those cool, overcast days when the sea and the sky look equally grey and inhospitable, and the general mood of the crew matched it. It was a combination of exhaustion, lack of proper food and far too many days at sea. At first I thought that Padraigh's absence might also have been blighting our spirits, but his loss was felt far less strongly than Crosan's. Though Padraigh had been a far fitter man, and therefore more useful with the oars and sails than had been the former jester, I think that many of the brothers, like myself, had sensed on a deep, unspoken level that Padraigh's goals had not been the same as our own. And beyond this, he had so often given the impression that he was contemptuous of us and our goal. We sought the Blessed Isles with a view towards eternal salvation; Padraigh – obviously – sought his happiness in this life.

We had left Padraigh and all he represented behind some . . . was it ten days now? The crew were growing restless; but, at this moment, I felt reasonably at peace with myself and the natural elements. Sunshine playing on the water and blue skies are a cheering sight; but the grey emptiness of a fog-locked horizon has always held its own fascination for me. How many times in Erin had I walked for hours along the shore in just such weather as this, feeling the chill, salt breeze on my face, staring into the misty horizon, feeling it pull me in towards it, wondering what lay beyond, what the clouds concealed? I've never had the bouts of longing for my home that most men seem to feel when away; no, my longing has always been for places I've never seen, though I've never been able to explain this fully.

Someone moved beside me and sat down. It took an almost conscious effort on my part to turn away from the sea towards him. It was Fiachra, looking very lonely and almost frightened. 'What's wrong?' I murmured.

'I wish we were home,' he whispered. 'I miss Clonfert terribly, Abbot. And my little milk cow – anything could have happened to her by now . . .'

'Clonfert will be much the same when we return, I promise you,' I said to him. What I did not say was how much he might find himself changed by our voyage.

'We are going back, sometime, truly?' Fiachra continued anxiously, looking so solemn that I almost felt like laughing.

'Of course we are,' I said.

'When?'

I shrugged. 'That is in God's own hands,' I said slowly. 'But I think we have completed much of our journey, and that what we seek draws nearer.' The truth was that I didn't know whether the Isle of Paradise lay over the next horizon – or the one beyond that, or over the next hundred horizons. But it was what Fiachra wanted to hear. 'You must not have such doubts, my son,' I added, attempting to frown.

'Forgive me, Abbot, but I did wonder if Padraigh chose to stay on the Isle of the Men of Strength because he thought we'd never return to Erin. I can't understand it, otherwise – to spend the rest of his life with alien folk, so far from Erin. He must be mad!'

'No, he's not mad,' Martyn said, dropping down beside us. 'It's just that his values differ from ours, and he held certain things more important than this voyage.' Martyn glanced across at me and smiled slightly, and then he turned back to Fiachra. 'But you'll see your little cow again; only I venture that she won't be so little. She'll have grown into a fine animal in your absence.'

This seemed to comfort Fiachra. He and the others had long

since guessed that Martyn was granted accurate glimpses into the future – doubtless they ascribed these to his druidical background. But every time he made some prediction or prophecy – large or small – the image of the Corr always came to mind.

On impulse, I turned to Martyn and asked, 'And what of me? Will this voyage bring me my heart's desire?' I deliberately kept my tone light, although my question was serious.

Martyn's dark, clever eyes looked at me and then seemed to glaze over for a few moments. When he finally spoke, his voice was so soft that I had to lean forward to hear him. 'Yes, Abbot, I am afraid that it will . . .'

A sudden shout interrupted us. It was Geoffrey who had the steering oar. 'We've been heading due west all morning,' he called out, his practical tone breaking the mood. 'Do you want to continue or alter course, Brendan?'

'Hold the course,' I ordered, standing up and stretching. It was not simply that everything I had gleaned from tales and legends suggested that the Blessed Isles lay far to the west; but with neither charts nor recognizable stars to guide us, I was terrified of sailing around in circles as we had done before. I glanced up into the sails; they were barely moving, so I added, 'We'll man the oars for an hour and make a bit more headway.'

The rhythm of rowing was soothing, and the exercise quickly warmed us; but I soon became uncomfortably conscious of a gnawing in my stomach, and my throat felt raw and gritty. Unfortunately our supplies were limited, and the magical flask we had been given earlier on our voyage would not renew itself till evening. I glanced into the heavens, trying to gauge the time: not yet noon. We had a long time to wait before the meagre rations would be distributed, and supplies were too low for an extra meal. 'Let's rest,' I called. 'We've rowed enough for the moment; the sea can carry us.'

I dozed fitfully, dreaming of the Isle of the Men of Strength. In my dream I heard once again the ceaseless, omnipresent noise of the boys' singing, and the shouts and roars of the men at their games. I was wondering if they were ever silent, when I slowly realized that it was my brethren around me who were shouting. And then hard fingers bit into my shoulders and

139

someone was shaking me awake. It was Fiachra; his long pale face was now ashen, and his eyes looked as if they were about to explode. 'What's wrong?' I demanded. He opened and closed his mouth several times, attempting to speak; and then finally he just turned me around and pointed. Coming up on us fast from the north was a huge bird.

'Wh . . . what in God . . . God's holy name is it?' he asked, shivering.

I shook my head, feeling my heart beginning to pound. I looked around the crew, until I finally found Martyn. He too was staring at the creature, shading his dark eyes with his hands. He seemed to feel me looking at him, because he turned and looked in my direction. 'What is it?' I mouthed above the shouts.

For once, even Martyn had no reply. He shrugged slightly, and then began to make his way down the currach towards me. 'I'm not sure,' he shouted. 'I'll have to wait until it gets closer.'

I glanced up into the sky again. The creature was nearer now, and I could begin to make out details. But its size alone was staggering; its wing-span was as wide as our craft was long, and at least twice as broad. I pointed up. 'What's it holding?'

Martyn squinted upwards, and then shook his head. 'It's holding something in its claws,' he agreed, 'but I can't make it out.'

There was nothing to do but watch and wait as it flew inexorably towards us. If it were inimical to us, we stood no chance against it. I crossed myself, and began to pray.

We could hear the slow booming of its wings, and then suddenly we were in deep shade as the creature hovered directly over us, its wings beating so slowly that I expected the bird to fall from the sky and crush us. And then I saw its talons uncurl and objects it had been holding began to rain down about us. There was panic as the brothers dived for cover – but on an open currach there was little enough of that. When the first object hit the bottom of the craft at my feet with a slight splat, only Eoin, Martyn and myself remained standing.

I looked down and found that liquid oozed, purple and sticky, around my toes, from the broken object. It was a ball – or rather a bunch of what looked for all the world like a bunch of grapes – but each grape was larger than an apple. More of the objects were falling into the boat. Three rolled down the decks and stopped by my feet, and I stooped down and looked closely at them. They still looked like grapes – giant grapes. I wetted my finger in the juice and held it to my tongue; the taste was that of grapes, but with a slight tang – sweet and sharp. I picked up an unbroken fruit and bit into it. It tasted delicious. I nodded to the rest of the brothers, who looked terrified, almost as if they expected me to fall down dead, poisoned by the fruit. 'Eat,' I commanded. 'They're grapes!'

They needed no urging. Obviously I had not been the only one with half a mind on his stomach.

I walked down the craft, still eating, while the great bird continued to hover, watching us. It looked like an eagle, a giant golden eagle, although its wings were broader in proportion and its beak was more hooked than any eagle's. It was a rich tawny colour, and the tips of its wings were a deep, almost metallic, bronze, as were its talons. Its eyes were hard and black. 'What is it?' I asked myself, unaware that I was speaking aloud.

'It's a roc,' Martyn said very softly. 'A giant bird supposed to inhabit the lands far to the east of Erin. They are sometimes called "God's Messengers",' he added with a smile. 'Look, it's moving!'

The roc flapped its huge wings and soared upwards almost as if it had been pulled. It circled once, and then it turned back towards the north, moving slowly. And then it described a second tighter circle and came winging in fast and low towards us. It circled the currach again a third time and then set off into the north once more. 'It wants us to follow it,' Martyn said slowly.

And this was one of God's messengers! It was a sign. 'Geoffrey, Eoin, alter course,' I ordered. 'Follow the bird . . .'

It was with some reluctance that the brothers put away the huge fruit and set to the oars. Eoin called the beat; but once the rhythm had been established, I saw some of the brothers grab quick bites of the grapes that were rolling around the deck. Indeed, I too was guilty of what nearly amounted to gluttony. The fruit satisfied both hunger and thirst; the flavour, I decided, was something between grape juice and wine, while the flesh was as fresh and tasty as newly made bread. Indeed, I was feeling quite light-headed on it; but I thought that was probably the result of our long fast on the ration of the magical bread and water. Behind me, I could hear Barran singing softly to himself, an old air in a dialect I could barely make out. There was something in it about a maid and a pagan courtship rite – rather a secular song for any monk, and especially for the puritanical Barran – but I couldn't muster enough energy to reprimand him. Besides it was a cheerful, pleasant sound.

And so we followed the bird for the remainder of the day. It continued to fly slowly, an obvious guide, and when it got too far ahead, it would make a huge circling turn that would bring it directly above us. But its home isle would not be too far, I reckoned. A huge creature such as this would stay close to its own lands, needing a secure nest and a certain supply of food to sustain its vast bulk.

We rowed, and we ate all the grapes that the roc had dropped into the currach. Spirits were high, and I felt my own humour improving with every stroke of the oar. Someone ahead of me – Geoffrey, I think – started an old sea shanty, and soon everyone joined in. What excellent fellows they were, really, I thought with contentment. They had their faults, yes – who did not – but a man could hardly ask for more stalwart companions. I felt a burst of renewed confidence: hadn't Martyn said that we would find the Isle of Paradise? Then we would return to Clonfert, where all would come to hear of our voyage, and I would become the most famous monk in Christendom . . . no, I must not think along such lines. That was Pride, the most deadly of sins. Strangely, this sudden thought served to bring me back to reality, although it didn't dampen my euphoria. To distract myself, I scanned the horizon as I rowed. The port side was clear, but there was a distant smudge off the starboard bow, which quickly shaped itself into an island. The roc seemed to pick up speed as we closed with the isle, as if it were eager to be home.

The current took us then, and a slight onshore breeze came up, both of which helped to push us in towards the shore. As we neared the island, all we could see was a mass of lush vegetation, with only a narrow strip of beach along the small cove towards which the bird had unswervingly led us. Once within the shelter of the cove, the wind dropped and the current died, and so we drifted up onto the beach in a gentle, almost effortless landing. The roc hovered overhead, making sure we were safely beached, and then, with a few flaps of its huge wings, it took off out of sight into the island's interior.

We looked around in growing delight. The island might not be Paradise; but for hungry mariners, it came very close. Grapes such as we had been eating were growing on vines with stems as thick as those of a young tree and leaves which would have been big enough to shelter under from the rain. Not that it rained now, or even looked like it; the roc had led us from grey skies to sunshine. Even the temperature seemed much higher than the time of the year would warrant. Amongst the vines grew tall trees bearing fruit of sorts I had never seen. Brown, hairy things the size of a man's head which did not look suitable for eating; long, curved fruits with smooth yellow skins. Others that, but for their size, might have been plums. Doubtless there was much here that was fine to eat; but without guidance, I was loath to risk it. However, we had eaten the grapes . . .

'Take the grapes and only the grapes; only the Lord Himself knows what these others are.'

'This is by far the pleasantest place we have seen in our travels,' Geoffrey said, as he finished with the last of an especially large bunch of grapes. His sandy-coloured beard was wet and stained with purple juice.

'A good . . . a good . . . place to rest and . . . refresh ourselves,' I agreed. For some reason I was having difficulty speaking – almost as if I were drunk, I thought dimly. Not that I have much experience of drunkenness, not since my youth, before I took holy orders, when I had often enjoyed too much wine and food and paid the price the following day.

Martyn came up and stood before us. Geoffrey and I were sitting back to back on the smooth sandy beach, surrounded by the pips and twigs of a score and more of the huge grapes. I looked up at him, and his dour expression and hard accusing eyes unaccountably made me want to laugh out loud.

143

'Should we not press on with our journey before darkness sets in?' he asked me.

I waved him aside. 'There's time enough, time enough; perhaps we'll stay the night here – build a fire, have a bit of comfort for a change. I think we deserve it, don't you?' I asked Geoffrey. He nodded solemnly.

I saw Martyn looking at me with a curious expression on his face, and then he turned to look at the rest of the crew who were scattered about us. Conn had fallen asleep a few paces from me, curled up into himself and looking very young and vulnerable; beyond him, Barran was slumped asleep sitting up.

'We'll rest,' I said and then added, 'We have spent uncounted months at sea, and who knows how many still lie ahead of us. Wha's . . . what's the harm of a little rest, eh?'

Geoffrey nodded. 'Aye, what can harm us here?'

'Well – that for one thing!' Martyn pointed towards the sea.

I turned my head slowly and with great care – and found a huge shape winging in low over the water towards us. 'What of it?' I asked impatiently. 'Its mate meant us no harm; why should this one?' I slumped back down onto the sand. 'Oh, Martyn, your druid craft has made you suspicious. Sit here with Geoffrey and me and have another grape.'

'Abbot!' Martyn's voice was shrill with urgency. He fell to his knees in the sand and held my face in both his hands, and then he twisted my head back towards the creature. 'Your sight is sharper than mine; look again. Look again, and tell me if what's approaching is the same as the bird which led us here.'

I shielded my eyes with my hand against the glare of the sun, and tried to focus on the distant bird. I first noticed that its head was similar to the first bird's, eagle-like with a vicious beak; but the body – dear God, the body – those weren't a pair of talons beneath the body, but four legs. And, as it closed with us, I could see that, despite the huge wings, the body was an animal's, not a bird's. The claws on its feet were shaped like talons, and the body was muscular and powerful under wings that beat noisily in the air. I tried to stand and found my legs unsteady, untrustworthy, and my sight blurred. 'What is it?' I asked, my voice cracking.

'I think it's a gryphon, though I never believed such creatures actually existed,' Martyn said in a tight, terrified whisper.

'Will it harm us?'

'If it can,' he said softly, grimly.

'We must rouse the others – we must try to defend ourselves,' I said. My brain was clearing, though my legs still seemed unwilling to obey me, and I felt as if the world were swaying slightly, like a ship at sea.

'How – they're all unconscious. I think the juice must ferment in these grapes as the fruit ripens. You're all drunk,' he accused.

'Well, we've got to try,' I insisted.

Martyn moved over to Eoin, and nudged him gently with his foot. 'Wake up; come on, now; wake up . . .'

Eoin drew his arms tighter about his body and rolled over. 'Go 'way . . .' he mumbled.

'Run to the trees,' I shouted. If we could get in amongst the thick matted vegetation then we stood a chance. The brothers were coming awake, but they were moving slowly, and their first reaction was to stand and stare at the creature in astonishment.

'We won't make it,' Martyn said, hauling Eoin to his feet, dragging one arm across his shoulder.

'We must,' I said, taking Eoin's other arm, and manhandling him towards the trees.

But the gryphon was already overhead, hovering hawklike as if it were assessing which one of us to take first. Its eyes were not brown, but blood-red, intelligent, almost human-looking in their fashion. It opened its beak, and I glimpsed a long snake-like tongue, and then its claws came down . . . It was going to dive . . .

Suddenly it looked away, its attention taken by something above and behind us. I heard the sound of a second set of giant wings – and then the giant roc exploded from the bushes behind us, its great wings pulling it upwards, until it was soaring over the gryphon.

As large and as fearsome as the gryphon was, its wing-span was less than half that of the roc. It turned its blood-red gaze back to us for a single pounding heartbeat, and then it drew in its wings with a terrific clap of sound and attempted to outrun the larger bird. With a contemptuous gesture, the roc folded its wings and fell down onto the gryphon, its weight bearing it down, its talons biting deep into its back.

There was a roar of frustrated rage and then a howl – which was curiously cat-like – of anguish. The great bird flew off clumsily with its prey, out over the sea; and then I thought I saw it drop the gryphon into the water. The battle – if indeed it could even be called that – had lasted no more than a score of heartbeats; but it had felt like an age.

The roc returned, flying over us without pausing, back into the centre of the island. The whole thing might never have happened. It could have been a drunken dream – except for the blood which had spattered the beach, in large red-black circles. Even at that, a few of the brothers around me were shaking their heads, as if they suspected that they might have been hallucinating.

But my head was clear now, and I realized Martyn had been right – the grapes had very nearly been the cause of our deaths. There was a lesson to be learned here without a doubt – although I wasn't really sure what it was. However, whatever else happened, I daren't allow the brothers to eat any more of the island's fruit.

'Only the stores in the craft are to be eaten from now on,' I announced.

There was a chorus of suppressed groans. With great restraint, I added, 'And we will pack no fresh supplies from this island!'

Chapter Fourteen

We left the island at first light, still slightly numbed by the events of the previous day – and by the effects of the intoxicating fruit. Heads were sore, tempers were short and the brothers seemed content to keep to themselves – which suited me. My own head was throbbing, my throat was sand-raw and I had to squint against the harsh light of the morning. I promised myself a penance for my drunkenness – then decided I was already doing my penance.

The brothers rowed strongly, if a little raggedly at first, and once we were out of the bay, Geoffrey, who had the steering oar, looked to me for directions. Ignoring the painful throbbing over my eyes, I made my way back down the craft and stood by him. He was disinclined to talk, and so we stood in silence while I attempted to discern our course. I judged that the great bird had led us due north on the previous day, so I eventually ordered a south-westerly course, hoping that it would take us back to our original direction.

Geoffrey relayed the order, his usually loud voice sounding strained and raw. Eventually a steady beat was established, and, despite a somewhat variable breeze, we maintained our course, using the sun to orient by. But we were not more than three leagues out, with the island just beginning to slip beneath the waves behind us, when low clouds formed on the horizon. Throughout the morning they thickened, and soon the sky above our craft began to cloud over. A thin mist descended on us, a damp greyness that clung to our robes, dusting them with silver, but biting deep into our bones. As the morning turned towards afternoon, the cloud thickened, and when I moved up to the prow I could barely make out the figures of Eoin and Geoffrey standing in the stern. The light breeze died, leaving the sails hanging uselessly, dripping chill moisture down onto the decks below. We could row, but until the fog lifted, it

147

would be a foolish, wasteful gamble. We could end up travelling eastwards as easily as west.

'Lower the sails and take in your oars,' I shouted; but the fog dulled my voice, robbing it of all volume. 'Let us pray for guidance. We will trust to God's will and drift with the current. It has served us in the past, and it will serve us now.'

I was looking for a miracle, a sign from God. Perhaps it was the drink still in me, but I half expected the mist to lift immediately. And so, in a strange and almost terrifying way, I felt somehow betrayed when nothing happened. If anything, the fog thickened. God had directed and guided us so far; He had protected and fed us ever since we had left Erin's shores; He had brought us safely through the terrors of this haunted sea, but now, now when the crew needed to row, needed to do something to work off the alcohol, needed to do something to forget the shame of drunkenness . . . what was happening? We were fogbound.

We drifted for two sunless days and two starless nights. If the truth is to be told – those two days tested my faith harder than any other ordeal I have ever undergone. The thick fog effectively isolated each man, and movement was limited – both by the obstacles aboard the cramped currach, and the danger of falling overboard. Spirits amongst the crew were low, for the inaction left us all with too much time to think; and I suspect we all came very close to despair. Had we been hungry or exhausted it would have been better, for the external discomforts would have distracted us; but we were as well nourished and fit as we had been at any point since we set out so long ago.

And how long ago was that? I tried to work out just how long we had been at sea, retracing our steps island by island. I knew roughly how much time we had spent ashore; but what about the long stretches we had spent drifting? Months, certainly. How many? A year? Two? More? I gave up, eventually; my mind could not compass it – at some point during our voyage time had become unreal, meaningless. Thinking back on it, it seemed as yesterday when we had set out so bravely and so hopefully from the foot of Didache. Then I considered where we had been and all that we had seen, and Clonfert seemed a lifetime away.

On the morning of the third day, we found the mist had lightened. I could at last make out the dull copper disk of the sun rising on the horizon, and so, turning our backs on it, and with our shadows dancing across the shifting banks of fog, we assumed a westerly course. 'Row!' I called, and it is one of the few times I can ever remember seeing my brothers actually happy to be rowing again. Eoin set up a stiff beat; and they rowed like madmen until the first exhilaration had worn off, then settled down to a more measured pace.

The fog lightened as the morning wore on, and by mid-day it had thinned to a gauzy mist – allowing us to see the bulk of land rising from the sea ahead, an island. It lay directly in our path, but there was never any question in my mind – or indeed, in any of the crew's, judging from their renewed efforts – that we would make for it.

The island had risen from the sea, looming large and ominously before us, when Geoffrey voiced the words that sent a chill into my heart. 'Brendan, there's something terribly familiar about the shape of that island.' He pointed. 'I could swear we've seen that headland there; and inland, that strangely regular formation of hillocks looks familiar also.'

I was loath to admit it, and I waited until we were close enough to the shore for there to be no doubt that we had seen this island before. 'We've backtracked or circled in the mists,' I said bitterly. Frustration welled up in me, and I felt as if I wanted to shout, to scream, to strike out . . . Every time, I thought, every time we seem to be drawing nigh on our goal, we are set back. Was there to be no end to it? Were we doomed to sail this sea for all eternity?

I walked down the craft and stood in the prow beside Eoin and Geoffrey, who were staring across the choppy waves towards the shore. 'What do you see?' I asked wearily.

'I can make out some ruined buildings,' Eoin said slowly, and then he added excitedly, 'It's that deserted island we stayed on . . .' He must have misinterpreted my horrified expression because he continued quickly, 'You remember, Abbot, the one that looked as if it might have housed a community of monks like ourselves. The wind and tide are

149

carrying us in – do we land there again?'

There was a sudden movement behind me, and then Martyn's small hard fingers bit into my forearm. 'Ailbe's island!' he hissed in my ear.

I nodded impatiently to him and then turned back to Eoin. 'I don't think we have the time to land,' I said. 'We've lost too much headway as it is,' I added.

There were soft murmurs of discontent from a few of the brethren who had overheard my remark. Geoffrey looked back at me and asked hesitantly, 'Would one more day make all that much difference . . .?'

Martyn's grip on my arm tightened and, glancing down, I found that his knuckles were white with the strain. He leaned close to my head and whispered with a soft, desperate urgency, 'Abbot, I would rather jump into the sea and drown than visit that accursed island again. Nothing will induce me to set foot on it again – I'll kill myself first.'

I turned, gripping his arm, pulling his fingers from my flesh, and then ushered him to one side. Eoin, Geoffrey and several of the brothers turned to watch us curiously, but I was past caring – Martyn's words had touched my one private terror. 'How dare you say that to me – your abbot! You're talking of mortal sin, eternal damnation! You must never think of suicide, for which there can be no forgiveness!'

Martyn's dark eyes were bleak. 'I do not hold much hope of salvation for myself. At least I would die as a Christian, amongst Christians, though I would be damned . . .'

'Even to contemplate suicide is to court damnation,' I interrupted him. 'And I'm not sure I follow your reasoning.'

'That which rules the island is more terrible to me,' he whispered; and I found that there was real fear in his voice. 'If we land on that isle, it will have us,' he promised.

'I will protect you – I did so the last time,' I said, almost coming close to boasting.

'This time you might not be so strong, or they might be stronger, more powerful and you would be consigning me and yourself to eternal damnation in the service of the sea-demon. And what of the rest of the crew – what right have you to risk their lives . . .?'

Martyn's words struck home without his realizing it, bringing back all the fears and terror-filled nightmares that had haunted me after my first ill-fated voyage, when I had asked that same question – what right had I to risk their lives? And always the answer came back – no right. I had made that mistake once, and two score of good men, close friends, boyhood companions, some of them not more than boys, had paid for that mistake with their lives. It was a mistake I would not make again.

'You need have no fear,' I said softly. 'I'm not going to endanger my crew.'

He looked into my eyes – and perhaps he saw something there, or perhaps his druid-trained senses allowed him to feel my hurt and pain. He looked confused. 'I'm sorry . . . I . . . have offended . . .'

'No, there was no offence,' I said, looking over towards the island. 'You reminded me of something.' I looked back at the pale young man and smiled reassuringly. 'You reminded me of my duty.' I turned back to the crew and when I spoke, I pitched my voice low, using all my authority, brooking no argument, no dissent. 'We will not be landing on this isle,' I stated flatly, looking at each man in turn. 'Now, I know you're all tired, exhausted after this long spell at sea; I'm just as tired, just as cold and chilled. But I saw and experienced certain things on that island that you did not. So did Martyn.' I had their attention now, and I suddenly knew how I would be able to lure them away from the isle. 'The isle is ruled by a creature called Ailbe, who dwells there with his followers. They have the shape and appearance of men, and their clothing and ways suggest that they follow the way of God. But it is all a sham. They are not men, and I'm sure now that they suit their clothing and manners to whatever race or class of men comes their way; they appeared as monks to us; to pirates I'm sure they would appear as such; and if a merchant ship were to land there, then I'm certain they would have taken on the guise of merchants.' I paused for effect before adding, 'To land there is death.'

A ripple of curiosity ran through the crew, quickly replacing the resentment of being deprived of landfall. Conn, ever curious, asked the obvious question, 'Then why did we see nothing, meet no one . . .?'

'When we are well clear of this area,' I promised, like a father persuading his children to behave with the promise of a treat to follow. As they rowed away from the isle, I sat in the prow of the currach and, with Martyn's occasional help, I related the events they had never experienced. The younger brothers' faces were open with wonder, although some of the older, more experienced men fully understood the danger the isle had held.

I'd set a course of west-north-west, which was slightly different from the first time we'd left Ailbe's island. These waters were obviously vast, and I wondered again where exactly we were – certainly not off Erin's shores, that was certain. But without charts all we could do was to trust to the will of God, hoping and praying that He would lead us to our ultimate destination. But somewhere, deep within me, a voice murmured insistently that we could already have sailed within twenty leagues of the Blessed Isles, unknowingly.

As we sailed on into the morning, the nature of the sea itself changed. The water was extraordinarily clear, and gaining in clarity as we rowed deeper into it. Looking over the side of the boat, it was difficult to work out where the air finished and the sea began – although, oddly enough, we still left a white froth in our wake, and our bow still cleaved the water, cutting two foaming billows on either side. There was no chance of our fetching up on a hidden rock here, for I could see down to the sea bed itself, despite the many fathoms of water beneath us. It was a glimpse of another world, silently and wondrously beautiful. Tall plants swayed in the gentle current, while fish – singly and in huge cloud-like shoals – swam in and about them. There were stretches of white sand, and rocks covered with green moss and then vibrant swatches of colour which contrasted with darker, stunted growths.

As we rowed on, fish began to rise to the surface, close to the currach, turning the by now invisible water to a shimmering, glistening sheet of iridescent scales. Then huge globes of jellyfish rose around the currach, beautiful, fragile-looking and deadly, while the slim shapes of eels twisted and circled through the mass. The sea-creatures swarmed around our craft, as if wondering what manner of being had invaded their territory.

I ordered the oars shipped, in case they were attacked by the fish, and so we drifted on the tide, with the brothers leaning out over the sides of the boat, fascinated by the sights. It was Eoin, the practical fisherman's son, who wondered if we should not try to catch some of the fish. 'After all, they're so numerous and so close I could just reach out and pluck them from the sea with my hands. Surely something like this is a gift from God – and they'd make a change from bread and water and dried fruits,' he added persuasively.

It was a tempting idea – and for that very reason I rejected it. 'And how would we cook them?' I wondered. 'Do you propose that we eat them raw? Or that we travel with a boat full of rotting fish till we reach the next landfall?'

Eoin looked so crestfallen that I had to smile. 'You're right, of course, I wasn't thinking,' he said finally.'It's just that to my mind there is nothing to compare with fish fresh from the sea. Sometimes in the past, in my early days at Clonfert, I felt guilty that the fast days were no great denial to me.'

'Well, your stomach has done penance enough on this voyage to make up for it,' I said cheerfully. He had reminded me of something I've often noticed – that monks who have successfully denied themselves the pleasures of a woman can yet retain a great sensual delight in food. I've never understood it; one meal is much like another to me, so long as it gives me enough sustenance and strength for my work.

A wind took up and our sails flapped and rattled. The currach listed slightly to one side – and the massed sea-creatures vanished, scattering like summer clouds before a stiff wind. We continued on into the east for the remainder of the day. Towards evening the crystal-clear sea began to darken, and it gradually returned to normal. The wind didn't let up during the night – if anything it became a little stronger, but not enough to be worrisome. However, the following day the wind remained with us – and the day after that, and the day after that . . . It blew for five days, never slackening, increasing slightly at night, not enough to do damage to the structure of the craft, but enough to keep the sails taut, and keep us all awake. There was nothing anyone could do during those days – except pray.

At last, on the morning of the sixth day, following our completion of the first offices of the day, I saw a shape on the horizon. I say a shape, because it was immediately clear that this was not just another isle. Far, far in the distance something rose tall and straight, connecting the sea and sky. As we neared it, our first impressions were borne out – it was a giant pillar. Its height was incalculable; from where we were, it stretched up into the low cloud-covering, which extended as far as the eye could see, and its shimmering length went down beneath the waves, presumably to the sea floor. I did not have to suggest a course. We were heading directly for the pillar, the strong wind pushing us from behind. Then we sailed into a deep current, which turned the whole craft like a child's toy, and then swept us once again towards the pillar.

I have sought God for most of my adult life, and in that time I have come to feel His presence, to know when He is near. I felt the presence of a god now – but which god?

As we drew nearer to the shining column, I saw that it was much wider than I'd supposed – from a distance its immeasurable height had misled my eye. The side we approached was something like three times the length of our craft in width at the base, though it seemed to taper as it rose. Nor was the pillar round, as I had first supposed; but, rather, it looked to be faceted – although I could only see three of its sides. Later I was to discover that it was octagonal. It looked to be of some sort of pure crystal, illuminated from within by a pale milk-white light that seemed independent of the sun.

It wasn't until we were quite close to the pillar that we discovered that it was surrounded by a silvery mesh, which was so fine as to be almost invisible. Each strand of this marvellous mesh looked to be no thicker than a man's finger – and yet I had no doubt that it would slice through the currach's skin like a hot coal through ice. As we approached, I thought the mesh would keep us from the pillar; but on nearing it I found that the gaps were wider than our craft, though not by any great amount.

When we were within perhaps three or four boat-lengths of the pillar, the wind dropped abruptly. Still the current kept pulling us in. The brothers scrambled to the oars, while both Eoin and Geoffrey grabbed for the steering oar, all of them recognizing the danger of the mesh. I leaned over the starboard prow, while Martyn took up position on the port side, and we both attempted to bring the currach safely through the opening.

As we reached the mesh, I shouted the order to ship oars. With Eoin's rock-steady hand on the tiller, we drifted through the mesh on the current, the smooth, almost translucent but deadly strands sliding past without so much as brushing us.

The current died once we were inside the mesh, although we were still nearly two boat-lengths from the pillar itself. It rose between us and the sun, an artificial cliff, smooth, polished, awesome.

I gave the order and the oars dipped, rose again and dipped, bringing our craft up to the pillar itself. And then I reached out, my hands trembling slightly, and touched it. It felt cool and very smooth, far smoother than any surface I have ever known, with no flaw or imperfection on its surface. It was like ice – although it was not so cold – a column of ice. I stared deep into its glowing interior, but I could see nothing except vague shadow-shapes, though these might have been a trick of the light.

We rowed around the pillar without speaking and Geoffrey's voice, as he called the beat, seemed loud, vulgar and too intrusive. My earlier feelings of being in the presence of some deity increased as did the impression that I was being watched. I kept seeing shadows moving within the pillar from the corner of my eye – although when I turned to look there was nothing there.

I resolved to look only straight ahead – but that too was a mistake, because at the edge of my sight, I saw leering, gibbering faces appear behind the clear crystal. And the faces were familiar. It took me a few pounding heartbeats to place them – but then one face spun into vivid focus. It was Crosan's. And then I suddenly recognized the rest of the faces – they were those of my dead friends and brethren, the brothers who had died on my first voyage, and those we had lost so far on this one. But when I turned around to look directly they disappeared; and so I spent the rest of our tour around the pillar staring straight towards it, unwilling to allow the reminders of my failures to reappear.

Three sides of the pillar were identical, smooth and indistinguishable from each other. However, a low carved ledge ran the length of the fourth side. Almost in the centre of this ledge, recessed into an oval niche, was set a silver chalice and a paten carved from the same crystal as the pillar.

I called a halt and the currach drifted to a standstill before them; and then, while the brothers trod water, with the oars keeping us in place, I examined the holy objects. The chalice was like nothing I had ever seen before; it was a long-stemmed, long-bodied, high-based cup of infinite beauty, while the paten was a perfectly circular disk, coming to a point in its middle.

'Who made these; who placed them here?' Fiachra finally burst out.

'I don't know,' I said absently. I was wrestling with the most terrible and overwhelming desire I have ever felt in my life. I had never seen anything as beautiful and wondrous as that chalice and paten. I had never seen anything I wanted so badly. I had to have them. For Clonfert. For myself.

'Perhaps the Lord Jesus Christ Himself made them,' Fiachra whispered.

It was a straw, and I leaped at it. Perhaps He had, I thought wildly. And perhaps He had brought us here to retrieve them and bring them back to the world of men. It was the excuse I was looking for. I reached out my hands and touched the chalice. A current seemed to run through my body, a tingle that numbed my fingers and set the muscles in my arms and legs twitching of their own accord. Not for the first time, I was afraid. But my desire was stronger. I reached across and wrenched the chalice which seemed reluctant to be parted from its crystal setting, then placed it in our boat. Next, I took the paten.

And suddenly the light within the crystal pillar began to dim. 'Back,' I screamed, fear and tension cracking my voice. 'Get us away from this pillar!' The brothers rowed frantically, pulling us away from it; but as I watched, it changed.

The very structure of the column altered, growing darker and more opaque . . . turning to stone.

I looked down at my precious treasures in the boat by my feet. But the chalice and paten remained as brilliant, still glowing with that soft internal fire. 'We must leave here – bear westwards,' I ordered. 'We have a voyage to complete.'

'Have a care when we reach the mesh,' Geoffrey added. 'It will be almost impossible to see at dusk.'

But when we reached where the mesh should have been there was nothing, no trace of it. There was only a grey and empty sea, above which the first few stars were beginning to rise.

I looked down at the chalice and paten again; I had destroyed something of incredible beauty to steal – yes, steal – these. My heart said it was worth it.

Chapter Fifteen

I felt no guilt about taking the chalice and paten – not then, anyway. Even now, after all that has happened, I can at times believe that they were truly meant for me, for Clonfert.

We had wrapped the treasures in a sack of oiled cloth which Eoin had hastily stitched together for me, to protect them from the rain and salt spray. I then wedged them carefully between some of the stores packed under the keel in the stern of the boat, where they couldn't roll about. I personally believed that they were indestructible – but it was a theory I was not about to put to the test. But even though I knew that they were as safe as we could make them, at least twice a day I found myself untying a corner of the cloth sack and pulling it back to assure myself that my treasures were still whole and undamaged. It was two days after I had taken them from the pillar before I discovered that the chalice would start to glow with a pure crystal light at the onset of twilight. The glow brightened as the evening progressed into night until, around midnight, the chalice and paten blazed with a cold white fire. Whatever doubts I might have had concerning the holiness of the objects vanished then; that light was pure. Just to see them and touch them brought me comfort. As marvellous as our voyage had been to date, we had nothing to show for it – nothing tangible, that is. But now, whatever else happened, we had something unique, something wondrous to show for our journey. A gift from God.

It was probably coincidence, but I imagined that since we had found the treasures, our days had become unusually well-ordered, almost as if we had resumed our monastic discipline and pattern, which unfortunately – if understandably – had lapsed somewhat. Our devotions were resumed with full vigour and even our simple meals seemed to be served more regularly, instead of when we felt hungry. The remainder of the time was spent in small repairs to the sails or hides or in rowing – and this was more for exercise than necessity, as we were running before a moderate and favourable wind. And thus eight days passed without incident.

We awoke on the morning of the ninth day to find the sky was dull and overcast and that the wind had freshened. Our course still remained westerly, but our speed had increased with the wind. The sea was leaden and choppy and the white-capped waves were chill. Even the least seawise amongst us knew that there was a storm brewing. But though the sky remained overcast, there was no sign of any storm clouds. Still, the very air tasted tart, and I felt the small hairs on the back of my hands and neck begin to crawl – a sure sign that the storm was not too far away.

I was moving forward to the prow to join Eoin and Geoffrey, when I thought I heard a distant rumble that sounded very like thunder. 'What do you think?' I asked them. 'Are we in for a thunderstorm?'

Eoin shook his head slightly, his hard eyes searching the sky for the telltale flicker of lightning. 'I don't think so,' he said finally. 'There's not enough heat in the air for it.'

Geoffrey looked less certain. In his careful measured tones, he said, 'I don't think so – although who knows what manner of freakish weather can be found in these parts? Still, I don't think that was thunder; but whatever it was, be it storm or something less natural, we're headed towards it at some considerable speed.' He glanced across at me, his clear eyes hooded. 'It might be as well to prepare ourselves . . . just in case,' he added.

Another low growling rumble trembled across the waves – the sound louder and nearer now. It seemed as if the decision had already been made. 'Tie everything down securely,' I ordered, 'and take up positions; we may need to change course against the wind.'

If our voyage had taught my brethren nothing else, it had made mariners of them, true seamen. I'm not sure if any other crew had ever spent as long at sea before; and even if they had, I'm certain their circumstances were different. The brothers lashed down the few loose stores and pots and then positioned themselves by their oars. I saw Martyn, who was so good with ropes and knots, turn his face to the wind and then move unobtrusively to stand next to the mainsail's stays. After that there was little else we could do but ride before the wind.

I remained standing in the prow, staring across the growing waves. There was another grumbling rumble, and this time I actually saw the shock wave ripple across the surface of the water, like a stone dropped into a pool. The currach bucked, and I lost my balance and staggered back. When I returned to the prow, the first thing I noticed was a dark point on the horizon. We were moving with such speed that I could actually see it growing while I watched. It was a mountain, an island that seemed to be nothing more than a mountain. It rose up out of the water like an accusing finger, black stone dark against the sky. There were clouds gathered above, heavy, almost solid-looking clouds, which suddenly glowed a bright orange-red. At the same time a series of similarly coloured lights blazed red- and white-hot about the base of the mountain, and another rumbling explosion of sound rippled across the sea.

The island grew even uglier as we neared it. Against the dark rocks, it was difficult to make out details, but I could find no tree, no hedge, not even a single blade of grass on its bleak surface; and at one point I actually thought I saw the very earth moving, like some huge sluggish worm. Smoke was belching from scores of fissures along its bleak coastline, with a noise like the hissing of serpents. The very air was thick with black ash, cinders and glowing sparks, which stung like insects.

'This is what Hell must look like,' I thought and quickly crossed myself. My brethren had fallen silent, although I saw some lips moving in private prayers as they contemplated the bleak, threatening land ahead.

I felt a hand on my shoulder and Geoffrey's voice said softly in my ear, 'The fires on their own might be natural; the booming also, but don't they remind you of something . . .?'

I shook my head slightly, 'I'm not sure . . .' I began, and then there was another roar of flame and smoke and the thunder boomed out once again. And I found the sounds were indeed familiar. 'It's a forge!'

Geoffrey nodded solemnly. 'It's a forge – but the size, man;

160

consider the size.'

I didn't have to. I didn't want to even think of a forge that size – or the inhabitants.

The onshore tides had us now, pulling us in towards the island's rocky shore. Eoin shouted behind me, and I heard the terrifying scrape of timbers against stone. It had only been a scrape, but it made me realize just how dangerous these waters were.

'We've two choices,' Geoffrey shouted as another terrifying crash boomed across the water. 'We can attempt to pull free – or we can land . . .'

'I don't want to land here, Abbot,' Ruarai suddenly blurted out from behind me. 'I'd rather stay at sea.' I turned and found he was ashen-faced, huddling down close to Barran, who was looking almost as frightened himself.

There was a quick murmur of agreement, and Martyn said coldly, 'Well, if we don't do something now, soon, we will no longer have a choice.'

I gave the order and the sails were dropped and the brothers began to pull strongly away from the island, but, with the current pulling us in, we made little headway.

Eoin suddenly shouted and pointed towards the isle. I turned and found that there were now tall figures standing at the shore, watching us, waiting. And then the wind dropped – and the sounds became clear. The noise which we had heard as distant thunder was all about us now, but now it was immediately recognizable as roaring bellows, followed by a sound like a giant hammer striking an anvil – but the size, for the sound to be that loud, the size was unimaginable. Was this entire island populated by blacksmiths? But to what ends? Tools or weapons? But no metal tools could till that lifeless soil, and there were no neighbouring islands upon whose people they might use weapons. And then the thought struck me – just what in fact did they eat on this dead stone island?

But smiths they certainly were, I decided, as the men at the shore ran down into the shallows, waving huge hammers and long bars of metal. They also wore the blacksmith's traditional dark leather apron, though aside from this, they were as naked as savages. Thick hair matted their legs and their powerful arms, and fell across their faces. There was something about their faces . . . something wrong . . .

The figures on the strand suddenly turned, and ran back up the beach, heading for the glowing, smoking crevices.

Ruarai spoke again, and I could actually hear his teeth chattering. 'Abbot, you know how I feel about the open sea, but anything is better than this. Let us go; we've seen enough.'

'There's nothing to worry about,' Barran said quickly, more to himself than to Ruarai. 'See how they fled when they saw us approach. We probably look as frightening to them as they do to us. We should pity them – not fear them.' Something changed in his voice, and he added slowly, 'Perhaps it is our duty to bring the Word of Christ to them, and that's why we're being pulled in towards this place.'

'I don't think so,' Martyn said quickly. He was huddled into his robes, shivering despite the waves of heat which the island exuded. 'This never was, nor ever will be a place for Christian souls. Our Christ holds no dominion here. They say a man's soul may be seen through his eyes,' Martyn said, with a glassy smile. 'Look at their faces, when they return, look into their eyes and tell me then what you see.'

'Superstition! And what you're suggesting smacks of heresy,' Barran hissed. 'Our Christ died for all men, not just those who are fair-skinned and civilized. Do you suppose that, because they are dark-skinned, hairy and unkempt, they do not have souls worth saving? I dare say our brethren back at Clonfert would be horrified if they saw us now, with our beards and our stained clothes. Shave them, wash the grime of the forges from their faces and I think you will find that they will be much the same as we are.'

Martyn smiled thinly. 'I wouldn't be too sure of that.' He shook his head. 'You're misunderstanding me; I never suggested that these creatures *should* not be taught the Word because they were dark-skinned – I said they *could not* be taught the Word . . .'

Barran threw him a contemptuous glance and, before I could stop him, stepped up to the prow, cupped his hands around his mouth and called out a long, loud, 'Hallooo . . . hallooo . . .'

A score of figures reappeared on the strand. They were

carrying long tongs, which held glowing ingots of white-hot metal. They fanned out in a long line on the beach, some of them actually moving out into the shallows. One of them raised his head, and brushed back his matted hair with a gloved hand . . . and Barran screamed in terror. He had seen their faces. I too caught a glimpse of them – and it was a sight I will carry with me to my grave.

Their heads were large, broad browed, with wide, almost lipless mouths and slightly protruding jaws. Their teeth were large and flat, and the incisors were longer than usual and pointed. Their noses were short, broad and flat, with wide flaring nostrils – and each man . . . but no, they were not men, each creature had just a single staring eye, directly in the centre of his forehead. The eye was huge and beastlike, black-centred, red-rimmed and blazing with a wild animal-like fury that I could almost feel from the currach. The creature threw back his head and roared, and then he lifted his long pincers . . .

'Row!' I screamed. 'Row!'

The blacksmith hurled his ingot directly at us. It missed the craft by no more than the measure of a man's stride, and the water exploded in a geyser of boiled steam where it struck. Hot spray scalded my hand.

'Row!' I shouted again, although my brethren needed no encouragement. Eoin called the beat, and then, as another glowing ingot hissed through the air towards us, increased it.

The ingot fell short, and the water foamed and steamed again; and then two more lumps of glowing metal were coming towards us. They splashed into the water on either side of us and waves of steaming water washed over our prow, scalding some of my brethren's feet. The creatures on the shore howled with rage, the snarling cry of animals suddenly deprived of easy prey.

I prayed then, calling out a Pater in a strong voice, knowing the brothers would say it with me. 'Our Father . . .' The men joined in, some softly, some with an edge of hysteria in their voices. And indeed, it was as much as I could do to keep my own voice level.

More of them had now massed on the shoreline, and the sea was a blaze of fiery ingots and boiling water. Some fell so close

163

that I knew it was merely a matter of time before a white-hot lump of metal fell directly into our craft . . . I called aloud to our Saviour for aid; and then, as if in answer, the wind changed direction!

It only took a score – maybe less – of heartbeats, before Martyn and Eoin had unfurled the sail, and then it snapped and cracked, and the currach lurched, heeled, righted itself – and we were out into the bay, with the shore dwindling rapidly behind us.

I dropped my oar and stood up, easing my cracking back. 'What did they want?' I asked Martyn, as we watched the tiny figures capering on the beach with their dreadful cries of anger and frustration drifting across the waves. Occasionally the water exploded in a tall fountain of steam, but we were well beyond their range.

'Us, I think,' he replied in a soft even voice.

'But why?' I wondered.

'There wouldn't be any sources of meat on that island, you know . . .' he suggested quietly.

His meaning was clear, and I shuddered. And then I knelt and crossed myself, and my brethren followed suit. 'Let us give thanks for our delivery from that hellish place . . .' I began, looking from face to face. The brothers nodded, relief evident on all their faces. Martyn's expression caught my attention, and his smile disturbed me. For a fleeting moment, I thought of druid wind-spells; but then something took my attention and the thought slipped away. Somehow I never got around to asking him . . .

Novices in the first throes of devotion could not have prayed with more fervour than we did then. So absorbed were we that it was not until the last Ave and Pater that we became aware that we were in the grip of a strong undercurrent. Once more we were racing along, as the wind and tides acted on our small craft.

I made my way to the prow, and stood, lost in thought, watching the phosphorescent waves foam about our bow. I was so absorbed that I didn't actually hear anyone come up beside me, and I was startled to find Martyn standing at my left hand. On impulse, I turned to him, 'Do you know where we're bound?'

'Not precisely.' His eyes were bleak, evasive.

'That's not an answer,' I said. 'Either you do or you don't.'

I could barely make out his features in the dimness, but I thought I saw him smile slightly. 'Do not press me, Abbot. My foresight is partial, fragmented, sometimes flawed. It is as if I had to grasp the whole of a manuscript from a glance at a single page.'

'Is there danger ahead?' I persisted.

'When has there not been?' Martyn countered.

I knew I would have to be content with that, although content was probably the wrong word – something was gnawing at me, making me more uneasy than even our encounter with the smiths would account for. I could feel my skin crawl, and all the hairs on my arms and at the back of my neck were rising. A sudden thought struck me and I hurried to the stern to check on the chalice and paten. They were safe, of course, but I couldn't resist the temptation to look at them once again. And while I was absorbed in their gleaming beauty, which seemed to ease my soul and soothe my fears, Eoin called out to me, 'Abbot, look ahead!'

I stood up slowly, and then followed the direction of his pointing arm. Yet another mountain rose out of the sea; but this time there was no land around it whatsoever. It was a bleak, sheer knife of a mountain, black as coal and as ugly as sin. Its summit was an inferno, spewing ash and smoke high into the twilight sky. It was a natural phenomenon – a volcano; I had read about such things in the writings of the ancients, and from mariners' tales; but this was the first time I had ever actually seen a fire-mountain. And it was terrifying.

There was nothing for us here, and after the last island I felt little inclined to chance even coming in close to the shore. As for the men, their oars were already out. 'Row away,' I commanded.

Nothing happened.

All the men began to speak at once. 'Abbot, we can't!'

'I know the current's strong against us, but you must try,' I said in exasperation.

'We can't move the oars,' Fiachra shouted. 'Try them yourself.'

I took my oar in both hands, and pulled back smoothly – a controlled, powerful stroke which should have propelled us forward. The oar dragged through the water as if it were thick honey and then it stopped. I pulled again, this time with all my might. The oar would not budge; it was locked so firmly that it might have been set in solid rock, not water.

I leaned over the side of the currach and plunged my hand into the murky sea around us. Though it was oily and unwholesome, my fingers moved freely. While I was staring into the rainbow-hued depths, the boat suddenly rocked violently and my brethren began screaming, terrified. I turned . . . and found that a winged creature hovered above our craft, its huge, almost translucent wings beating slowly, a sour, rancid odour wafting down into our craft. Its body was that of a man – a youth, really – but scaled, like a serpent, and its feet ended in cloven hooves. Perhaps there was a tail behind, but I did not see one. But its face was beautiful; its cheekbones high and defined, its hair tightly curled and golden, its nose straight and imperious. Perhaps its lips gave a hint to its true character, for they were fleshy, wet and slightly parted. The eyes were terrifying; pale amber, wide and staring, and looking into them was like staring into the source of pure evil. There was never any doubt what it was; my life and training had taught me to recognize the demon-kind.

'Welcome, Brendan of Clonfert.' The voice was ice cold, and seemed to bite deep into my skull. The creature hadn't spoken with his lips, but yet I had heard him clearly, and understood the menace and authority in his voice. 'I have waited long for this meeting.'

'Be gone, damned creature,' I commanded aloud. 'We are Christian monks, men of God – you have no dominion over us!'

A laugh snarled in my head, making me shiver. 'Hell has dominion here, not your god; you have no control over me.'

'What do you want?' I demanded, my fingers finding the small wooden cross that hung around my neck.

'I have come for you; yes, you, Brendan, abbot of Clonfert. You are to join us. And rich will be my Master's reward for such a prize.'

'I do not belong to you, nor ever shall. My life and my faith

166

have prepared me for Heaven, and your kind have no hold on me!'

'Beware the sin of pride, Brendan. It is one my kind know well.' Again the laughter, as if the creature were spinning out its delight and triumph. Its huge wings beat, and beat again. 'Though you are in the confines of Hell, yet you could have passed through safely, had greed not corrupted your heart . . .' Perhaps he could sense my surprise, because he continued, 'What price your pretty toys now, eh, monk-man? They'll decorate your pathetic building in Clonfert, but you shall never celebrate your services with them.'

'The chalice, the paten, I was meant to have them . . .' I whispered.

'Many things are meant,' the voice hissed, 'though not all of them come to pass. Perhaps you were always meant for me.'

I turned, looking wildly at my brethren, whose faces were frozen with terror. The hellish voice continued, 'They cannot save you, they cannot even hear me . . . But part of my delight will be to let them wonder why I have come for you only; they will know then that you must have sinned, and how they will speculate on your hidden vices, holy abbot!' Suddenly his expression changed, hardening, and he sank his talons into my shoulders. Hot pain that was like a preview of the torment of Hell lanced through me, and I screamed. Dimly I heard a human voice shout, 'NO!'

And then Eoin was beside me, wrestling the talons from me, struggling with the demon. 'Not the abbot. You will not take him, fiend. Take me if you must have one of us!'

The demon released his hold, allowing me to fall to the deck, and then he spoke, his voice clear and almost musical. 'So be it – for now,' he snarled. 'But we will converse another time perhaps, Brendan. And you can take the memory of this day home to Clonfert with your other treasures.'

The demon wrapped its arms and legs around Eoin and rose up, his huge wings beating furiously to gain height. It circled the currach once and then flew directly in towards the top of the mountain. Eoin's screams filled the air as the flames began licking around him and then there was only a terrifying silence as the demon dropped down into the cone of the volcano.

167

Chapter Sixteen

'Brendan, you must eat.' Geoffrey's voice was soft and insistent. 'It's been two days and nights since you've broken your fast with us. You can't go on like this.'

I don't want to go on, I thought; not with another death on my conscience. The cost is too high; too many deaths, too much pain. But when I looked up, I found my old friend's face creased with worry. I forced myself to smile in reassurance. 'I'll be all right. Just leave me alone for a bit . . .'

He squatted down before me, proffering a cup of water and a small piece of bread. 'Just take a little now,' he coaxed, like a mother to a fretful child.

I was too tired and too ill to argue with him, so I smiled my thanks and took the food. I sipped at the water; and as I drank, I realized just how parched and sore my throat had become; but when I chewed and tried to swallow a mouthful of bread, my stomach heaved and I gagged. I spat it out over the side of the boat, and took a gulp of water. Geoffrey held a hand against my forehead, and I had to steel myself not to flinch; I wanted no man's touch, nothing to remind me of my loss . . .

'There's no fever, thank God,' he said, his soft grey eyes staring deep into mine. 'But you're ill. If only we had some milk or broth or even an egg that would give you nourishment without making you sick.' He shook his head. 'I'm not sure what we can do for you.'

'Just let me rest for a bit,' I begged. He began shaking his head. 'Please!' I insisted.

Reluctantly, Geoffrey moved away and I closed my eyes. And the images that haunted my sleep and waking hours came flooding back. I saw it happening again and again; I saw the demon's mocking smile, saw Eoin being carried off in its long-taloned claws, saw them dropping down into the volcano's gaping mouth, into the flames. I heard Eoin's screams again

168

echoing and re-echoing around in my head, until I felt as if my skull were about to burst. And Eoin of all people. Why Eoin, Eoin, who was blameless, loyal, trusting – whom I had been closest to amongst my company. He had reminded me of everything I once was; even having him aboard pushed back the years, made me a young man again. Why would I not be sick? Sick with sorrow, sick with guilt. He had been taken in my place, and I should have been taken, because I had stolen the chalice and paten . . . I had killed him.

Lost in my thoughts I didn't feel the morning slip away; and all too soon it was time for the mid-day meal, and once again I could feel the brothers murmuring amongst themselves, watching me. Something in my face must have kept the others from pressing food on me; and to emphasize the fact that I wished to be left to myself, I bent my head and pretended to doze over my oar.

However, I actually did fall asleep, and when I awoke, the afternoon had moved on. The meal was long finished and I found Martyn sitting by my side. For a while he merely rowed silently; then, when the rhythm of the beat had been established and the others were talking idly amongst themselves, he glanced sidelong at me, and said softly, 'Do you remember when we came back to Ailbe's island? The matters we spoke of then?'

'Yes,' I answered indifferently, gazing out to sea.

'You told me that despair was sinful, and that even the very thoughts of suicide placed my soul in mortal jeopardy,' he persisted.

'Yes, yes,' I snapped. 'What of it?' I glared at him, feeling a dull pounding at the base of my skull. 'Why do you bring this up now? Are you still bent on self-destruction?'

'No,' he said very softly. 'But you are.'

'How dare you even suggest that!' I wheeled around on him, rage boiling up in me like the lava from the volcano that had swallowed Eoin. I saw some of the brothers look up curiously, and then look away, leaving me alone with the young man. It was only afterwards that I realized that they might have had instructions not to interfere.

Martyn's dark, clever eyes met mine evenly. 'Then tell me what you are doing? You are the most experienced sailor of us all; you have spent more time at sea than you have on dry land, I'll wager. Even the druids have a name for you: they call you the Navigator, and it is a name used with respect. So you of all people should know what will happen to you here on the open sea and exposed to the elements if you take no nourishment. Your muscles will go, you will be unable to pull an oar; your sight then – Brendan's famous sight, that can count the feathers on a bird's tail at a hundred paces – that will leave you. Then waking dreams will follow, and you will rave and scream, become more of a beast, less of a man. Is this what you want? Is this how Brendan the Navigator will die?' His voice had hardened, becoming contemptuous. 'For you know you will die as surely as if you had cast yourself into the sea. But not only will you be killing yourself – with neither spiritual leader nor captain on board, you'll condemn us all to a slow, lingering death. Do you want another shipload of men on your conscience, Abbot?' I winced as he almost spat the last word; he had made it sound more of a curse than a title. 'None of us can afford the luxury of your grief, Brendan.'

The rage within me blazed white hot, and I felt an almost uncontrollable urge to strike this pale-faced, tight-lipped young man. I had to make a deliberate effort to unclench my grip on the oar; my knuckles cracked and popped as I straightened them. Some part of me recognized that Martyn was right, yet – and God forgive me – I needed to vent my anger and grief, to strike out and hurt. 'Why did you not tell me what would happen, why did you not warn me? I asked you, and you would say nothing. What use are the powers that you paid so dearly for?' I saw the pain in his own eyes, but I hurried on, triumphantly. 'It was a bad bargain you made – an innocent creature killed and eaten – and for what?'

Martyn nodded. 'A bad bargain indeed, Brendan; and I pay for it in ways you could not even begin to comprehend, every day of my life,' he said softly. 'Yes, I saw danger to you, but I did not see its nature nor the outcome.'

'Did you not have some idea of what would happen?' I demanded.

'Yes, but there must always be free will; those with the Sight can only suggest paths or ways to follow. Man's will alone determines his ultimate destiny. Eoin chose to save you.'

'Don't speak his name to me,' I whispered. Tears were coursing down my face. I drew the hood of my robe up and lowered my head, that the others might not see me. 'You don't understand . . .'

Martyn deliberately looked to the stern of the craft to where the chalice and paten were stored and then he turned back to me. 'I understand all too well. And I understand that no father can love all his sons equally, that there is always one who holds a special place in his heart. You are like a father to us all, and Eoin was your special son.'

I began to shake my head, but Martyn interrupted me. 'Surely you did not think yourself above other men, without flaw? Will you now add pride to the list of sins you flail yourself with?'

'I won't have you speaking to me thus. I am still your leader!'

'Then you must act as such,' Martyn said simply. 'For unless I am mistaken, we are still within a place where Hell holds sway.'

He stood up and bowed to me and then made his way down the length of the craft, leaving me with my thoughts. His words stung, rankled, hurt – but there was still enough honesty left in me to recognize the truth in them. Pride. Yes, I realized I was proud. But perhaps pride was necessary for a journey such as ours and was not always a sin, I argued with myself. The men needed a proud, courageous leader such as I had been; they needed someone to follow, someone they could trust – and blame, when something went wrong. I had been all those things, and could be again, if I trusted to the Will of God. Our goal could not be far away, and I was needed. When we were home again at Clonfert, I would offer up mass daily for Eoin's soul. Until then I would put him from my mind and concentrate all my will and energy to our search.

It all sounds so simple now, a rational, straightforward decision arrived at logically; but in truth it took me the remainder of the day, and involved much soul-searching. But the decision – when it was made – brought a sense of profound peace to my soul. When the evening rations were brought out, I took my share along with the others. As I soaked the bread in the water and sucked carefully on the paste, I stared out over the level, seemingly motionless waves, and I decided that even if we never reached the Promised Land, I had found something even greater: I had found peace within myself. It almost made the voyage worth it.

I was crouched in the prow, somewhere close to seven or eight days later, still vainly attempting to construct the chart of these enchanted waters, when, on glancing up, I saw what looked to be a small sailing craft in the distance. There was a shout behind me; someone – Barran, I think – had also spotted the boat. There were cries of excitement, and then the currach listed in the water as the brothers all moved to the port side.

I couldn't share their excitement; had someone else then gone forth on the same mission as ourselves? And had they found the Promised Land? Even the thought of it was unbearable – to have come so far and have endured so much . . . There was a powerful temptation to swing away, to order the brothers to the oars to pull us away from the tiny, insignificant – yet utterly terrifying – boat.

'Abbot?' Geoffrey asked, looking to me for instructions.

I looked again at the small craft – and I knew I had to know. 'Bring us in,' I ordered.

As we drew nearer, the size of the craft in the water before us became more obvious – it was tiny. How remarkable, I thought, that anyone could have ventured so far from land in such a craft. And what was even more peculiar was that it didn't seem to move, although the water we were in was far, far too deep for anchorage. Perhaps it was grounded on a sand bar; but I could see no change in either the waves or their colour that might indicate one. I felt our craft heel, and then we veered slightly to the starboard side of the little boat, so that a sudden swell wouldn't crash us into it. Then we made a swift, though careful approach, coming around in a wide circle.

'It's not a boat at all!' Ruarai cried out, even as I realized the same thing myself.

It took us a while to work out exactly what it was. If it had looked peculiar at first, it became absolutely fantastical as we made out more and more details; for there, effectively in the middle of nowhere, was a naked man sitting on a rock. Before him – what we had at first taken for a sail – was a white cloth, held up on either side by what looked like two large iron cooking forks. As we moved in, we could see that the waves were lapping in over the man; and even as we watched, one especially large wave swept across his body, completely submerging the rock. We were close enough to hear him coughing and spluttering as the water receded.

But what was he; a hermit – one of those who lived out their lives in secret valleys, on inhospitable mountains, or on almost barren isles? I've always thought them to be foolish people, wasting their lives, instead of filling their days in the physical work devoted to the glory of God. Or was he a stranded sailor, I wondered, some poor wretch whose craft had foundered and he the only survivor? But whatever he was, it was our clear duty to rescue him, unwilling though I was to have a stranger in our craft.

We rowed to within a few feet of the man, and then the brothers gently worked the oars to maintain our position, while Geoffrey, Martyn and Barran moved forward to speak to him. It was difficult to make out his features for the fine, pale, bleached hair that covered most of his face and matted his body. What we could see of his flesh was as pale as death and puckered with the cold, while most of his toes and at least half the fingers on either hand had succumbed to frostbite. Compassion overcame my earlier hesitation about having a stranger on board. 'Just stay where you are,' I called out. 'We'll have you off that rock and into our boat directly.'

Shock appeared to have left him speechless, for he made no reply but only stared at me with wild, frozen eyes the colour of rusty metal. Hoping that he could understand our language, I tried again, and then repeated my message in Latin and Greek, saying, 'Don't be afraid. I don't know how you came to be here, but we'll rescue you. You're saved now.'

He laughed then, a strange, frightening sound that had no mirth but only pain it it, and when he spoke, he used my own native tongue, although with a harsher, barbaric accent. 'Come no closer, brothers. I thank you for your offer, but I must stay where I am. It is ordained that I remain on this rock until sunset.'

He spoke slowly, like one who had long been unaccustomed to human speech, but his words had the force of certainty to them and were not the ravings of a man gone mad from some disaster at sea.

'What have you done to be punished in this manner?' I asked.

'This?' He gestured to the rock and the cloth and the iron forks on either side of him. And then he laughed again, long and high, and I felt an ice-cold chill settle in at the base of my neck. 'This is no punishment, not this, no, not this. This is my indulgence, my boon, granted to me by the Lord Jesus Christ in His infinite mercy on the Sabbath and on certain holy days.'

'But this water is freezing,' I cried.

He nodded, smiling like an idiot. 'This water chills me; but it is balm compared to the fires of Hell, where I must stay in everlasting torment, save when I am granted respite on special days, holy days, blessed days.'

'Who are you?' I whispered.

'I am Judas Iscariot!'

'Accursed Judas, who betrayed our Lord Jesus Christ!' Barran said wildly.

'My lord as well,' Judas cried. 'My lord, my god – before you ever took Him as your god, my lord whom I loved above all else until . . . I did what I did. Guilt and horror made me take my own life, and that, coupled with my ghastly sin, ensured that there can be no end to my suffering. Nor should there be – eternity is not long enough for me to atone for what I did.'

I had been taught to meditate on Christ's suffering, and sometimes I had wondered what kind of fiend could have betrayed the Christ after sharing the joy of discipleship to the incarnate God. I suppose I had built up an image of what that man must be like. But now before me was not the monster of my imaginings, but a pallid, pitiful wretch, tormented not only by eternal damnation and hellfire, but also by the memory of

174

his deed. A thought teased at my brain, something I had read in the Scriptures or had been told, perhaps. I asked, 'Were you not accounted the closest of all the disciples to our Lord?'

'And so I was,' Judas said, not boastfully, but in a tone of terrible longing. 'Up to the end, in life, I served Him well and comforted Him; and even when I did what I did, I did it believing I was saving Him. I wanted to save Him – truly I did,' he cried. 'Truly! The coin meant nothing to me. Perhaps that is why he grants me this indulgence – or perhaps my destiny was ordained in some way that He could see but not prevent, and that is why I am spared so much. During my tortures in Hell it gives me some little comfort to realize that Christ lives because I betrayed Him!'

I knew I should detest this creature, whose very name was anathema, and yet, against my will, pity stirred in me. To cover the confusion of my emotions, I pointed to the length of cloth. 'What is that, what does it signify?'

'That is the cloth that in life I gave to a leper.' Judas reached to touch it, but the breeze wafted it from his grasp, the stumps of his fingers closed on empty air. 'Those iron forks are those I gave to the priests of a temple to hold up their cooking pots. And this very rock upon which I sit was one that I used to fill a trench in the public road. These small things stay with me throughout eternity, and they are a constant reminder of my past and what might have been . . . what might have been . . .'

The silence lengthened and I found I could think of nothing to say – nowadays, of course, I have constructed volumes of questions I could have asked Judas Iscariot – and so, I said, 'Tell me, have you seen other voyagers pass this way?'

Judas shook his head. 'None. You are the first mortal men I have conversed with since my punishment was meted out to me. Should I ask what brings you to these hellish parts?'

'We are Christian monks, and we have been journeying for longer than even we can remember, in search of the Promised Land. In my heart, I think the end of our voyage is near, but I don't know which way to venture next.'

'You are indeed close to the Promised Land,' Judas said softly. 'It is part of my torment to be so close to that which is eternally unreachable for me.'

'Can you tell us the way?' I asked eagerly.

'In part, yes.' He paused and moments were lost as he sat absorbed in his own thoughts. I did not press him; surely all this was part of a greater pattern, else why were we here? If, as I suspected, this voyage was a lesson, what were we supposed to take from this meeting with Christ's betrayer?

At last Judas said, 'When the sun sets this evening, the demon who watches me always will come to carry me back to Hell. If you and your brethren were to stay here by me through the night, I could have another day's respite, for he could not take me in your presence . . . A day for me would be an eternity . . .' He added, his voice dead and hopeless.

Without hesitation, I said, 'It's a bargain.'

Barran tugged at my sleeve, and hissed, 'Abbot, remember with whom you treat!'

Before I could reply, Judas shook his head again and said, 'I do not make bargains any more. I will tell you your course, such as I know it, whether or not you stay with me. Head south, and you will come upon another island a day's – perhaps two days' – sail from here. A hermit lives there; perhaps he will help you – if he thinks you're worthy. For myself, I ask your favour out of any pity or charity you might find in your own hearts for a damned soul.'

'We will stay the night here.' I turned to the others, first looking directly into Barran's face, and allowing my eyes to mirror the contempt I felt for his behaviour. 'Can we fail to show to this man even a fraction of the compassion which our crucified Saviour has shown him? Remember that this creature has never harmed us in any way.'

Barran said, 'He wronged us when he wronged all mankind! We cannot stay here.'

'Without his wrong, there would be no Christian Faith; there would be no blood sacrifice at the Holy Mass; there would be no holy orders of men following the Way,' Martyn said, his voice ice-cold and dismissive.

'We will stay,' I said loudly. 'And, Barran, remember, there can be only one captain on this craft. I will seek and listen to advice, but no one will question my authority.' Many of the men looked startled at hearing me speak in so blunt a manner;

176

but Martyn, I noted, smiled approvingly. Well, I did not need his approval any more than Barran's sullen anger.

Despite my brave words, I felt the same unease as the rest when darkness approached. The wind that rose, though our craft did not move, was tainted with the stench of resin, smoke and burnt flesh, and its howl was like that of an animate thing, furious and evil. Now, in the shadows I could make out shapes whirling around us, too numerous to count. As it grew darker they began to take on form, gaining substance from the night itself. But these weren't like the creature which had taken Eoin; these were red-hued, winged demons from my most terrifying childhood nightmares.

The first voice I heard was like a breeze speaking – soft, insidious, cajoling and completely inhuman. 'Go away, man of God. Judas is of our company, not yours; but we may not approach him while you are near. Do not deny him to us; our Master calls for him, and we dare not return without him . . .'

With more courage than I felt, I stood up and shouted into the whirling demon-filled breeze. 'Begone. He is under our protection and that of the Lord Jesus Christ!'

A different voice – or perhaps the same one without the attempt at being pleasant – rasping and angry, said, 'How can you invoke the name of Him whom this creature betrayed? Leave him. He is ours.'

'The Lord protects him and us for this night,' I said, then turned to my brethren and called them to prayer. 'Glory be to God . . .'

As our prayers rang out across the water, the keening and howling around us grew, but never managed to drown out the sound of our own devotions. All night we prayed, with the demons attempting to shout us down. We finally stopped towards dawn, hoarse and exhausted. In the silence that followed, one of the fiends spoke again, but even his voice sounded hoarse as if the night's struggles had weakened him. 'Man of God, we curse you and your coming here and your journey that is before you, for great will be our Master's wrath towards us. Our suffering will be doubled because of you.'

Martyn spoke before I could reply. 'Your curses are as nothing to us; for a demon's curse to be effective, one must believe in it!'

'Go then,' another voice shouted. 'Judas' punishments will be doubled because of this night's work.'

I laughed, suddenly realizing that we had won; we had defeated Hell's minions; and it filled me with confidence such as I had not felt in months. 'It is not within your power to alter such things, you are powerless. Go then, go face your master, and tell him how you were defeated by men of God.'

The demons swooped, and a thick fog rose up out of the sea like smoke and swallowed the tiny islet. Our sail cracked and snapped as a breeze filled it, pushing us away from the place where the island had been. When we looked back, the sea was clear and the rock had vanished; but we still heard the demons' howling and Judas' screams long into the morning . . .

Chapter Seventeen

I think it was only as we rowed away that the full impact of what we had just encountered and witnessed sank in. Perhaps it was fear, or just a desire to be safely away, that lent us strength. The brothers rowed at a furious pace, Geoffrey calling a quick double-beat, pushing them at what I judged to be a foolhardy pace – although I gladly joined in. Most of us had the sleeves of our robes rolled up; but even though the air was cool, we were bathed in sweat.

Eventually, when I felt the dull pounding in my chest, and a score of black points swam lazily before my eyes, I let my own oar rest in the water. I looked down the craft, contemplating those who remained of our original group. How old we had become – and I don't mean old in years, but experiences. The time we had spent on this voyage had marked us, had etched lines and furrows onto all our faces, made us cynical, made us wary, distrustful. There were other changes, just as noticeable, but of a physical nature: even the fairest skin amongst us had now been deeply tanned by the wind and weather to a colouring that would not easily fade, even in the poor light of winter. Ruarai, who'd barely needed to shave when we set out, now sported a thick red beard, and his hair had lengthened and thickened. The last vestiges of darkness were gone from Geoffrey's hair, leaving it entirely grey, and my own had thinned down to wispy strands. In the early days of our voyage, Eoin had kept our hair and beards trimmed with his knife . . . but that had been a long while ago now and it was best not to think of Eoin at this time.

I looked over at Fiachra; his youthful features were set into something harder and older now, the fat gone from his cheekbones and jaw, giving his face an almost skeletal appearance. Conn had left Clonfert a boy and – God willing – would return a man. Ultan and Tadgh, who were of an age and whom I had thought of as young men, had matured and quietened, and were now wont to think more before acting. Indeed, we had all changed for the better in one other way: we were now fitter than we had ever been. Bodies had grown strong and muscles bulged impressively – I'm sure that, but for our habits, we looked more like a band of warriors than of monks. I smiled at the thought and wondered what our brethren would think when we returned to Clonfert. My mood had changed and lightened and I never even considered that perhaps we would not be returning to Erin eventually.

My brethren were still rowing furiously, pulling at the long oars in a sort of frenzy, as if they were attacking the waves themselves. At this rate they would exhaust themselves by the evening, and then even their strong limbs would stiffen and cramp, and all would be sore and weary in the morning. Now, with our ultimate destination so near, I wanted them fresh and alert.

'Geoffrey!' I called. He looked up and I shook my head, pointing to the oars. He looked puzzled for a moment, and then he nodded, and stopped calling the beat. The brothers carried on for a few more strokes, but then, with their rhythm broken, their stroking became ragged, and the currach began to flounder. 'Rest awhile,' I called. 'Save your strength; we've nowhere to go in a hurry.'

'But what about this hermit's island?' Barran called, his voice coming between gasps.

'Will a few hours or even a few days more make much difference after all that has passed?'

'How much further away do you think this island is, Abbot?' Fiachra asked me.

'A day, two days perhaps, depending on the wind and tide, but certainly not much more.' I had once been asked a question like that before, and then, as now, the answer had come to me unbidden. The hand of God, I decided, and crossed myself.

'And there will be a man there who really knows the way to the Promised Land?' Fiachra persisted.

'So Judas told us, and so I believe,' I answered firmly.

Only Barran looked doubtful, almost mutinous. 'We are

placing trust in the word of a man who was the greatest traitor the world has ever known!' he said.

'Judas had a destiny, just like you all have a destiny. Yours is to follow me; his was to follow the Christ. And yes, he betrayed our Lord; but that too was his destiny, and I believe that he had no more control over that than we have over the wind and waves.' It came close to blasphemy, I knew; but it was what I firmly believed. 'Judas is no longer a man,' I added. 'He is damned, a soul in perpetual torment, and far beyond human treachery. Now, let us hear no more about it.'

The lengthening silence that followed was broken by Geoffrey. 'We'll row again, but in shifts and at an easier pace . . .'

No wind rose to hasten our journey; but its absence also meant that we were moving through a calm sea, and it was a simple matter to maintain a course due south. My brothers took it in turns to row, and we kept a steady pace all day and on into the night, pausing only for our brief spartan meal, and prayers. On the morning of the third day after our encounter with Judas, I awoke to find the horizon was smudged with the blur of a small island, still a few leagues south of us. I made my way to the prow and stood there, straining to make out its shape through the damp mists of dawn; and it was only the obligation of morning offices that took me from my position.

I returned to the prow after we had broken our fast, and had I not been possessed of an inner certainty that this really was the island we sought, my heart would have sunk as it rose up out of the sea and into clear view. It was naked rock, as dark as flint and as bleak and lifeless as the island of the terrible blacksmiths had been. But no hellish fire punctuated the smooth cliff which rose from the sea, and when the first rays of sunlight broke through the clouds this gave it a strange austere beauty, while also revealing the oddly uniform proportions: the length, breadth and height of the rocky isle were roughly equal. A sudden mad, impossible thought struck me that the island was artificial, man- demon- or god-made.

We rowed slowly around the stony strip of coastline, looking for a safe place to beach our craft. But sheer, glass-like cliffs came straight down to the water's edge and nothing offered itself to us except a narrow cleft in the cliffs – a crevasse – which went back into the island itself, reminding me of the fjords of the icy Northlands. Within this gorge, the sea boomed and roared, tossing spray high against the dark cliffs. At the end of the opening there seemed to be a broad flat ledge; and beyond this a thin winding line, pale against the dark of the stones, wound up and disappeared into the cliffs.

Geoffrey pointed. 'A path.'

I nodded; I had been thinking the same thing. 'Bring us in,' I said. Bringing the currach into the fjord, with its shifting, twisting currents, swells and cross-swells, proved incredibly difficult and hazardous. Twice we actually brushed the cliffs, ripping sections of hide away, down to the wooden framework. But luckily the current was onshore, and actually drove us straight down the length of the gorge, up onto the gravelled ledge! Gravel crunched, and the hide covering screamed and cracked; and then we stopped. In the silence that followed, the currach began to creak and groan like an old woman. I felt water around my ankles and looked down to find a twisting rill of dark liquid coming in through the hides. We had made land – but at what cost?

Geoffrey was first out over the side, followed by Martyn. They both knelt in the shallows and examined the damage to our keel. I dropped down beside them, gasping with the icy chill of the water. Geoffrey looked up, smiling grimly. 'I hope this hermit is worth it,' he said, moving aside and allowing me to see the damage. It was bad – the hide covering had been ripped away and the framework either snapped across or cracked in a score of places – but it could be repaired.

'Start work on it immediately,' I said, nodding to a thin line of weed further up the beach. 'We're well below the high-tide mark. I'll head inland and see if I can find this hermit . . .'

'I'll come with you . . .' Martyn began; but I shook my head firmly.

'No, you'll stay here with Brother Geoffrey and the others. Give him whatever help he needs with the repairs.' I stared into Martyn's dark eyes, hoping he understood what I was trying to say. For a moment I saw his face close in with a sense of rejection; but then he frowned and – almost as if he were

182

reading my thoughts – smiled. He nodded. If anything happened to me, Martyn would help Geoffrey lead the others back to Erin.

Perhaps Geoffrey had sensed something of the unspoken exchange, because he looked up at me, frowning slightly. 'There might be danger here – let someone else go in your place.'

'There is no danger here,' I said confidently, and, bleak and cheerless though the isle was, I instinctively felt that it was a holy place. But, although I felt that there was nothing malevolent here, the island itself was treacherous. The pebbled beach was ice-smooth, the stones polished and rounded by the tide; and as I climbed up through the narrow gorge my eyes were almost always at my feet, partly to avoid bruising my toes on the broken bits of stone and rock that were everywhere and partly to see if there was any form of plant life here. There was none, not even the lichens which cling to the most barren and inhospitable mountain tops in Erin, and which I have encountered, in one form or another, in just about every land I have visited.

The passage was steep and rough, and so narrow that the glass-smooth cliff walls on either side pressed against me at points. I was so busy concentrating on keeping my footing that when I eventually paused to gain my breath I was surprised to find that the boat and my companions were out of sight. The path – if it was a path – was taking me not only upwards but deeper into the isle, and the stillness and silence were absolute.

At last I reached what I gauged to be the summit, although the rock walls were still too high on either side for me to see out over the island. But above me there was only the clear sky, and the path I was following now curved downwards. I continued to follow the path.

It twisted, serpent-like, and then suddenly led out onto a broad circular opening; it reminded me of a clearing found suddenly in a forest, except that it was surrounded by walls of rock rather than by trees. The cliffs were pocked with openings of all shapes and sizes; but directly opposite me was a cave, larger than the rest, and the path I was following led straight into it. I heard sounds then, the first sounds I had heard since we had landed on the island; and when I went to investigate, I found a tiny spring bubbling up from the ground a little to the right of the cave. I lay flat out on the ground and bent my head to it. It was ice cold, and fresh, and I allowed the bubbling water to wash over my head, to ease my salt-dried skin. When I opened my eyes again, I found I was looking at a pair of dirty feet!

I scrambled backwards with a shout of alarm, frantically brushing water from my eyes . . . and I found myself looking at an animal! At least, that was my first impression; but then the creature spoke. 'Welcome.' It was a man. But he was the hairiest man I have ever seen in my life, and beneath his hair he seemed to be naked. I say seemed, because only portions of his face, hands and feet were actually exposed. The rest of him was entirely clothed in thick white hair. Hair from his head and beard reached down to his ankles, blending with his luxuriant body hair into a covering that was more like an animal's pelt than anything else.

At last I found my voice. 'I am Brendan, abbot of Clonfert, in Erin.'

'Yes, yes, of course you are. I've been expecting you – well, not particularly you, but someone like you, someone mad enough to go in search of the Isles of Promise, for quite some time now.' He rubbed his small hands together briskly. 'You are mad; you know that, don't you? Only a madman would undertake this voyage in the first place.' He spoke in a high-pitched, breathless drone. 'I suppose you've left a boatload of men down by the shore? Yes, yes?' I nodded. 'Well, we'd best get you back to them, don't you think? They'll be wondering what has happened to you, I don't doubt.' As he spoke he moved around me, dancing from foot to foot, his eyes bright and darting. 'Well, perhaps you had better rest a moment or two more. It's a steep climb if you're not used to it. I do it every day myself, of course, but . . .' He paused for breath, then snapped his fingers together. 'Oh dear. I forgot to mention my own name. I was called . . .' He hesitated. 'Paul, I think. Yes, I'm sure it was Paul. I suppose I still am, come to think of it, except that it's been such a very long time since anyone called me anything.'

184

'Are you the hermit of this island?' I asked.

'Well, there's no one here but me, which I suppose makes me a hermit . . .'

Before Paul could launch into another speech, I managed to ask, 'How long have you been here?'

'Oh dear, let's see . . . why, it must be ninety years, now; which must make me a very old man, for I was fifty when I left my own land,' he added, with a touch of regret in his voice.

Perhaps if I had encountered this mad hermit earlier on our voyage I might have disbelieved him, and scoffed; but if the voyage had taught me anything, it had taught me not to judge too quickly. And so, accepting the fact that he might well be one hundred and forty years old, I asked, 'Do you know why we have come here?'

'Yes, yes, of course,' he answered impatiently. 'You're in search of the Isles of Promise and you want me to tell you the way; why else would you come here?'

Whatever doubts I might have had vanished, and I accepted him for what he was, a slightly mad, ancient hermit. But there was something troubling me. 'What have you sustained yourself on all these years?' I asked. 'Nothing grows here, surely?'

'Ah, you've noticed that,' he said, nodding slightly, as if I had made a particularly intelligent observation. 'God has looked after me.'

I crossed myself. 'How?'

'Well, for the first thirty years my food was brought to me – by an otter! Truly!' he added, seeing my look of astonishment. 'Every third day an otter would come swimming in from the sea with a big juicy fish in his mouth. Then he'd scramble out of the water in the fjord just where I expect you've wedged your boat, and drop the fish at my feet. Then away he'd go. After a while I learned to ration myself, and I'd eat a third of the fish each day, so that by the time I finished the fish, the otter would have returned with another. At least I assume it was always the same otter, for I can't believe that there would be two who would behave in such a fashion . . .'

'You said that was the first thirty years; what happened after that?' I prompted.

Paul smiled, showing an astonishingly full set of teeth. He pointed to the spring I had been drinking from. 'This burst forth from the ground. Drink some of this water,' he suggested.

'I already have,' I said.

'But it's almost noon now,' he said, with a secretive smile. 'What about it?'

'Drink the water,' he repeated.

I bent down and cupped my hand, filling it with the ice-cool water. And then I saw that while only a few moments earlier, it had been sparklingly clear, it was now discoloured with tiny brownish flecks. I was about to empty my hand, when Paul said, 'Drink it!' Not wishing to upset the crazy old man, I drank. It tasted different! It was still cool, but now it was marvellously sweet, with the faint traces of herbs in it. Strength flowed back into me as I drank. I took some more, then rose. 'It's excellent,' I said.

'It has sustained me for sixty years,' Paul said simply. 'Before you leave bring your flasks here and fill them – the water will give you strength and stamina for the final part of your voyage. Your bodies must be purified by fasting before you enter the Promised Land; but this will ensure that you will not be weakened through lack of nourishment. But you can only fill your flasks at noon – only then does the water take on its magical properties. But come, come; it's time we returned to the others.'

As we descended in single file down the path through the gorge, I asked curiously, 'How did you come to this place?'

The hermit looked back over his shoulder, his mad bright eyes sparkling. 'Ah, well, that is a story; oh dear, yes,' Paul answered, reverting to his earlier manner. 'I was a monk, like you – does that surprise you? A monk, yes; and I lived in a community, like yourselves. The monastery of St Patrick, on the southern coast, it was; and a fine place, too. I wasn't anybody very special, not an abbot, like yourself. No, my job for the most part was tending to the cemetery, and very pleasant work it was too, with the grass and the wild flowers all about. Not like here, of course . . .' His voice trailed off; but then he continued quickly, 'There was always death, of course

– name me a monastery where death is not a constant visitor – but one summer something like a plague passed around our community. Everyone was affected, and the older and weaker amongst us succumbed. Strangely, I didn't catch the sickness – perhaps it was because I spent so much time away from the rest of the brothers. But the dead had to be buried – and quickly, I should add, because it was a warm summer. You can't imagine how hard I worked, by day and by night.' Paul's voice trailed off again as he relived the past, and then he glanced sharply back at me. 'So there I was one evening, digging a grave for poor old Nessan, when a brother I'd never seen before comes up to me and tells me not to dig there, because it is his own burial place, if you please!'

' "And who are you?" I ask, not recognizing him at all. "Don't you know your own abbot?" he says to me. Well now, our abbot was a small, plump sort of man – very fond of boiled fowl and mead he was – while this man was small and thin, with a large nose, and he spoke with a strange accent. So, I called out to one of my brothers, who was a hundred paces away, to see if he knew this man. And do you know, he didn't even look up. He didn't hear me, and a bit later he brushed right past us, as if he didn't see me. "And just who are you?" I demanded. "I am St Patrick," he says simply, as if I should have recognized him immediately. What could I do? I had to believe him, although he didn't look at all like what I'd expected.

' "What do you want of me?" I asked, for it was clear he had something in mind.

' "Go down to the sea," St Patrick tells me. "You'll find a boat there, and you must put up the sail and let the wind take you. You will be guided to a place where you will await your own death in a holy manner, according to God's will."

'Looking back on it, I realize now that perhaps I was just fever-struck; because I did what he said without question, and the odd thing was that I wasn't at all frightened, even though I'd been very happy in community life. It turned out well, though, and I've been very content here. I've missed the company at times, but I've wanted for nothing – except clothing.' He glanced back at me and smiled. 'But I suppose that's the purpose of all this hair.'

At once I felt ashamed of myself for my earlier thoughts on Paul's appearance: had not the Lord God given him covering, while we were dependent on clothes made by man?

As if divining my thoughts, Paul said, 'It does occur to me that I must look very strange to you and your men. But I have no choice – God did not see fit to preserve my robes as he has yours.'

Now, for the first time, it occurred to me that although our habits were stiffened by salt, they were more or less as they had been when we left so long ago from Didache – the wear and tear that even ordinary life would have produced was not visible. I thought of mentioning this to Martyn, but perhaps he had already noted as much.

When we reached the beach – and the almost repaired currach – I watched with amusement my brethren's reaction to the small hairy man. But whatever they thought of him was overwhelmed by the fact that he greeted each of them by name.

'How did you know which of us was which?' Ruarai asked, assuming that I must have told him the names of my companions, whilst coming through the gorge.

'I don't know how I know you, but I do seem to know you. Perhaps we have met before – but no,' he shook his head, smiling shyly, 'that would be impossible. But now you must hurry . . . the tide will soon shift and come roaring up this gully . . .'

'What about our flasks?' I asked. 'I thought we were to fill them in your spring.'

For a few moments Paul looked confused, and he hopped from foot to foot. 'Oh dear, oh dear . . . Go!' he said decisively. 'Do not drink from your flasks until after mid-day on the morrow. When you open them again, you will find they will be filled with the spring water.'

As the brothers took up their positions, Paul turned to me and, in a graver voice than before, said, 'Now you must sail east, keeping a straight course. There will be no opposing wind to hinder you, no reefs to bar your way – nor could you lose your way now, in any case. The Steward will take you to that which you seek.'

'The Steward?' I asked. 'Who is he? Where will we find him?'

'He guards the way to the Promised Land – and there is no question of you not finding him. He is directly in your course.' He stepped back away from me and raised a thin furred arm in formal farewell. 'Go now, Brendan; the end of your voyage is in sight.'

Chapter Eighteen

'Brothers – the next land we encounter will be the Isles of the Blest. Row!'

With the promise – and lure – of Paradise so close now, the brothers took turns rowing, while both Geoffrey and I kept us to a steady course. The water and the air were so still that I sometimes wondered if we were moving at all; but I think this was an illusion of the smooth and featureless sea, or the result of our fast, for lack of food will bring strange fancies to a man's mind.

I had followed Paul the hermit's advice, and neither I nor any of my brethren had eaten since we had left his barren rock; and yet I felt none of the gnawing incessant hunger which always attends the beginnings of any fast; the water from his island seemed wholly sufficient to our needs, and the provisions still stowed in the stern of the boat remained untouched. Nevertheless, I felt as if I were receiving all the benefits that fasting brings – a sense of lightness, clarity, purification – but without the pain and weakness which always eventually results from any prolonged period of abstinence.

I looked around me. My movements – and those of my crew – seemed slow and deliberate, studied, almost ritualistic. Everything had taken on a fragility, a delicacy. It was a sensation I had experienced occasionally before in fasting, but never with such intensity. I looked into the sky; it was the colour of washed silver, and so close I fancied I could reach out and touch it. The sky was a shell, a bird's eggshell, blue and translucent. The sea was cloth, smooth damask, worked with threads of pale needlework . . .

I realized what was happening, and bit my lip, the pain bringing me back to my senses. When the dreams began to seem real and, more frighteningly, were accepted, that was the danger sign. I have seen fasting men injure themselves because they believed in their own dreams. What I needed now was sleep – true sleep, not this half-waking daydreaming.

I closed my eyes, and immediately images began to float behind them, images at first strange and utterly alien; but then they seemed to shift and suddenly became recognizable. I saw myself as a young boy, walking around my father's prosperous farm with him, while he showed me all that would be mine in time, and knowing, even then, even at seven or eight years of age, that the houses and lands meant nothing to me, that I wanted both much less and far more . . . Myself as a young man on my early voyages, standing in the prow of my frail craft, proud and eager for adventure, with a young man's strength, arrogance . . . and stupidity . . . I saw that same young man, but slightly older now, and still voyaging, studying the stars and their movements, and loving the cut of the salt spray in my face, the exhilarating speed of the groaning, creaking, crackling – talking! – craft as the wind snapped at the sails . . . There I was, while still a comparatively young man, laying the first stones for the single building that would eventually grow to become the monastery at Clonfert . . . And then I saw the broken body of Fionnbar, my cousin, and heard again his tale of the Promised Land . . . I fancied I could still hear his voice – and then the voice became clearer, sharper, more insistent, and familiar.

I opened my eyes and found Geoffrey was bent over me, roughly shaking my shoulder. 'Brendan! Abbot! Wake up – there's a bank of fog ahead, stretching from horizon to horizon. What should we do?'

'Go around it,' I mumbled, images from my dream still swimming confusedly around me.

'I can see no end to it.'

I squeezed my eyes shut and then opened them again and rolled to my feet. I found that we were still under clear skies; but directly before us, stretching from horizon to horizon, was a dense wall of white fog, through which nothing could be seen. Or could it?

'Abbot . . .?' Geoffrey said hesitantly, pointing away to one side.

I nodded; I had spotted the same thing. To the port side,

something was visible through the shifting wreaths. 'Bring us around slightly,' I said quietly.

'Are you sure?' Geoffrey said, very softly, his broad face creased with worry.

'I'm sure,' I said.

The mist-hidden shape took on form and definition as we approached. It was a rock – a single tall pillar of black stone rising from the sea to about the height of a tall man. The front section of this pillar had been torn away, leaving a sort of natural cavity, an indentation in the stone. And sitting in this natural stone chair was a man.

The figure – his features still blurred by the shifting fog – rose to his feet as we drew near.

'Who is it?' Ruarai asked, voicing what I'm sure we were all wondering.

'Another traitorous lost soul?' Barran suggested defiantly; but his voice was hesitant, uncertain.

'I think not,' Martyn said. 'For we are well outside the confines of Hell, now.'

'Not every demon lives in Hell,' Barran snapped. He turned to me. 'Perhaps it would be better if we avoided this creature . . .?'

'Perhaps it would,' I agreed, 'except I don't think we have any choice in the matter.' A strong current had taken our boat, pulling us directly in towards the pillar stone and the standing figure. As we neared the pillar we could see that he was an old man, so old that I could not begin to reckon his age, although the outward signs of age lay lightly upon him. Something within him radiated an aura of serenity, of timelessness, of age. His hair and beard were long and white and his skin had the thin, translucent quality that I've always found in those who have lived far beyond their allotted span of years. But of his features I can remember nothing. I do remember that he was clad in a simple woollen robe that seemed only slightly darker than the grey mists surrounding him, and which was tied around his waist with a white cord.

When he spoke, however, his voice was as strong as a young man's, deep and musical in texture. 'Bring your boat by me that I may board,' he commanded. The tone he used was from one accustomed to absolute obedience.

'Who are you, and by what right do you demand passage with us?' I countered.

'I am the Steward,' he answered, and then he pointed off into the dense, shifting fog wall. 'Without me to guide you, your voyage ends here, Brendan of Clonfert.'

'What is your name; where are you from? Of what are you the Steward?' I pressed, suddenly unwilling to enter that blanket of whiteness.

'My name? I have long since forgotten it,' he answered dismissively. 'I have even forgotten the land of my birth. I am the Steward who guards the way to the Promised Land, and without me none will find it. You may call me whatever name pleases you; names are of no import here.'

'The Promised Land,' I breathed, hope once again surging within me. 'Are we close to it now?'

'As men measure distance, you have been close to it most of your life; and during your voyage, Christian Abbot, you have come close enough to touch it several times.'

'That's not possible . . .' I began, but the Steward ignored me and continued on.

'You have not seen it because it is always shrouded from mortal eyes. Sometimes men need to be shown what is clearly visible to them. I am your guide.' And then he stepped – indeed, almost seemed to glide – into our currach. He brushed past me without saying another word and moved to the stern, where he took the helm from Ultan, and turned us into the fog.

Time – which had always been difficult to calculate on our voyage – was lost utterly, and I had no way of knowing for how long the Steward guided our craft through the shifting, twisting, writhing banks of fog. After what seemed an eternity, the mist suddenly thickened, so that I could not see from one end of the currach to the other; and then, just as quickly, it began to thin – and then it vanished . . .

We were on a flat, motionless, deep blue sea. The sky was the colour of polished iron and cloudless . . . and before us was an island. When we first looked upon it, it looked like just another isle; there was a single tree-covered mountain rising tall and proud in the centre of it, and a golden thread of a beach at its foot. Then the Steward spoke a single word – and at once the isle seemed to burst into flaming sheets of colour, vibrating and shivering on the still morning air. We felt heat then, summer's warmth; and we could taste the odours wafting out from the island: freshness, growth, scents from a score of plants, flowers and herbs.

And that word was, 'Paradise!'

My brethren and I sat stunned and motionless, hardly able to breathe, let alone speak or take oar. We sat in silence as the boat which had been our home for so long drifted into the shore and up to the shimmering sands of the Promised Land, where it shuddered to a halt.

'You have reached your destination, Brendan of Clonfert,' the Steward said harshly. 'Your voyage has ended.'

I hesitated. Was this indeed our journey's end? Had we reached Paradise? And as I looked around at the sparkling, shimmering sands, the lush green – vibrantly alive – vegetation, and felt the peace and serenity of the place, I knew that in truth we had reached the Isle of Paradise. And I felt nothing! Yes, there was joy and happiness that we had accomplished what we had set out to do; there was sadness at the brothers that we had lost on the way . . . and there was also the realization that this was not what I wanted!

'Come out,' the Steward repeated. 'We have arrived.'

I felt the men staring at me, looking for guidance; and I realized that they too were unsure. Perhaps despite all our faith and all our dreams, none of us had ever in his heart fully believed in this moment. Paradise was not for mortals. And yet here we were. I turned – and found Martyn beside me. Looking into his eyes, I found a great sadness, a loneliness there. He touched my elbow, his hand telling me that I must do something.

'My brothers,' I said rising to my feet and moving to the prow, 'let us thank God,' and then I stepped out into the shallows. One by one, the others followed.

When the entire crew had disembarked, I turned, reaching out to help the mysterious Steward to the ground. But he shook his head slightly. 'I may not enter the Promised Land; for it is my bane to wait just outside the gates of Paradise, but never to enter them. I have duties to perform elsewhere, and I must go. But you may wander where you will here, and eat and drink your fill. Everything you have ever wanted, every dream you have ever had, every desire can be fulfilled here. This is Paradise.'

'The currach . . .' I began.

'Have no fear for your craft – it will be here should you ever need it again.'

'Will we ever see you again?' I asked our guide.

'If you have need of me, I shall appear,' the Steward answered. 'But why keep your eyes fixed on me, man of God? This is what you have come for; look around you and see what few men have ever seen in mortal life. This is Paradise,' he repeated, and then added, 'where everything is and is not what it seems.' He bowed slightly and then spread both hands, indicating the pebbled beach.

'The beach,' Fiachra exclaimed. 'Abbot, look down at the stones beneath our feet!'

'Not stones,' Ruarai breathed. 'Diamonds, rubies, pearls, sapphires . . .'

'. . . Amethysts, opals, emeralds, corundum,' Martyn continued, 'topaz, quartz, jasper, agate, aventurine, amber, jade . . .' His voice trailed off to a whisper. 'Every precious stone in the world must be scattered on this beach, and there are some here I've never seen before . . .'

I bent down, and lifted a king's ransom in my cupped palms. All about us sparkled. And, on closer inspection, even the grains of sand turned out to be powdered gold. It was dazzling – almost painfully so – and I felt my eyes beginning to water. I looked away, up the beach towards the trees that lined the upper reaches of the beach. They looked so cool and enticing. I let the jewels trickle through my fingers and straightened up, walking towards the greenery, walking on the wealth of a world.

When we stepped into the cool and moist shade of the trees overhanging the beach I stopped and turned, looking back down the beach. But the Steward had vanished, although our craft remained.

'Father Abbot . . .?' Someone – Martyn? – called, and I

turned away, and led my brethren into Paradise.

A lot of what we saw and experienced on that blessed island I have forgotten, or, and this I think is closer to the truth, I cannot possibly convey in simple terms. I can say that it was cool beneath the tall trees, but that does not convey the sense of security we felt in their shadow, nor the emerald shafts of light that filtered down through the leafy canopy, nor the rich odours of life and growth.

But parts remain, and my brothers all seemed to recall different aspects of the island; indeed, some of their accounts differ so wildly from each other that I came to the conclusion that they each saw Paradise exactly as they had expected Paradise to be. Naturally, being Christian monks, and followers of the Christian faith, their images, their differing visions of Paradise, were remarkably similar; but the differences are there.

Some of the memories I retain of the island are remarkably clear. I remember the forest particularly. Although the sky was that of high summer, the trees were that of autumn fruitfulness. The trees themselves were familiar – achingly so, bringing with them memories of my childhood, and the wood which had surrounded our fort. There were no strangely shaped or monstrously large fruits on these trees, either, but the apples, pears and plums were in a state of ripe perfection, without sign of blemish or insect. I remember reaching out my hand and taking a plump pear from the tree nearest me. I had barely touched it, when it moved into my hand, and the texture was like butter as I bit into it; the juice might have had honey mixed in with it. Was it a fruit such as this that Adam had eaten in Eden before he took that which was forbidden, I wondered? And if the fruit in the Garden had been like this, I could see how he might have been tempted!

I turned, and found the brothers watching hungrily, eyes fastened on the half-eaten fruit in my hand. I took another bite, and then dragged my sleeve across my chin which was running with juice. 'Eat,' I shouted. 'Eat!'

I watched them almost attack a tree, stripping its lower branches bare of the shining, smooth-skinned fruit, but when I looked again, I found that the same branches were still laden.

Shaking my head, I strolled over to another tree a short distance away and helped myself to some plums of a deep, luxuriant purple. They tasted like nectar, with a faint tartness to cut the almost cloying sweetness. The brothers moved over and joined me. 'Eat lightly,' I cautioned, 'since we have only just broken our fast.'

'I don't think you need fear stomach cramps from this fruit,' Martyn said softly to me.

He was right, of course, this was Paradise – nothing could harm us here.

'How large is this island, Abbot?' Ruarai asked.

I shook my head. 'I don't know.' Looking over at Martyn, I asked him, 'Have you any idea?'

'As large as need be,' he said enigmatically, and then he turned away.

It was an answer that in normal circumstances would have angered me; but on this day, in this place, nothing was important, and I was at peace with the world, and with myself. I glanced over my shoulder at Ruarai. 'Let us walk the fields of Paradise.'

I cannot describe what we saw; my words would be poor things. Had Padraigh remained as one of us, perhaps he could have produced illuminations to make all men marvel. Had we taken a bard, perhaps he could have written words to make men weep with joy and longing. But even those powers would not be able to render the scent, the texture, the absolute beauty and peace that we beheld and experienced. I can say that we passed small streams, and that they sparkled in the sun, and that the sound of them rushing over sapphire and emerald rocks was the most beautiful music we had ever heard, a choir singing an eternal pæan to heaven. I can say that the crystal water tasted of milk and mead, but I cannot capture in words that taste; nor can I convey the sounds and scents of Paradise. I can say that though we wandered for untold hours, there was no dusk, no night, but only an unchanging golden light that had the freshness of dawn and the warmth of afternoon in it. Nor did we tire and sleep. It seems to me that there were times when we rested, but they are grey, hazy memories. In all our wanderings, we did not reach either end of the Isle, nor did we meet any other men; but I often thought I saw figures moving just out of sight, shadows moving from the corner of my eye. Yet when I turned there was nothing there and the only movement was a branch trembling in the light breezes that sometimes played through the air.

We wandered along the coast, keeping just within the cool, scented vegetation, with the sea on our left-hand side, until we came across a broad natural roadway that seemed to lead in to the centre of the island. As we moved inland, the trees became strange, though not unnatural, and Martyn was able to put a name to some of them: 'exotics,' he called them, from the warm lands far to the south of Erin. The ground underfoot was soft and pliable without being marshy, a mixture of moss and grass unmarked by either leaf or twig; and we found ourselves in a long tree-lined corridor through which the light slanted in, catching patches of surprising colour and throwing the spread of flowers into sharp relief. In one sense the scenery varied barely at all; but it was this very sameness which allowed us to notice the minute details of leaf and twig, bud and flower. It was a cathedral, a huge living cathedral.

The forest seemed never-ending, and I was beginning to wonder how big the island was. By my reckoning, we should now have reached the single mountain that we had spotted from offshore. I was about to order the brothers to turn back, when we heard the sounds of running water. The sounds, faint at first, grew in power and intensity as we approached; and then suddenly the track dipped into a hollow and we found we were standing on the banks of a great river, a torrent of silver-hued water that reflected the light so brilliantly that it blinded us to the riverbank on the other side.

I stopped; but Ultan pushed forward, heading straight for the water. 'Wait!' I commanded.

He paused on the bank and looked back up at me, his broad open face reflecting a green tinge from the forest. 'What harm can come to us in God's Kingdom?' he asked.

He was right, of course; but I still hesitated to attempt to cross the vast expanse of water. 'We don't know what lies beyond,' I said.

'Paradise,' he said simply.

'Paradise,' I nodded. I turned back to my brethren. 'Well, what should we do?'

Some of the brothers – Fiachra, Barran, Ultan – were in favour of striding into the water; but others were less certain. While we were attempting to come to a decision, I thought I saw movement out of the corner of my eye. I ignored it initially, expecting it would vanish if I looked directly at it; but when I turned around moments later, the movement was still there. I turned quickly – and a slim and rather fair youth, clothed in a simple shimmering tunic on which colours ran like liquid with every movement, stepped out from the bushes. He was tall and thin, his skin deeply tanned, his eyes startlingly blue against the dusk of his face, and his hair was yellow-white. His features were strong and handsome, and, as with the Steward's face, I retain no clear memory of them.

'Brendan of Clonfert,' he said simply, stepping up and embracing me. He then went to each of my brethren in turn and embraced and addressed them by their own names.

'You know us, but I am afraid I don't know you,' I said when he returned to stand before me.

'A name is but a label,' he said, shrugging his thin shoulders, while his tunic flashed colours.

'Can you help us?' I persisted.

'Ask,' he said.

'Should we cross this river and if so, by what means?' I asked him.

'It is easily done – if you wish,' he replied in a grave but friendly manner. 'You have only to step into the water and walk across; it is fast but shallow. As to whether you should, only you can decide. If you cross, you choose to remain here in the Promised Land with us forever. If you turn back without crossing, you can still return to your own land.'

'And if we go back to Erin, will we ever return here?' I asked.

'With God's grace,' the youth promised. 'But not in mortal life.'

I turned to my brethren. 'What would you do?'

No one spoke at first; then Geoffrey said quietly, 'You have led us this far, making what decisions needed to be made –

difficult choices, but always the correct ones; and so now we leave it for you to decide, Brendan.'

Something like terror gripped me. 'You cannot ask me to make this decision for you!'

'We have found what all men seek; and yet it may be that we have found it too soon.'

I turned back to the river, feeling the dull pounding of my heart, the tightness in my chest. I had the deaths of many on my conscience. But what now; what if I made the wrong decision and brought what remained of my crew away from Paradise? And what if I took another choice and doomed them to Paradise for all eternity?

Yes, we could cross the river to what surely must be eternal bliss – no more struggling, no further temptations from grace, no more effort, no more suffering. Or we could return to Erin, to Clonfert, to mortal matters and mortal sorrows. Only a madman would go back; and yet . . . was it not our duty to tell others of all that we had done and seen? Was it not part of my destiny to continue to preach – and this time with certainty – of Paradise and God's goodness? We still had a purpose to fulfil. Our voyage was not completed when we reached the Blessed Isle – rather it would only be over when we had returned to Erin with that news.

I turned to the youth – but he had vanished; indeed, I wondered if he had ever been there. 'I will go back,' I said slowly. 'And those of you who wish will come with me. I would not have them thinking back home at Clonfert that we were lost at sea.'

I expected at least half of my brethren to elect to stay, but all chose to come with me.

'We have seen enough, then; let us go,' I said, and turned away before I could change my mind. Although our decision was made, I felt my sense of loss increase with each step that took us closer to the jewelled strand and our currach. It was not that I was tired; but my feet moved more heavily as my eyes tried to take in everything we passed, to fix it in my mind's eye and keep it with me always. Once beyond the forest, we hurried down the clattering, dazzling strand towards our craft; and the sight of the currach once more brought a lift

200

to my heart, like seeing again an old friend. As we drew near, I was unsurprised to see the Steward of the Blessed Isle waiting by the prow.

I held back as the rest of my crew climbed into the boat. 'Where now?' I asked the Steward.

'You have made your decision?' he asked, his voice flat and emotionless.

'We will return to Erin,' I said softly, gazing back into the interior of the island.

The Steward nodded slightly. 'That may be a wise decision,' he said. 'Even the greatest voyage is not in itself preparation for Paradise.'

I too nodded, silently agreeing; and then I climbed into the currach. He set his foot against the prow and pushed us offshore. 'Set your sails,' he commanded, 'and allow the wind to guide you through the mists to your own land. Once through the Gate, you are but a day's travel from Erin.'

'You're not coming with us this time?' I asked anxiously, thinking of the fog.

'You will not need me now; only those coming to Paradise have need of my guidance,' he replied. Then, as the currach drifted out towards the enveloping whiteness, his voice drifted out across the waves. 'Farewell – till we meet again!'

The fog closed in and we allowed the barely perceptible wind and invisible currents to guide us through the silent waters. Our appreciation of time once again disappeared, and it seemed to be days later – certainly we slept twice – when we suddenly spotted a break in the fog wall. It was a gap, a curiously regular opening, which resolved into a perfectly formed archway rising from the sea. And it framed clear blue sky.

I think we all went blind as we sailed through that fog-woven archway; certainly there was a blinding burst of light, which left shimmering afterimages on our eyes . . . and when we could see again, the sea had changed. It had become familiar; it was as choppy and grey as the waters which washed Erin's shore. Exhaustion struck me then, a mortal bone-weariness; and I felt every one of my sixty and more years.

A wind struck up from behind us, snapping our sail open,

pushing us in towards the distant grey line of a shore. I turned and looked over my shoulder towards the archway – but there was nothing there; there was only a sky of blue with rain-clouds far off on the horizon.

'Where now, Father?' Martyn asked.

'Take me home; take me back to Clonfert.'

And so now it ends . . .

Epilogue

'Our sainted abbot has now returned to the Promised Land –
and returned in all the honour and glory that he surely
deserves.

'Following his return to Clonfert, he laboured night and day
to fashion a record of his travels so that men might know of the
lands to the west and the Lord's infinite glory and goodness.
His one regret was that he could not properly describe the Isle
of Paradise; but there are many things which are beyond man's
comprehension.

'His last act was to lay the foundation stone of a new
community at Didache, to mark the spot where he first set out
in search of the Blessed Isle.

' "Lest men forget," he said; but no man will ever forget
Brendan of Clonfert, Brendan the Navigator!'

Brother Martyn, this day, the Second of Advent.

Select Bibliography

ASHE; *Land to the West; St Brendan's Voyage to America* (Collins 1962).

DILLON & CHADWICK; *The Celtic Realms* (Weidenfeld and Nicolson 1967).

GINNELL; *The Brehon Laws* (West 1917).

GREGORY; *A Book of Saints and Wonders* (Dun Emer Press 1906, John Murray 1907, Colin Smythe 1971).

KENNY; *Sources for the Early History of Ireland: Ecclesiastical;* vol. I (Editions Tailliuira 1980).

LITTLE; *Brendan the Navigator* (Gill 1945).

O'MEARA; *The Voyage of Saint Brendan; Journey to the Promised Land* (Dolmen Press 1978).

SCOTT; *A Celtic Odyssey: The Voyage of Mailduin* (Sphere 1985).

SELMER, ed.; *Navigatio Sancti Brendani Abbatis* (Univ. of Notre Dame Pr. 1959.)

WESTROPP; *Brasil and the Legendary Islands of the North Atlantic* (Proceedings of the Royal Irish Academy, vol. XXX, 1912).

BENEDICT KIELY

Nothing Happens in Carmincross

Benedict Kiely's latest novel tells the story of a journey to his childhood home undertaken by Mervyn Kavanagh, a man in middle age who has been living and teaching in America. The wedding of a favourite niece takes him travelling back across the Atlantic and Ireland to Carmincross, the small town in Ulster where he was born. As he journeys towards this family celebration he repeatedly encounters people and events from his own and his country's past, while the constant flow of news of contemporary acts of terrorism and counter-terrorism invades his consciousness more and more insistently. Somewhere, it seems, the past and the present are bound to collide. . . .

'Even readers who know of Mr Kiely's comic gift from his previous novels may find it hard to see much scope for comedy in such material. Yet the first thing to say about *Nothing Happens in Carmincross* is that it is often brilliantly funny . . .'
John Gross *The New York Times*

'Written with zest and grace, humour and irony in a style that is totally individual . . . It must be read by everyone interested in Irish writing and the peculiar tragedy of the Irish situation.'
Kevin Casey *Irish Times*

'Richly, grimly funny . . . At its best this is a remarkable study of a man struggling to come to terms with the country he thought he'd left behind him and with his own complicity in the troubles.'
Margaret Walters *The Observer*

'I have been waiting for a novel as full of rage about contemporary Ireland as this one. And this is the book I have been waiting for.'
Frank Delaney *BBC World Service*

'[A] dark and compellingly troubled meditation on our contemporary situation. Read it.'
Terence Brown *Sunday Independent*

BENEDICT KIELY

A Letter to Peachtree

'A masterly collection of new stories' *Irish Press*

Benedict Kiely is one of those rare writers who can portray the unexpected, the comic and the tragic sides of life, often in the same person and in the same moment of hilarity and doubt. In this, his fourth collection of stories, he teases his readers as happily and as wickedly as ever.

'There are fine things all over this collection, lives to brood about and glorious gallops down every interesting looking diversion . . . There are so many Irish people who write short stories, and so few who are real storytellers. Ben Kiely is one, and he should be preserved in aspic or crowned high king or just bought in huge numbers.'
Sunday Independent

'This is a splendid collection, confirming Kiely as a master of the oral tradition.'
Irish Press

'They are as much occasions of sin as any Ben Kiely story ever was'
Irish Independent

'The stories are full of the sort of verve you would expect from Ben Kiely, overflowing with wit, erudition, a sense of the absurd, a tenderness for beauty, whether of people or places'
Evening Press

'Sheer magic'
Dominic Behan, *Dublin Evening Herald*

'Stylish, gabby, using language like a fallen angel, he mixes his feelings with a true storyteller's verve that looks like superb skill but is in fact something better. Call it instinct.'
Norman Shrapnell, *Guardian*

MAEVE KELLY

Necessary Treasons

When Eve Gleeson joins the women's movement in Limerick, she finds it is a largely disregarded concern. Young, naïve but grimly independent, she begins to work for a battered wives' refuge, and her increasing anger and pain at women's lot – especially among the ill-educated poor – is matched only by her growing frustration at the movement's limited resources and support.

Set against this is her relationship with Hugh. Twenty years her senior, he clearly sees in Eve the chaste and tender bride he has always wanted, and is baffled by her more 'modern' side and her growing resentment. To complicate things there are also his four possessive sisters and lonely ancestral home; and the attractions of unthinking, rigid matronhood begin to dwindle considerably while what Hugh calls Eve's 'hobby' becomes an issue of central importance.

'Maeve Kelly writes with a kind of bitter elegance . . . Her descriptions of modern Limerick with its shoddy affluence and its comfortable contempt for 'social' issues are vivid and accurate.'
The Listener

'Ms Kelly's insights . . . are shrewd, her style incisive . . . A fine, provocative first novel from a writer already noted for her sharply individual short stories.'
Sunday Independent

JEREMY LELAND

Bluff

'Mr Leland writes like an angel'
Guardian

Conor de Burgh is in retreat from life on his remote farm in County Clare. But his solitude is invaded by a number of women, each like yet unlike the other, who could all be the same person. The last of them, journalist Nel Farrell, seems to be on to a scoop which could overturn political life in the Republic.

Baffled and aroused, Conor attempts to untangle the traumas of his own life through his relationships with these women. But when Nel disappears, Conor is forced to act. . . .

'Confident and poetic . . . here is another [Jeremy Leland book] that deserves the spotlight'
Irish Times

'*Bluff* is a superbly written book and Mr Leland an entrancing author'
Times

Methuen Modern Fiction

While every effort is made to keep prices low, it is sometimes necessary to increase prices at short notice. Methuen Paperbacks reserves the right to show new retail prices on covers which may differ from those previously advertised in the text or elsewhere.

The prices shown below were correct at the time of going to press.

☐ 413 52310 1	**Silence Among the Weapons**	John Arden	£2.50
☐ 413 52890 1	**Collected Short Stories**	Bertolt Brecht	£3.95
☐ 413 53090 6	**Scenes From Provincial Life**	William Cooper	£2.95
☐ 413 59970 1	**The Complete Stories**	Noël Coward	£4.50
☐ 413 54660 8	**Londoners**	Maureen Duffy	£2.95
☐ 413 41620 8	**Genesis**	Eduardo Galeano	£3.95
☐ 413 42400 6	**Slow Homecoming**	Peter Handke	£3.95
☐ 413 42250 X	**Mr Norris Changes Trains**	Christopher Isherwood	£3.50
☐ 413 59630 3	**A Single Man**	Christopher Isherwood	£3.50
☐ 413 56110 0	**Prater Violet**	Christopher Isherwood	£2.50
☐ 413 41590 2	**Nothing Happens in Carmincross**	Benedict Kiely	£3.50
☐ 413 58920 X	**The German Lesson**	Siegfried Lenz	£3.95
☐ 413 60230 3	**Non-Combatants and Others**	Rose Macaulay	£3.95
☐ 413 54210 6	**Entry Into Jerusalem**	Stanley Middleton	£2.95
☐ 413 59230 8	**Linden Hills**	Gloria Naylor	£3.95
☐ 413 55230 6	**The Wild Girl**	Michèle Roberts	£2.95
☐ 413 57890 9	**Betsey Brown**	Ntozake Shange	£3.50
☐ 413 51970 8	**Sassafrass, Cypress & Indigo**	Ntozake Shange	£2.95
☐ 413 53360 3	**The Erl-King**	Michel Tournier	£4.50
☐ 413 57600 0	**Gemini**	Michel Tournier	£4.50
☐ 413 14710 X	**The Women's Decameron**	Julia Voznesenskaya	£3.95
☐ 413 59720 2	**Revolutionary Road**	Richard Yates	£4.50

All these books are available at your bookshop or newsagent, or can be ordered direct from the publisher. Just tick the titles you want and fill in the form below.

Methuen Paperbacks, Cash Sales Department, PO Box 11, Falmouth, Cornwall TR10 109EN.

Please send cheque or postal order, no currency, for purchase price quoted and allow the following for postage and packing:

UK   60p for the first book, 25p for the second book and 15p for each additional book ordered to a maximum charge of £1.90.

BFPO and Eire   60p for the first book, 25p for the second book and 15p for each next seven books, thereafter 9p per book.

Overseas   £1.25 for the first book, 75p for the second book and 28p for each subsequent
Customers   title ordered.

NAME (Block Letters) ....

ADDRESS...

....